Raina's FANTASY

JO CARLISLE

ELLORA'S CAVE
ROMANTICA PUBLISHING

What the critics are saying...

༠

Third Place, 2007 Night Owl Romance Award for Best EBook Paranormal Erotica!

5 Hearts "Okay ladies and gentlemen get ready for one hot, exhilarating and oh yes passionate story from a debut author. I'm shocked that this is Jo Carlisle's first paranormal erotica for she has got in all the basics for a great erotica. [...] Awesome job and can't wait for more from this talented, imaginative and passionate author. Not only does she know how to create strong, virile, handsome men, but knows when to take them far beyond just vanilla sex." ~ *Night Owl Romance Reviews*

Joyfully Recommended "*Raina's Fantasy* is the real deal, a complete treat from start to finish [...] vampires, demons, slaves, conspiracy, and mind blowing sex all wrapped up and tied with a big, red hot bow." ~ *Joyfully Reviewed Reviews*

"I couldn't put this book down [...] a very talented, passionate author with a gift to bring her story alive. [...] Jo Carlisle, she is at the top of my list from now on."
~ *ParaNormal Romance Reviews*

"A spectacular story, RAINA'S FANTASY will intrigue, entice and drag you willingly in its grasp to the final, breathtaking scenes." ~ *Romance Reviews Today*

An Ellora's Cave Romantica Publication

www.ellorascave.com

Raina's Fantasy

ISBN 9781419957635
ALL RIGHTS RESERVED.
Raina's Fantasy Copyright © 2007 Jo Carlisle
Edited by Raelene Gorlinsky.
Photography and cover art by Les Byerley.

This book printed in the U.S.A. by Jasmine–Jade Enterprises, LLC.

Electronic book Publication August 2007
Trade paperback Publication June 2008

About the Author

ജ

When award-winning author Jo Carlisle developed a lucrative side business in the third grade writing and illustrating stories, then charging classmates twenty-five cents each to buy them, she discovered a calling that would last a lifetime. Breathing life into the colorful characters crowding her head and sharing their dark, decadent world with her readers proved a temptation too powerful to resist.

Jo's erotic tales, whether paranormal or contemporary, carry readers on a fast-paced ride of danger and forbidden passions. Tortured, dashing heroes fight for the love of the strong-willed mates who melt their emotional and sexual boundaries and free their souls.

Jo invites you to leave your troubles behind, step into her world, and lose yourself in wicked pleasure for a while. She'd love to hear from you. Jo Carlisle lives in Texas with her own dashing hero and two children.

Jo Carlisle welcomes comments from readers. You can find her website and email address on her author bio page at www.ellorascave.com.

Tell Us What You Think

We appreciate hearing reader opinions about our books. You can email us at Comments@EllorasCave.com.

RAINA'S FANTASY

છા

Chapter One

১৩

"Rough crowd tonight, sweet cheeks. Sure you wanna go through with this?"

Johan stared at the young woman awaiting his answer. A girl, really. Once-pretty features already hardened beyond her years, dark eyes that had seen too much. Silver studs adorned her nose, lower lip and, unless he was mistaken, her tongue. Her black skirt barely covered the firm globes of her rear, and the taut circles of her large nipples were clearly defined underneath the wife-beater shirt. His gaze swept to her feet— *combat boots?* —and up to her skull.

Bright pink hair flew in tufts from her head as though trying to escape the entire horrid picture. She was smacking gum as though her life depended on it, a bored *I don't give a shit* expression fixed on her face when Johan knew from experience nothing could be further from the truth.

"Yes, I'm sure."

Dread coiled in his gut, a serpent waiting to strike. Poisoning him with fear he could not afford. More than his own life hung in the balance, and he ruthlessly squashed the useless emotion.

More smacking, the arch of a fuchsia brow. "Once your fine ass is up on the slave block, it's too late to book out. Like, your soul is toast. You get that, right?"

"Yeah, I get that."

Feel nothing. You have no choice.

"What about your friend?"

Johan's gaze flicked to the sofa, where Zane had collapsed to rest. His lifelong best friend. The only person left in the world who gave a damn about him, and vice versa. Sweat trickled down his friend's lean cheeks, dampened his sun-streaked brown hair. His breathing was raspy, getting worse by the hour.

One more night starving in the bitterly cold streets of St. Louis, sick with pneumonia, and Zane would die.

Zane raised his head and nodded, mouth drawn into a grim line.

No choice. "He gets it, too. And we are sold together, or no deal," he reminded her. Gods, the worst thing would be for Zane to suffer alone, ill and at the mercy of a tyrant.

The girl braced her fists on her slim hips. "Gotcha. But he'll have to be able to stand, or he can't go on the block."

"He will." *Even if I have to hold him up.*

"Drakkon is sitting in front with the bidders. You've heard of the creep? The shapeshifters used to get a kick out of stealing the choice slaves he'd picked. Until he started eating our furry friends." She paused for dramatic emphasis. Blew a noisy bubble. "No one outbids the nasty demon anymore."

Oh, fuck. "I appreciate your honesty, but we won't change our minds. Let's just get this over with."

"All right," the girl sighed. "It's your virgin ass. Take off your clothes."

Confused, Johan opened his mouth to protest that he wasn't a virgin...then realized what she meant. In spite of his resolve, a prickle of fear raced down his spine. Gritting his teeth, he forced himself not to ask questions when the answers didn't matter.

Johan removed his clothes and tossed them aside, along with the hand blades, dagger and sword he'd carried for as long as he could remember. The weapons of a warrior. Protector. Reduced to a pathetic joke.

He and Zane would stand upon the block in their skin, allowed no comforts save what their new master deemed them worthy. A wave of misery swamped him, and he fought to hold steady as the girl began to oil his body. Preparing to show his assets to the best advantage. The more beautiful the slave, the higher the bid...and more money lining the pockets of Club Lash's mysterious owner.

Nakedness didn't bother Johan. But tonight, his and Zane's nudity before bidders and gawkers alike symbolized their plummet to the dregs of society. A slave. Lower than any other creature. Less than nothing.

He stood, legs spread as the girl worked the aromatic oil into the muscles of his arms, chest, shoulders, back. She massaged his legs, then began spreading the stuff all over his cock and balls. Kneading with gentle fingers.

"Relax. You gotta show off that impressive package, sugar. You want to snag an appreciative master, don't you?"

No. He wanted to run screaming from the building. "Is this necessary?"

She moved away for a moment and returned, holding out a glass half full of burgundy liquid. "Drink up. It will help."

Johan downed the contents as she gave some to Zane also. Wine? If so, it wasn't like any he'd tasted. The vile fluid burned a path clear to his toes. His body heated like a torch...and his cock...*great gods*.

He'd been set ablaze from the inside out. Blood filled his shaft, lifting his erection up and away from his body. Turgid, painful. He groaned, instinctively reaching for himself.

Which earned him a swat on his rear and a swift reprimand. "Hands off, big boy," Pinky smirked. "The audience expects a sexy show during the viewing and that's what they'll get. And if you're not primed and ready for your new master, the consequences will suck."

Johan had heard the stories. Didn't want to venture a guess as to which ones to believe. After tonight, his master could do anything he or she wished to him and Zane. In the eyes of the law, one can't rape or torture the willing. And they'd bartered their bodies and souls willingly, at least on the surface. No one, not even the highest-ranking Superior of Exodus, would be able save them. Ironic, considering their former employers were responsible for bringing them to ruin in the first place.

Anger threatened to choke him. Useless and debilitating, like the fear. With iron determination, he blanked all thoughts of betrayal and the trial to come. Which left only his rampant prick to keep his attention, no relief on the horizon.

Zane was standing now, holding on to the end of the sofa, shaking with the effort. The laced wine seized him in vicious talons as well, and his friend moaned in misery. The girl oiled his skin everywhere, taking obvious pleasure in saving Zane's thick erection for last. Fingers stroking the slickened, blue-veined length. Suddenly she stood, leaving him aroused and desperate.

The decadent sight of his friend's straining body did nothing to quell Johan's rising lust.

Zane closed his eyes. "Please," he rasped. "Help me…"

"Sorry, stud. If you're a good slave, maybe your master will let you off the hook. Let's go, boys." With a cheeky wink, Pinky led them out of the holding room directly onto a large, slick stage.

The deep crimson curtain edging the stage was drawn closed, but Johan could hear the festive noise of the crowd beyond. Anxiously awaiting tonight's tasty fare at Lash.

He and Zane were the treat.

His heart sank as he spied two sets of silver poles. Each set consisted of two poles about eight feet high, silver chains with manacles attached to the top and bottom. One restraint for each wrist and ankle. The simple contraption was fixed upon a round section of flooring that would rotate slowly, showing all angles of their bodies to the audience. Letting the bidders savor every inch their prospective new slaves.

So much for helping Zane stand upright. But the restraints would help bear his weight without being too obvious.

Don't think of tonight, and all the nights for the rest of your life. Don't imagine what this master will do to us.

Johan swallowed hard, standing between the first set of poles as the girl instructed. In moments, she'd fastened his wrists and ankles, spreading him wide in a letter "x". She secured Zane, then left without wishing them luck. Not that any amount of fortune could help them now.

Turning his head, his gaze locked with Zane's feverish one.

"Forgive me," he whispered.

"We were outcast, and fresh out of options, old friend. Whatever comes, we'll face it together, just as we always have." Zane sent him a weak smile, then faced straight ahead, stifling a raspy cough.

Regret speared Johan as he did the same. His friend was gentle and far too forgiving by half. For all his deadly skills as a warrior, Zane possessed a big heart.

The curtain began to slide open. Johan had known what to expect, but this final debasement, complete vulnerability, came as a shock nonetheless.

Bodies, a mass of them, crowded around every available table. Standing room only, all the way to the back of the room, around the bar. Smoke hung heavy in the air, a human habit. Lights filtered through the swirl, creating the ghostly image of bodies rising from Hell. At least he couldn't see individual faces. A small comfort.

They cheered, stomped, pounded on the tables. Shouted obscenities, lewd suggestions.

And one of them would own his body and soul by the end of the evening.

Shame cut off his breath, shriveled his heart. He didn't look at Zane again. It was done.

He'd consigned them both to a fate worse than death.

Johan, seasoned warrior, revered champion, was no better than a whore.

* * * * *

A vampire Queen with the Millennium itch? Be careful in there, my lady.

Raina paused outside the trendy nightclub, a ghost of a sad smile hovering on her lips. Alexi, her lone coven member and loyal companion, knew her too well. Did she dare? And why not?

Because she was saving a part of herself for her future mate, the great passion of her existence? The sexy, dominant male whose steely will and insatiable appetites exceeded her own?

Right. At her age, the chances of finding this elusive paragon of male perfection were infinitesimal. And to be fair, she readily admitted to her own flaws, which had contributed to her continued failure in the mating pool.

She'd always been far too picky in her choice of males, demanding, dominant and basically self-centered. Not traits that had endeared her to the males of her acquaintance, save for steady, gentle Alexi. But those were the traits of their Vampire Queen, and Raina couldn't afford to bow to anyone, to show weakness. Not even to her mate.

Which made her a very lonely Queen, though she'd adored Alexi madly ever since she'd plucked him from a hellish existence fifty years ago. She and her young vampire gave one another friendship—and yes, pleasure—but he wasn't her *mate*. And though he tried to hide his emotions from her, she sensed Alexi's restless longing as well.

If not for her treasured fantasies and her handsome companion, she might've sought the sun long ago. Every one hundred years, she treated herself to an indulgence. A fantasy held sacred, to be savored until the time had come to celebrate the passing of another endless century. Surely, a girl's Millennium birthday was deserving of her greatest, most deliciously wicked fantasy-made-reality.

Before the end of this night, she would own two males. Two men she would bond as her blood slaves. As such, they would exist only to satisfy her every desire, at her beck and call. Two cocks filling her, making a yummy Raina sandwich. Make that three whenever Alexi chose to join them.

Her new slaves would be spread naked before her, helpless to prevent her from doing whatever she wished to them. Learning to pleasure their Queen and each other, in every possible manner.

Raina nearly moaned aloud. Her sex heated, throbbing and hot between her thighs. Failure tonight was not an option. She may have buried her dream of finding a mate, but very soon, she and her companion would add a blazing fire to dispel their dreary nights. Determination boosted her flagging spirits, propelling her into the gloomy interior of Lash.

Millennium itch indeed, though what quality of slave she could expect to acquire was in serious doubt, in spite of her positive outlook. Not because of the establishment—Lash was as polished and sleek as any club of its kind—but because of supply and demand.

Fine, attractive specimens were too few, and were snatched quickly off the blocks by only the wealthiest of masters. Highly coveted, these slaves were used for food and sex. If very lucky, they enjoyed a normal life span serving a benevolent master like herself.

The unlucky ones sold to cruel masters like Drakkon who abused them mercilessly, without remorse. Under his rule, all slaves eventually suffered hideous deaths. And by law, a master could do as he or she pleased with them. Thinking of Alexi, her heart nearly broke all over again.

The lesser creatures sold at a low price and became food, consumed and discarded. Harsh times, but that was the way of the world. Nothing wasted. The weak perish. The strong survive.

The thick crowd parted in deference to Raina's passage. Drawing her long cloak tightly around her shoulders, she ignored the whispers floating on her heels. She bit back a sigh of annoyance, reminding herself that glimpsing royalty among any of the species was considered a rare occurrence and cause for excitement. She'd never understood why.

Pushing to the front of the room, she located a perfect table at the edge of the stage. Unfortunately, it was situated next to Drakkon and his three unhappy sentinels, which explained the unusual vacancy. *Damnation.*

Resisting the urge to pinch her nose against the odor of his rotting, bloated carcass, she took her seat. Why didn't he assume one of his handsome forms, for pity's sake? Probably to frighten his potential competitors. The day one of Drakkon's warriors became powerful enough to oust the Demon King and take his throne, wild festivities would abound throughout the city. Cheered by this lovely idea, she chose to ignore him.

Tonight, however, the demon was having none of it. "Raina, my dear. What brings you out to play this night?"

She stiffened and looked him in the eye. That he'd addressed her as *my dear* rather than "my lady", "Highness", or another appropriate term would have been acceptable if he were a close friend. Coming from Drakkon, it was meant as public disrespect. She arched a brow, opting for a noncommittal reply.

"Drakkon."

"Come now," he laughed, causing all three of his chins to wobble. "Tell us what's behind this rumor that the Vampire Queen has been haunting every slave auction within five hundred miles these past few moons."

"What's with the rumors that you've been devouring your competition in the bidding arena? Sore loser?"

He sent her a sinister smile that didn't reach his dead, black eyes. Dirty, yellowed fangs split his gaping mouth. "Only the pesky shifters. I could think of a much more pleasurable punishment for you, Raina."

Ick. "I'd rather be eaten, but thanks anyway."

Anger darkened his ugly features. A stab of satisfaction zinged through her as she dismissed him, facing forward.

A voice over the loudspeaker announced the start of tonight's auction. The crowd quieted as the curtain began to slide open. A momentary pause as the room held its breath and then...a collective gasp of stunned appreciation.

The predictable jeers and rowdy merriment began, but Raina stared in mute awe, jaw hanging open. Blinking, she studied the gorgeous vision before them all. They were the two most beautifully formed males she'd ever seen, human or not. Naked, every inch of tanned, gleaming skin a feast for the senses. Strong thighs, ropy arms and deep, broad chests corded with muscle.

Her gaze strayed to the apex of their thighs. Both men were huge with arousal, their cocks thick and long, arching to kiss their six-pack abs. A pearly drop of pre-cum had seeped to the purple tip of each broad head, heavy balls taut, evidencing what must be true sexual agony. The fire in her sex grew worse, the knowledge that these men *would* be hers, no matter whom she had to battle, making her hopelessly wet.

Chained with their arms and legs spread wide, the position accented their sheer strength and perfection. And heightened everyone's awareness that these magnificent creatures would soon serve a lucky master's every desire. That they'd given themselves willingly to do so.

Last, she studied their faces. *Oh, my, yes!* The male on her left sported a head of shaggy brown-gold, sun-kissed hair brushing against his neck and falling into bright, glassy green eyes. His cheeks were lean, as though he'd lost a little weight. Sweat beaded on his face, and her preternatural hearing

17

discerned his wheezing breaths. With a start, she realized the man wasn't just aroused. He was very ill. But no matter. A few drops of her blood and this sexy male would be good as new in no time. And the other...

Every cell in her body stood at attention. Her nipples puckered against the filmy blouse under her cloak.

This male personified raw power and defiance. Quite a feat for a human. The proud tilt of his dark head, the leashed rage in his golden gaze, struck her like a million volts of electricity. He may as well have shouted *I will not be broken*, so clear was his arrogant challenge.

Intrigued, she studied him. If the human harbored strong animosity toward bondage, why had he cast his fate to the wind by placing himself upon the block, knowing full well that few of his prospective masters would show him any mercy? Indeed, what could've driven two impressive men to such dire straits?

"Don't even think about it, my dear," came Drakkon's gravelly voice. He smacked his ample lips. "These two will satisfy my appetites far better than your loyal companion ever managed. How *is* Alexi these days?"

Masking her anger, she flicked her cool gaze to his. "Fuck off, demon."

Drakkon's face colored purple with rage, but she focused her attention on the stage once more, ignoring him. She had the coin to outbid the demon, as well as the ancient power necessary to deflect any attempt at retribution on his part, and he knew it.

She lifted her chin and smiled.

The circular portion of the stage each slave stood upon began to rotate, pausing briefly at each quarter turn.

Left side view, emphasizing the firm, hard lines of their bodies. Straining, erect cocks and heavy balls.

Back side. Broad shoulders roped with even more muscle, trim waists. Chiseled buttocks. Powerful thighs.

Her attention scanned north again to the small tattoo each man sported in the center of his lower back. About three inches in length, the design boasted a dagger with an ornate handle, razor-sharp tip pointed downward.

Stunned, she gasped in sudden recognition. "Warriors of Exodus."

Another quarter turn, and the men faced front once more. The viewing had ended, and bidding would begin.

They were the fallen warriors of Exodus, the ones branded as traitors. What creature had not heard of their banishment? The implications left her mind reeling.

Exodus had been formed using the strongest among humans, vampires, demons and shapeshifters. The elite. A warrior's job entailed forcing all creatures, both fanged and furry, to play nice. Or else. They were respected, feared...and most of all, hated.

The lewd shouts and jeers directed at the pair on the block took on sinister new meaning. A great many in this crowd would covet the rare opportunity to enslave a fallen warrior, wield terrible power and control to beat down once proud men.

First in line, the Demon King who, according to hushed whispers, gleefully persuaded his fellow Council members to ban the pair in disgrace.

The auction master stepped onto the stage. Beside her, Drakkon chuckled with confidence, the stench of lust pouring off his putrid body. His sentinels glanced at the block and each other, sympathy for the humans etched on their faces.

She straightened, awaiting the signal to begin bidding. For the present, all thoughts of self-indulgent fun and games vanished. With an effort, she crushed the unfamiliar and unwelcome surge of apprehension.

Blazing Hades, she couldn't remember the last time she'd been truly afraid of anything, but knowing the horror these men would suffer in the wrong hands—especially Drakkon's—knifed her heart.

Raina looked to the beautiful raven-haired warrior, his head high, silently defying any creature in the room to conquer him. Compassion stirred in her breast, and fear unlike any she'd experienced in centuries.

Yes, many here tonight would pay dearly for the privilege of breaking these two. Damn the price and the consequences. She had never learned to be a good loser and she would not start now.

Even if she had to flash-fry Drakkon the Disgusting and send him to Hades.

Chapter Two

കാ

The shouting pounded Johan's brain until he thought his skull would explode. He could only imagine how poor Zane must feel.

Would this humiliation never end? Gritting his teeth, he glared at the crowd he couldn't see, blinded as he was by the flood of stage lights. He'd tried to keep his expression blank, but hiding the ferocity of his emotions wasn't one of his strengths. About as useless as attempting to douse the flames licking between his legs.

The viewing ended and the final leap into the unknown began. The jeers quieted and somehow, that frightened him more than any part of this wretched evening. It signaled the end of his and Zane's freedom, the beginning of a lifetime of servitude, perhaps under horrid conditions.

In spite of the carnival atmosphere, the sale of a soul was a serious event and silence afforded the remainder of the proceeding the grim reflection it deserved. Two great warriors were reduced to little better than vermin, a brutal reversal of fortune none present would wish upon themselves. Johan wanted to be sick.

Bidding began in the thousands, a paltry sum for even the lowliest slave, but rapidly climbed into the tens of thousands. When the price reached one hundred thousand, a murmur of discontent swelled in the room. All except the wealthiest patrons had been shut out of the running, which meant Drakkon was driving the price out of his competitors' range.

Johan dared a glance at Zane. His friend's head dipped, brown hair damp and curling, sweating body limp save the forced erection. *Damn you, hang on a bit longer.* Gods, if they didn't hurry—

"Two hundred fifty thousand for the pair."

Drakkon. So, he'd decided to end this farce. Who among these jackals had the balls to oppose him? Johan swallowed hard. The Demon King wouldn't kill them right away. No, he'd make sure they suffered for a long, long time.

A weighty pause.

"Going once," the announcer called. "Going twice…"

Gods, no.

"One million. *Each.*"

A shocked, collective gasp practically sucked the oxygen from the room. Heart thudding, he wondered who'd spoken. A female to be sure, her clear, firm bell tone ringing through the stunned crowd.

The announcer repeated his last call.

No one, not even Drakkon, had pockets deep enough to match such an outrageous bid. Johan marveled at her audacity, even as he gave dubious thanks to whatever star had guided her to Lash this night. This mystery woman had not only purchased two new slaves, she'd bought herself a dangerous enemy.

"Sold!" the man cried with no little enthusiasm. "The human males, Johan Stone and Zane Ramsey, to Her Highness, Queen Raina Zharov, for the sum of two million dollars!"

The audience sent up a roar of excitement.

"Holy shit," he breathed. The Vampire Queen. He racked his brain for information.

What did he know of Raina? Precious little, as their paths had never crossed socially—*yeah, right*—or on any official Exodus business, since she did not hold a seat on the Council. He did know she was an Ancient, and a filthy rich one. A regal, flame-haired, mouthwatering wet dream.

Along with the currently imprisoned Vampire King, Zoltan, she ruled all vampires with an iron will tempered with fairness. She and Zoltan were not mated, indeed had never been involved, if rumors were true. The King and Queen need not be mated to rule as the strongest male and female of their kind.

What else? Nothing, except some vague memory of a story he'd once heard involving the Queen treating herself to some sort of celebration every one hundred years. Useless trivia.

The curtains closed, shutting out the revelry. Pinky returned and began to release him from the manacles, but his mind continued to drift. He and Zane had dodged a bullet tonight in avoiding Drakkon's clutches, but to what end? He ought to be grateful, yet the cloying rage returned.

Bought and sold. A whore destined for better surroundings, but a whore nonetheless.

Freed of his shackles, he rubbed absently at his wrists. He watched Pinky unlock the restraints on Zane's ankles, trying to gain control of his roiling emotions before the Queen arrived to take them. She could kill them both at the first hint of insubordination, and be well within her right to do so. Losing her investment wouldn't deter an Ancient who'd dropped a cool two million with no more thought than purchasing a steak dinner.

He didn't give a damn about himself. Death would surely be preferable to whatever degradation lay in store. His friend, however, was in no condition to make such a choice. Leaving his boyhood companion alone was not an option, and never had been.

A sharp curse from Pinky snapped his attention to Zane lying crumpled at her feet, on his side. In four long strides, he crossed to his friend and rolled him gently onto his back. Zane's jade green eyes were half-open, glazed with fever.

Johan laid a palm on his burning forehead, pushed back his wet hair. "Hang on, buddy. Our new mistress will have you healed in no time, I promise." He prayed that wasn't a lie.

"Johan?" he rasped. "I'm sorry. If it wasn't...for me...we might have made it—"

"No! The blame is mine." Guilt rose, hot and bitter. "It was my decision to go against the Council without solid evidence of Zoltan's innocence. I should never have included you in my foolish actions."

"Stubborn..." Zane attempted a weak smile, but his eyes drifted closed. His labored breathing had grown much worse.

He looked around, his worry increasing. Blazing Hades, where was everyone? Pinky had disappeared, apparently unconcerned he would change his mind and try to escape. Where would he go, even if Zane weren't an issue? Nowhere. If either of them had family, anyone at all who gave a goddamn about their plight, he and Zane wouldn't have come here. They were all the family each other had.

A brilliant flare of blue light blinded him for a moment, startling him as it always did when a vampire or demon flashed into his presence. He hated the disorienting glow, for the simple reason that the dazzle temporarily stunned a warrior's defenses, rendering them vulnerable to the first strike in an attack.

But when the spots cleared from his vision, a tall, redheaded beauty was kneeling on the other side of Zane. *The Vampire Queen, come to collect her playthings.* He shoved aside the hateful thought. Her attention was focused on his friend, slim brow furrowed in concern. She reached from beneath her black cloak and brushed slender fingers against Zane's cheek.

Without saying a word, the Queen laid a palm flat on the center of his chest and grew very still, gazing at the spot as though pinpointing the sickness inside his friend's body. Elegant blood-red fingernails pressed into his chest, her paleness contrasting with his tanned skin. Power hummed around her, crackling like an electrical current barely leashed. The air seemed to breathe.

The examination—or whatever it was—lasted only a few seconds. Gently, Raina smoothed his friend's brow. The unexpected sight of her tenderness did something strange to Johan.

"The human is dying," she murmured.

Dying! His heart lurched into his throat. "Please, you've got to help—"

"Remove your hand from my arm."

Johan blinked. He certainly had her full attention now. She raised her head, jeweled eyes sparking cool cobalt fire in her angular face. Gods, he'd grabbed a royal! The Queen, and their mistress, no less. Slowly, he unwrapped his fingers from her wrist.

"Forgive me." The apology burned his tongue like acid. "I meant no disrespect. Zane is all I have left, and if I lose him..."

To his horror, his voice wavered and unshed tears burned his eyes. Warriors took their blows without flinching, meted out harsh justice to those most deserving. They did not fucking cry.

The Queen's face softened. "I won't allow your friend to die, warrior."

He cleared his throat. No matter her unsavory motivations, he couldn't allow stupid pride to jeopardize Zane's life. "I...thank you."

She nodded, glancing at his friend again. "We must hurry." Taking a deep breath, she yelled, "Alexi!"

Another blinding flash, and a lean, well-built young vampire stood at her side. He was stylishly dressed in dark pants and a fitted, long-sleeved black shirt that hugged his toned body. White-blond hair was pulled back into a chic ponytail, revealing expressive pale blue eyes set in an exotic face. He carried himself with an air of dignity and grace, and Johan was struck with the notion he might have been a prince in a past age.

Alexi's eyes widened at the tableau before him. "Yes, my lady? Do you need me to have George bring the limo around?"

"No, there's no time for a leisurely ride home. I've pissed off Drakkon."

Johan's brows lifted. Never had he heard a royal use the term *pissed off*. Not that he knew many royals.

The two vampires exchanged a knowing look. Alexi's face darkened. "I'll bolt George and the car home. Do you need help with the sick one?"

She shook her head. "I've got this under control. Meet me in my chambers after you prepare the adjoining guestrooms."

"As you wish." He bowed slightly, then vanished.

Johan stared at the spot where Alexi had been. St. Peter's balls, his life had become a fast trip into eternal hell.

Still kneeling, the Queen gathered his limp friend into her arms as though he weighed nothing. "Have you ever zone surfed before?"

"Once. It made me a little queasy." He didn't mind admitting it. *Zone surfing*, the layman's term for vampires and demons "bolting" instantly to another location, disagreed with most humans' systems. They simply weren't designed for warp speed, and required magical assistance to accomplish the task.

"Then you know the discomfort will pass rather quickly. Take your friend's hand."

He did, and not a moment too soon. An explosion of crimson light rocked the room an instant before Drakkon appeared only ten feet away. And he was, indeed, extremely pissed.

"Raina!" he roared, flying toward them. "You bitch, I'll—"

A deafening hum of electricity cut off the demon's tirade. Whirling blue light enveloped him with dizzying force. Zane's hand was gripped tightly in his, but he lost all sense of time and place. The vortex sucked at his body, threatening to turn him inside out.

Seconds later, he found himself deposited on the floor of a vast bedchamber, along with Zane and the Queen. Nausea from the bolting threatened to send up the laced wine, but he fought it down. Ironically, he was thankful he hadn't eaten in two days.

"Are you well, Johan?" Her Highness studied him in concern.

"I'm fine," he lied. "Where should I put Zane?"

"There, on my bed," she gestured, indicating the huge, four-poster bed gracing one wall. White, gauzy material flowed from the canopy and encircled the mattress, giving the Queen's place of rest—and sport—a seductive charm.

He scowled, lifted his friend into his arms and strode for the bed, glancing around. Never had he seen such a palace. His entire former apartment could've fit into Raina's bedchambers. A place he suspected he and Zane would come to know well, whether they wished it or not. The lava in his balls churned and his tormented penis twitched at the reminder.

Pushing the filmy material aside, he laid Zane on her bed carefully. His friend didn't stir. In fact, he'd become worse. His face was colorless, every breath a struggle. Johan's hands fisted at his side in impotent fury. Damn Drakkon and his corrupt cohorts on the Council. They'd pay for this!

Raina sat down beside Zane, waving him off. "He'll be all right, warrior. Go with Alexi. He'll get you settled while I attend to your friend."

Johan glanced across the room. The younger vampire stood in the doorway to an adjoining chamber, waiting. Well, he'd fucking wait. "No. I'll see Zane's improvement for myself."

Alexi's brows shot up. Raina pushed from the bed and slowly straightened to her full height, which put her looking

Johan in the eye. Her expression remained serene, deceptively so. Power crackled around her, evidencing her anger. Like a true royal, however, she'd assert control with cool, ruthless logic.

"Insubordination, after a mere five minutes in your Queen's presence? You are either remarkably brave or incredibly dim-witted."

Shit. He'd made a serious tactical error in the face of terribly one-sided odds. His jaw tightened. "Do to me what you will, but I won't leave him until I'm certain he'll be well."

Raina crossed her slender arms. "You will if I reduce you to a pile of ash, which I'm now within my right to do," she pointed out.

"Do it," he challenged. Cold fear gripped him, but he kept his face impassive.

"Or I could have you flogged until you can't stand, punished until you scream for mercy."

"I don't care."

Her cobalt eyes narrowed, and her lips turned up. "Oh, I think you do. Perhaps not for yourself, but your friend is another matter."

He swore, closing his eyes as she continued.

"Your love for Zane is your greatest weakness, which you revealed to me the moment we met. You are loyal to a fault and would do anything for a loved one, else you'd not be my slave now. No, death is too easy an out, and physical punishment would teach you nothing of submission."

He opened his eyes, dread balling in his gut. "My lady, I—"

"You have much to learn. And learn it you will. I'll have your word as a warrior, or I'll cast you out of the city this instant. You'll never again speak to your friend, never know of his fate. Or I can hand you over for Drakkon's pleasure and solve the problem I created for myself tonight."

"Raina," Alexi breathed in apparent shock, gripping the doorframe.

She held up a hand to silence her companion. "No. In my position, I can ill afford to suffer opposition from a human slave. Johan must stand by his decision and learn to serve me or leave his friend." She gave Johan a hard stare.

"And even now, your arrogance kills him as you waste precious minutes."

She wasn't bluffing. She could send him to Drakkon, where he had no doubt he'd learn the true meaning of hell. His gaze fell upon Zane, fighting to live. He knew, just as he had when they'd gone into Lash, there was no choice to be made. He sank to his knees before the Queen and bowed his head. Begging, with no shred of pride. This is what he'd come to.

"Please do not send me away," he choked. Misery tightened his throat. "I was a warrior, Majesty. I don't know how to submit, but I will try to learn."

A pause, then she touched his hair. "I believe you are being truthful." She cupped his chin, raising his eyes to hers.

"You have much to absorb in your new position, the first being how to survive in my household with your balls intact. One, do not dictate to me, ever again. You must respectfully ask permission to do everything except breathe. Two, you'll kneel in my presence when I enter the room. Three, you'll not offer an opinion unless I ask. I'm afraid these alone will provide a challenge for you, and there's much more. Are you ready?"

"Yes, my lady. May I please stay while you see to Zane?" The humble request seared his soul. He'd never bowed to anyone in his life.

"Rise, Johan. You may stay."

He pushed to his feet and she resumed her seat at Zane's side. Hovering at her elbow, he watched tensely as she tilted his friend's head back, exposing his throat. Next, she smoothed back his damp hair, murmuring soothing words. When she bent to his neck, fangs flashing, he panicked.

"What are you doing?" he snapped. She sat up, gave him a pointed glare. He changed his tone. "I'm sorry, this is all new. May I ask what you are doing?"

"Of course." She nodded. "I'm about to perform the blood exchange that will seal our bond as master and slave. I'll take a bit of his blood, then give him some of mine in return. In his case, my blood will cure his illness and bond him to me as well."

"He won't turn vampire?"

She forgave his natural curiosity. "No. In order to turn him or any human, I'd have to drain him to his death. When you go with Alexi, he'll explain to you how the blood bond works. I'll perform the exchange with you after I see Zane is resting comfortably."

Turning away, she focused her attention on Zane once more. He didn't interrupt again, but watched in fascination as she bent, flicking her pink tongue, licking the delicate skin of his neck. Her lips parted, sharp fangs emerging...and she sank them into his friend's throat.

Zane moaned in rapture, arching his back, eyes closed. His hips lifted, erection seeking, stabbing the air. She drank, her fiery hair spilling across his chest.

"Ohhh, yesss..." Almost immediately, Zane's cock began to pulse. Semen spewed onto his belly as he thrashed, helpless. At last he stilled, his member far from limp thanks to the drug they'd been given. Poor guy probably thought he was dreaming.

Johan's own erection was close to erupting. Gods, what torture. He'd seen vampires drink, but never like this. Never drinking from his friend, knowing he'd be next, knowing this decadent ritual meant a lifetime of being bound in sexual servitude. He panted, staving off an orgasm.

Raina released his friend, sat up and quickly slashed her wrist using her fangs. "Open your lips, Zane," she commanded, voice husky with desire. He complied, and she pressed her wrist to his mouth.

Zane's eyes opened, glazed and unseeing, and his body stiffened. He grabbed her arm and latched onto her wrist, pulling, sucking greedily. She allowed him a few draughts before denying him more.

"That's enough, Zane. Release me," she said softly, pulling her wrist away.

"No," he groaned, his dusky lashes sweeping down.

She smiled. "There will be more, I promise. Sleep, darling, and all will be well when you awaken."

Mesmerized, Johan almost believed her. She'd been so tender to Zane, yet harsh with him. He sighed. That had always been the way of things. Zane possessed a special charm he'd never been able to compete with, even when the little shit was unconscious.

"Johan, you will go with Alexi now. As you can see, your friend is already making a rapid recovery."

He studied Zane. It was true! Normal, healthy color had returned to his cheeks and his breathing came much easier. No raspy wheeze. The Queen could have let him die, especially after his impulsive rebellion. *He will live.* Gratitude nearly sent him to his knees again.

"I don't know how to thank you," he managed. "I have nothing to give in return for Zane's life, save my promise of loyalty to you."

"And that, warrior, is everything. I require nothing more. Alexi? Prepare our new slave."

Her companion, who'd been observing the drama, motioned for Johan to follow him. And this time, he proved himself capable of learning at least one of Raina's many lessons.

He kept his fucking mouth shut and left.

Chapter Three

ဢ

Johan trailed Alexi into the next room, where the vampire closed the door behind them. This bedchamber was as stylish as Raina's but not as vast. The furnishings were a masculine, dark mahogany rather than light and feminine like hers.

"You'll sleep here in the daytime," the vampire announced, turning to face him. He pointed to an entrance on the far wall. "Your friend's room connects with yours, through that door. At night, whenever the Queen does not require your presence, both of you are free to roam the palace and surrounding grounds, or retire to these chambers. Whichever you prefer."

Slaves who lived better than most highly paid gigolos. Fantastic. Yet he knew guys who'd give their left testicle to be in his position. He eyed the vampire.

"Would she really have sent me to Drakkon?"

"Raina was turned one thousand years ago. She's been Queen of the vampires for the past eight hundred. Tell me, do you honestly think she held the position for eight centuries by being a pushover?"

"Good point." He studied Alexi. The guy appeared to be several years younger than himself. "How old are you?"

The question provoked a small, sad smile. "Seventy-five in human years. Raina turned me when I was twenty-five."

"Yeah? Looking good for an old man."

Alexi laughed, the wistful expression vanishing. He didn't comment or offer to tell the story of how he came to be a vampire. Instead, he took a black velvet bag from the dresser, worked open the drawstring and removed several items.

"So, how does this blood bond stuff work?" Johan prodded, eyeing the strange contents. A sharp needle, two gold rings, a scrap of sheer black material, a bottle of oil…and a large marble phallus, carved to impeccable realism. Gods!

The young vampire picked up the needle and shrugged. "Simple. When any vampire takes a bit of a human's blood, then immediately allows the human to drink their mingled blood in return, an unbreakable bond is formed. The human slave is bound to his or her master until death…or for eternity, if the vampire chooses to turn the slave."

What in the hell was he planning to do with that needle? He shook his head. "Unbreakable, how?"

"Say you try to escape, a very foolish move. The blood bond won't allow you or Zane to travel more than a few miles from your mistress before you are compelled to return. You won't be able to help it. Nor will you and Zane be able to part from one another once Raina performs your bonding. Ever."

He blinked. "Because I'll have his blood flowing in my veins, too."

"Exactly."

"But he won't have *my* blood," Johan mused.

"Yes, he will. You see, after the bonding, the slave must partake of the master's blood each night. Tomorrow night, he'll receive your blood when he drinks from her, and the circle is complete. All the master really has to do in order to punish you for any infraction is withhold the blood reward from you. Believe me, the agony is excruciating—even deadly." He lifted a golden brow. "But the ecstasy of receiving it is without measure."

Despair swamped him. Raina truly had him and Zane by the balls. "We'll be no better than fucking addicts."

Alexi rolled his eyes and came to stand before him, gleaming little saber in hand. "Good grief. Even if she never turns you, as her human blood slave you'll live at least another one hundred and fifty years. You'll never be sick a day. That's the power of vampire blood."

One hundred and fifty years as a slave? This was supposed to comfort him? "What are you doing with that damned needle?"

"You'll see. Relax and close your eyes."

"No."

"Unless you'd like to tell Raina you've broken your word—"

Snarling a curse, he closed his eyes. The vampire laughed, and he felt warm breath blow across his left nipple. Stunned, he stood still as Alexi's tongue teased it, flicking, sending delicious impulses to every nerve ending. The nipple hardened to a taut peak. Stood out in even greater relief when the vampire pinched it to full attention. In horrified fascination, Johan realized his erection was pressed firmly against the telltale bulge in Alexi's black pants.

And the sensation, much to his shock, was far from unpleasant.

Pain seared his nipple, shattering the interlude. "Shit!"

"There we are," the vampire declared, triumphant.

Johan looked down at himself, and scowled. The smaller of the gold rings now adorned his pierced, throbbing tit. "That was damned sneaky."

"But effective. Now for the other."

The vampire turned and picked up the larger gold ring, and Johan took a step back. "Forget it. You're not getting away with that again."

"Oh, Raina has something quite different in mind for this one." He grinned. "Spread your legs."

"Wh-what? Why?"

"Come on, don't tell me a warrior such as yourself has led such a dreary, sheltered existence." Alexi closed the short distance between them, twirling the shiny object on one finger.

"It's a cock ring, a simple yet immensely pleasurable little device that is fitted—"

"I know what it is and what it does, damn you." And where it *goes*. Heat flooded his face. The helpless anger he'd been fighting for the past few days churned in his aching stomach. "Your Queen wants to debase and humiliate me, probably because I stood up to her. No. No fucking way."

The vampire's amusement fled, replaced by...what? Sorrow? Yes, that was it. The quiet reserve of before settled over his features again. A deep, dark sadness lurking in his pale blue eyes.

"You are wrong, human. Her Highness is not a cruel mistress. She is passionate and headstrong. Quick to anger, but compassionate. She's—"

"Great gods, someone hand me a tissue before I start bawling!" he laughed, the mocking sound bitter to his ears. "She's a slave owner, for pity's sake. What makes her so different from Drakkon?"

Alexi leveled him with an intense stare, filled with such pain that Johan sucked in a breath.

"Pray you never learn the answer to that question." He sighed, lowered his gaze. When his eyes met Johan's again, the serene mask had slipped back into place. The anguish buried. "Let's get on with this, shall we?"

The vampire knelt before him and looked up expectantly. Face burning, Johan spread his legs. "Why the fancy adornments?" he gritted.

Alexi's expression softened. "Sensuality is a revered skill, Johan. Lovemaking, a fine art that takes practice. I suppose a warrior such as yourself is used to satisfying his base needs without too much fuss or finesse."

"True enough. And I've never had any complaints," he felt compelled to add, his pride bruised.

"I'm sure you didn't," the vampire murmured with a small smile. "Now, relax."

Right. He'd been aroused to the point of severe pain for so long, his balls were turning purple. He didn't need a damned cock ring to prolong the agony. Was Raina trying to kill him?

No. Just asserting her authority—and reminding him of his place.

Alexi's nimble fingers brushed against his groin, and the electric jolt nearly blew off the top of his head. Though the effort cost him, he held steady, clenching his teeth. The cool metal ring slid down his erection. Warmed instantly in response to his heat.

"How will that fit around me?" he rasped, looking down. "It isn't big enough to—to—"

"Magic," Alexi grinned. "Watch."

The vampire cradled Johan's aching sac in one hand. Before Johan's astonished gaze, the metal stretched to accommodate his large package. Alexi eased the ring over his balls and the base of his cock. Then the metal tightened, shrank, pushing his balls and penis forward. Squeezing deliciously.

Johan's knees threatened to give out.

"Gods!"

"Feels wonderful, doesn't it?"

He ignored the smug pleasure in the vampire's voice. "How often will I have to wear this thing?"

"You may remove it when you sleep. Otherwise..." The vampire shrugged, rising to his feet.

Johan screwed his eyes shut, clenched his fists. He'd be expected to suffer complete sexual torment every waking hour. Ready for whatever escapade the Queen desired. When he opened them again, Alexi had the black scrap of material in hand.

The young vampire held the thing up, stretching it out to reveal...underwear? No, this tiny triangle could not hope to cover even the barest essentials. Alexi ran his hand inside the crotch, wiggling his fingers, then flipped it around for the back view. Enjoying the hell out of this.

To his mortification, the crotch was made of sheer, see-though gauzy stuff. The back, a string. Nothing more.

"What is that?" Dumb question. He'd seen a g-string before.

"Your uniform."

"You can't be serious!" he croaked.

"In the top dresser drawer, you have them in almost every color," Alexi went on, unruffled. "Her favorite is black, of course."

He sat hard on his new bed, feeling like he'd been gutted by a hand blade. In fact, disembowelment would've been kinder.

The vampire tossed the "uniform" at him. "It's not so bad. You learn to love the sensual freedom of your body."

He crumpled the filmy thing in one fist. Freedom in enslavement? What an odd viewpoint. "*You're* clothed."

"I'm not a slave," Alexi replied gently. "The sooner you stop fighting the inevitable, the more content you'll become. You and your friend are here for Raina's pleasure."

Impotent fury clogged his throat. Despair. He'd never cease fighting her seductive lure. Would not allow himself to enjoy whatever she did to him and Zane.

But recalling how his friend had writhed in ecstasy at her slightest touch, how the she-devil had milked his straining cock simply by drinking from him, he knew himself for a liar. This was one battle a simple warrior had no idea how to win.

"My companion is right."

Raina glided into the room wearing a short black dressing robe. The silk clung to her tall, lithe body, teased her taut nipples. The robe hit mid-thigh, revealing mile-long, toned legs, slender calves. Peaches and cream skin he'd love to —

She arched a brow. Belatedly, Johan remembered to kneel. He slid off the edge of the bed to his knees, shifting them slightly apart, keeping his hands at his sides. Lowering his head, he tried to blank his mind. To think about anything other than what was about to happen. About his body spread naked and vulnerable to her wishes. He stifled a groan.

She touched his hair, running slender fingers though the strands. "Rise, Johan, and lie down on the bed where you'll be more comfortable. Alexi, you will witness the bonding."

With a nod, the young vampire retired to large, overstuffed chair nearby and flopped into it. Biting back a sarcastic retort, Johan did as told, settling himself in the center of the huge bed. She moved to his side with feline grace, sank onto the mattress beside him.

He hated how his body hummed with anticipation. She leaned over him, burnished hair cascading around her shoulders. Reached out to caress his cheek, then tilted back his head, exposing his throat. Her gaze held his for a moment, gone red with hunger.

A flash of her sharp fangs sped his pulse, and she bent, tongue swirling against the delicate, vulnerable skin. He shivered. She laughed softly.

And sank her long canines deep into his throat.

He gasped, but the lance of pain was brief, quickly drowned in a tide of warmth. The warmth became heat that spread to his heart. Between his legs. *Good, so good.* Her mouth pulled, sucking, stealing his essence. Taking his life. Delicious.

Dark and wicked. *Can't fight it. Don't want to.*

The heat burst into flame and he moaned, arching his hips. *Ohh, yes. Take it all...drain me.* Had he whispered that aloud?

The release he'd been denied all evening boiled, gathered for the coming storm. She continued to suck, the rhythm stroking his cock as surely as a hand. His balls tightened, and his release exploded, his cock pulsing on and on. Helpless, he could do nothing but ride the waves of ecstasy. Distantly, he wondered whether Zane had felt this forbidden joy, too.

"Yes...gods, yes..."

She pulled away at last, her lips crimson with his blood. For some reason, that didn't repulse him as he knew it should. Out of morbid curiosity, he tried to lift a hand to touch her mouth, but his arm was leaden.

Alexi's concerned voice drifted from the corner. "Raina..."

"Easy, warrior," she murmured, a frown of worry marring her lovely brow. "I got a bit carried away. Let my blood fortify you and complete the bond."

She slashed her wrist with one sharp fang. Through a haze, he watched as she held the wound to his lips like she'd done with Zane. Her delectable honey-almond fragrance filled his senses, darkly sweet, like amaretto. Droplets fell onto his tongue, so good. He swallowed and—

Unbelievable fire. Rocketing to his limbs, searing every nerve ending. Five shots of whiskey in one draught, making him drunk and lusty for more. Fastening his mouth to her wrist, he suckled like a babe at his mother's breast. Swallowing all he could, until she finally pulled her wrist from him.

"No, please." Was that his voice, so filled with sorrow at being denied more?

She smiled down at him. "That's enough for now. Do you feel the bond growing?"

He blinked, concentrating. Did he feel different? Yes, there it was. A golden light moving through his body, under his skin. An unholy glow demanding to be fed, stretching an invisible cord between them.

"Yes. It's like a living thing inside me. Why?" he choked in misery. "Why have you done this to me? I gave my oath of loyalty to you, and I'd never go back on my word, bond or not."

She tilted her head, eyeing him. "So you say, exiled warrior of Exodus. Accused traitor, banished to the streets."

In spite of himself, he blanched at the pain that scored his soul. "I fought for what I believed in, and so did Zane. And I'm not giving up on proving Zoltan's innocence of the killings. He's the Vampire King, your ruling counterpart, for pity's sake. Don't you believe he was set up, as we were?"

For a long moment, she was silent. "Rest," she commanded, giving away nothing. Soft fingers smoothed his brow. "Tomorrow evening we begin your training in earnest."

Whether she'd compelled him to sleep or he simply gave in to exhaustion, he didn't know. Nor did he care. Trying to survive for weeks while taking care of Zane had exacted a heavy toll. And to have their struggles come to this? He wanted to sleep for a day. No, forever.

Because tomorrow evening, if not sooner, he'd awaken as a blood slave.

Once, he'd been a great warrior. Now Raina, the Vampire Queen, would be his conqueror. Mind, body and soul.

Better to die with honor, a hand blade shoved into my heart.

On that unhappy note, he sank into blessed darkness.

Chapter Four

ဢ

I'm not dead.

That amazing knowledge resounded through Zane's head as he opened his eyes. The second fact to penetrate his brain was that he felt...good. No, *great*. Better than he had in weeks. Years.

What magic was this? He'd been certain death awaited his next sigh, and then...what?

A woman. He remembered a stunning vision with dark red hair, talking to him. Soothing his fears. Biting him, bringing him untold ecstasy. Or had his fevered, dying mind conjured the whole glorious episode?

Becoming aware of his surroundings, he blinked in confusion. Saint Peter's balls, where was he? He was lying on his back in a massive, comfortable four-poster bed draped with gauzy netting. The sheer panels of material inhibited his view, so he sat up, letting the sheet fall to his naked hips, and pushed one panel aside.

Great gods. He'd never seen such a room. The vast feminine chamber was fit for a sultan's palace. Soft and cool. Beauty and light. A refuge for the world-weary soul. Not a place of evil if looks were any indication. Which they typically weren't.

Cautious, he reached out with his mind, probing his surroundings. Utilizing the ability Johan had jokingly called *The Probe* since they were kids, a dubious gift no one else knew about. Not even the Council, because too many beings with too much information could become a dangerous thing. And considering how badly their tenure with Exodus had ended, thank the gods he and Johan kept the secret between them.

Zane detected no trace of evil here. No black stain of malice, no danger. Though this relieved him, worry for his oldest friend ate at him. Johan was nearby, he knew. He felt the man's presence, but couldn't connect with his mind. Johan must be unconscious, yet was alive and well.

Now what? He recalled standing in Lash upon the slave block, so sick and weak he could barely stand. Since he'd awakened healthy and whole, he must be in his new master's bedchamber. A slave. And a pampered one at that. No cold dungeons or hungry rats here, boys and girls. The idea was too odd — and yes, dammit, welcome — to wrap his mind around at the moment.

A strange itch seemed to crawl under his skin. Well, not an itch, exactly. More like a living thing flowing in his blood. Electrifying his body like a thousand miniscule points of wonderful light, pulsing. Craving. Almost an entity of its own, demanding to be fed. *Fed*? How, and with what?

Shaking his head, he peered down at himself, and stilled. "Sweet Virgin," he breathed.

His left nipple had been pierced and decorated with a thin gold loop. A symbol of ownership and his servitude. No doubt Johan would be enraged at the trappings of submission. For his part, Zane couldn't help being intrigued. Curious.

A strange pressure surrounding his aching balls crept into his awareness as well. Flinging back the sheet, he stared between his legs in astonishment.

His groin had been shaved smooth as a baby's bottom, a cock ring gracing his shaft and sac. He didn't know which was more alarming, the sight of his naked balls, devoid of the soft, golden-brown pubic hair...or the fact that someone had done this while he'd lain unconscious and vulnerable.

The gold metal device squeezed his shaft and balls, thrusting them eagerly forward, emphasizing his impressive size. Keeping him semi-erect, ready to pleasure and be pleasured. His cheeks heated in embarrassment. Seemed their new master had been quite busy during their slumber.

"Don't worry, you'll get used to it."

Zane jerked his startled gaze up to find a tall, beautiful redhead crossing the room toward him. The woman's knee-length dressing robe of midnight blue emphasized her lithe, graceful movements. The part of the robe revealed a hint of full, pale breasts. Her calves were long and toned. Careful not to alert the newcomer, Zane reached out with his senses. Not a human woman. *A vampire.*

Zane sighed. "And if I don't *want* to get used to it?" Too late, he realized the impertinence of the question, coming from a slave. Now that his rank was only slightly above that of an earthworm, he could earn severe punishment for speaking to anyone in a flippant tone, especially his mistress.

Gods, was this regal creature his new owner? The uncertainty of his new situation crashed in, and he felt the blood drain from his face.

But instead of becoming angry, the vampire smiled. Gods, what a gorgeous creature, unnaturally so. Long hair of deep coppery red framed her oval face and tumbled unbound halfway down her back in an unruly waterfall. Fathomless cobalt eyes regarded him with warmth and a bit of mischief. The vamp couldn't have been more than twenty-five when turned, but held herself erect with the maturity and grace of a queen.

"I *am* a queen," the vampire revealed, her bright smile widening at Zane's start of surprise. She pushed the netting aside and sat on the bed.

Zane eyed her, wary. "You read my thoughts."

"Easily enough, though that was rude of me, wasn't it?" The humor sparkling in her eyes belied any real apology. "I do have some manners, however. I'm Raina, and you may address me as such when we are alone. In the presence of guests, you must call me 'Highness' or 'my lady' in deference to our positions."

Zane blinked, scrambling to form an intelligent response. Raina, the legendary Vampire Queen, was the fiery beauty sitting next to him. The one who'd saved his life. Unbelievable.

"I wasn't dreaming. You bit me, and I drank from your wrist," Zane murmured.

Raina's smile gentled, her expression soft with compassion. "Yes, you are bound to me, as is your friend. Do you understand what that means?"

Eternity. He swallowed hard. "I've heard the stories, secondhand."

"And I suspect they're true, for the most part. Fortunately, you and Johan will find me to be a fair mistress. I have never mistreated those in my service, and never will." The flicker of mischief returned. "Unless, of course, you *wish* to be on the receiving end of my flogger. That is another matter altogether."

The vampire's sly reference to bondage caused Zane's cock to twitch, and did nothing to relieve his earlier embarrassment. Without a clue what to say, he changed the subject. "Where's Johan? Is he well?"

"Your friend is resting in his quarters, and he's fine. The events of last night took a toll on him, given all the two of you have been through. Now that the sun has set, he will awaken soon."

Thank the gods. "When will I see him?"

"Shortly, I promise. For the moment, you're stuck with me." Concern furrowed her lovely brow. "How are you feeling now? Are you well?"

Studying the ethereal creature, he digested this. *Stuck with* wasn't the term he'd have used, and he wasn't as bothered by the idea of being her slave as he would've thought. She seemed kindhearted, for a royal.

"I am, thanks to you. Though a simple thanks hardly seems appropriate. I could've died of pneumonia, or worse, ended up in Drakkon's clutches. I was sick, but I remember that much."

"Oh, don't sing my praises just yet. My motivations aren't completely altruistic, Zane," she laughed, low and seductive. "Perhaps I received the better bargain...or maybe we'll all benefit. Come, sit with your back to me."

"What are you—" He squelched the protest burning his tongue and did as told, imagining a wall around his thoughts. Seemed like Raina was among the rare few able to read them. Wouldn't do any good to take a chance of the vamp learning he held the same gifts, perhaps to a greater degree. And he knew better than to provoke the anger of the Queen by refusing her.

A warrior no longer, but a possession.

Saints help him, he wasn't sure he minded.

Raina's nipples brushed against Zane's naked back through the silk robe, two little points of delight, making him shiver. Hot breath tickled the bend of his neck and shoulder. Gods, she smelled so damned good, like almonds and honey. Did she taste dark and sweet as amaretto?

"You were a seasoned fighter, a man to be reckoned with. But to me, you are an innocent, handsome and ripe for picking. I am very much going to enjoy my part in your education."

Slender fingers buried themselves in Zane's hair, tilting back his head until he was leaning fully into her soft curves, back to front. Excitement laced with fear caused him to tremble.

"Yes, Zane, relax into me. Just like that. Do not be afraid."

Lean into me. I won't hurt you.

Raina's smooth voice spoke in his head, compelling him, taking the edge off his fear. His muscles went liquid as the vampire's hands encircled him, skimming his chest and flat stomach. Grazed his ribs to his hips. Caressing. One hand slid between his thighs, her warm palm gripping his hardening cock.

Zane sucked in a breath, but made no attempt to escape her hold. "What are you doing?" Stupid question, idiot.

"Beginning your teachings, love. Just because you are my slave doesn't mean you can't enjoy my feedings."

"Please, I..." The vampire's skillful fingers stroked his turgid erection, cutting off his thoughts. Blowing reason to bits, seducing him.

"Am I hurting you?"

"N-no." Except his heart, pounding painfully in his breast.

"Then tell me how this feels," Raina demanded in a soft whisper.

His throbbing length filled his mistress's hand, aching for more. The grip around his cock tightened deliciously, almost to the point of pain. Pumping up to the leaking tip, then down again, to his tight balls. The opposing pressure created by the cock ring nearly made him explode. "Good...s-so fucking good."

A woman—no, a female vampire—was touching him intimately. Arousing him beyond reason. *And I want her to do me.*

Stunning, but true. As a warrior, he'd always been careful to avoid falling under the spell of vampires and demons. All highly sexual creatures, all dangerous. Now those reasons for caution no longer existed. He was under the total control of a seductive creature that could kill him. Make him come, begging for more even as he died. And he didn't care.

Raina's hot, wet tongue traced his jugular. "Sweet slave, you are mine."

He closed his eyes, shivering. "Yes."

"Easy," she soothed, stroking his hair. "This will only hurt for a moment. Just a taste, love."

With that, razor-sharp fangs tore into his throat, burying deep. His heart clenched, seized by a giant fist, twisting. Zane cried out in agony, tried to struggle free, but was held fast. Raina's mind touched his, abating the terror.

Don't fight. Feel your blood flowing into me. You are Chosen, and you give me life.

Chosen? The term carried serious meaning he couldn't puzzle out right now. The fist twisting his heart loosed, and the beat settled into a slow rhythm. The sensual pull of the vampire's mouth at his throat, drinking his lifeblood, seemed…right. As did the expert touch between his legs, rousing him to insanity.

"Ohh, gods…don't stop. Please, whatever you need."

She lapped at his neck in time to his heartbeat. Taking more and more, devouring his soul. The flames licking his cock become unbearable. Fire, in his gut, his balls. Searing him like the center of the sun…boiling hotter…

"Yes, yes! I can't stop—" His ass lifted off the bed, hips bucking as Raina moaned her approval. Hot ejaculate rocketed from his balls, spilling over the sheets, her hand. Pulsing until he'd been wrung dry and lay panting, his head resting on the vampire's shoulder.

Reason returned with cruel swiftness. For a few moments, he'd become a mindless toy in the hands of a dangerous female. Fallen prey to her allure, willing to do whatever she desired. And yes, oh gods, he already craved that wicked feeling again. The overwhelming need to be…did he dare admit it?

The desire to be dominated.

A groan of despair escaped him. What did that say about his true, hidden nature? How could he have been so weak at the core and not known it?

He closed his eyes, deeply ashamed.

Raina withdrew her fangs, whispered in his ear. "No, do not. I selected you and Johan for your strength and courage.

You will need to employ both to come to terms with your destiny, I think."

"Stay out of my head," he snapped, forgetting his place. He pushed out of the vampire's arms to stand beside the bed and glared down at the beautiful creature, who arched a serene brow.

Raina stood, somehow managing to look down her nose at Zane though he topped her by inches. She reached out, cupped her slave's cheek. "Oh, I'm going to delve into much more than your mind, dear man. Now, go to the kitchen while I see about Johan. Hope, my housekeeper, will make you something to eat. You'll want to keep your strength up, handsome."

She smiled, the teasing statement carrying an undertone of steel, belying her angelic face. Her cobalt eyes radiated a quiet strength, an iron will Zane couldn't fight. Caught in that magnetic gaze, he was powerless to look away. Felt himself drowning in their depths.

The sensation lingered as Raina turned and strode from her chambers toward a connecting room he presumed to be Johan's. Incredulous at the entire situation and his lack of resistance, he swiped a hand down his face. Wherever the seductive vamp planned to lead him and Johan, he had no doubt about one thing.

His training as a slave had begun.

And he wished with all his soul that the idea didn't make his cock lift in anticipation.

* * * * *

Propped on one elbow, Raina stretched on her side and watched in unguarded fascination as the human slumbered on.

Johan Stone. A man among men. Every bit as sexy as the dear, sunny Zane, but his polar opposite in personality. Johan was proud, tough. Unyielding.

Right now he appeared vulnerable as a boy, sensual lips parted in sleep. Thick black lashes such as she'd never seen on any male curled against darkened cheeks hollowed by fatigue and weeks of hunger. Midnight hair tumbled around his shoulders and into his eyes. Unable to resist, she brushed the stray lock from his face.

"Like spun silk," she murmured, rolling the strands between her thumb and forefinger. "My, what a lovely man you are."

But not too pretty. A prime example of his species, Johan oozed raw masculinity. No doubt he'd vanquished many a foe and enjoyed more than his share of willing sexual partners. The man possessed a raw, untamed quality about him. A proud spirit she must be careful not to break.

And as Vampire Queen, she could break him if she desired, in spite of all that marvelous strength. Physically. Mentally. That was her right. Even so, the idea of Johan—or his handsome friend, for that matter—being harmed in any way made the ancient feral bitch inside her growl in warning. No, she wasn't anything like the foul Drakkon, and her virile young slaves would not come to harm. Ever.

Zane's gentle spirit and innate, untapped sensuality had surprised and pleased her. A wellspring of suppressed, dark secret desires, ready to overflow. He'd prove a most willing pupil, that one. In contrast, she'd very much relish the challenge of bending Johan's steely will to hers. Forging his fire into something new and more accomplished in the erotic arts than he'd ever dreamed possible. Fascinating, delicious pair.

Beside her, Johan stirred and stretched with a groan. Much like a big jungle cat awakening from his nap, replete. The fringe of his lashes fluttered, swept upward, and striking golden eyes heavy with sleep blinked at her.

A sleepy half-smile curved his sensual lips, and a low rumble of satisfaction purred in his chest. "Mmm, baby, again? You wear me out…"

In an instant, he'd rolled, pinned her with his big body, hard muscle and solid strength surrounding her.

Pushing against his shoulders, she let out a squeak of surprise. "Johan—"

Long, tapered fingers buried themselves in her hair as he dipped his head and captured her mouth with his. Whatever protest she'd been about to make drowned in the heat of his tongue, sweeping past the seam of her lips, tasting. Reason incinerated in a ball of flame as he seated himself between her thighs, cock hard as an iron spike.

Johan groaned, began to grind his hips. The impressive length of him rubbed against the slickened folds of her sex, her clit, sending wonderful little waves of pleasure whirling to every nerve ending. The broad head of his shaft probed her entrance, seeking sanctuary as he kissed her deeply, their bodies all but joined as one.

When had she stopped pushing him away, twined her arms around his strong neck? Great gods, she wanted this man to take her in the dirt like a conquering barbarian of ages past. Fuck her as though his very life depended on it.

Ah, who is the master and who is the slave, Highness?

Tearing her mouth from his, she began shoving in earnest. "Get off me!"

"What?" He froze and lifted his head, staring down at her, dazed.

Angry with herself, she used the preternatural strength that seemed to have deserted her before, and tossed him aside. "What willing female did you imagine was underneath you, warrior?"

Beside her, Johan sat up and scrubbed a hand down his face. "What in Blazing Hades…"

Her face heating, Raina gripped the sheets to keep from ripping out his throat. "Rolling over for a nice morning fuck with the first warm body you encounter? How charming."

His gaze snapped to hers, confusion and lust morphing to abject humiliation. The blood drained from his cheeks and he looked away, a muscle jumping in his jaw.

"My lady," he said hoarsely, frustration creeping into his tone. "I didn't mean to offend you. What is the protocol now? Do I kneel at your feet? Beg your exalted forgiveness?"

"Lie back on the pillows and lose the attitude, unless you'd like your punishment to be more severe than I'd planned."

Helpless anger darkened his eyes. He opened his mouth, but obviously thought the better of provoking her and closed it. Why that should bother her, she couldn't fathom, but he complied without a word. He settled on the pillows, his mounting rage a palpable, living thing, throwing off such blistering heat that had he been a vamp or demon, he could've fried her on the spot with no effort.

"Grab the headboard behind you." He did, hooking his fingers backward over the top, the position emphasizing his ripped biceps, shoulders and chest. "Good. Now spread your legs."

His knees fell open, and she resisted the impulse to suck in an appreciative breath. The man was absolutely stunning. Tousled black hair framed a gorgeous, angular face. His long, thick cock, nestled in a light dusting of dark curls, lay hard against a ropy thigh. Smooth, heavy balls accented nicely by the cock ring rested between sculpted legs that stretched forever. A heart-stopping, mouthwatering bad boy ready to be gobbled up.

"Like what you see, Highness?" His expression darkened, glittering with an emotion far more dangerous than rage.

Gods, yes. Chilled, she schooled her features to reveal nothing. "You'll do."

On hands and knees, she crawled between his spread thighs, allowing a ghost of a smile to play on her lips.

"What are—"

"You are not permitted to speak," she purred. "In fact, you must not make even the slightest sound, no matter what I do to your delectable body. Nod your understanding, slave."

At her deliberate reminder of his lowly position, Johan's mouth flattened into a grim line. His amber gaze sizzled as he inclined his head, the desire to snap her slender neck telegraphed from their depths.

If armed with his warrior's weapons to even the odds, this man would lop off her head without thought or remorse. Somehow, that knowledge only served to make the fire between her legs stoke higher and caused her nipples to pucker against the silken robe.

A good fifty years had dragged by since she'd enjoyed so much as an invigorating skirmish—wresting Alexi from Drakkon had amounted to mere child's play—and damned if she wasn't spoiling for a challenge.

"Excellent." Kneeling, she let her breath tickle his groin, a cascade of deep red tresses trailing over his lap. "No sound, no movement…and you may *not* come."

In spite of her warning, Raina half expected a sharp retort. But he held still as she cradled his heavy sac in her fingers. Squeezed and caressed the velvety orbs, marveling at their tremendous size.

Experimentally, she flicked the delicate skin with her tongue, loving the dark flavor of salt and man. "Mmm, yes."

She laved the sac in slow, torturous circles, working behind his balls and up to the base of his cock. Down again, licking, sucking. They tightened in response and his breathing quickened, but he uttered no sound.

How long until Johan broke?

He remained silent, even when she suckled him, rolling his balls in her mouth all the way to the gold ring, pulling harder. But he wasn't unaffected. A peek at the sheen of sweat forming on his face and chest revealed the truth. He was fighting damned hard to obey her command.

Her tongue blazed a hot, wet path the length of his shaft to the broad, purple head. Beautiful. How many had known the decadent pleasure of him?

She took him between her lips, sheathing him deeper, deeper, until his cock was stuffed down her throat. A lovely skill, and one she excelled at, if Alexi's fervent praise upon occasion was any indication. Johan's body tensed as he sucked in a lungful of air. Oh-so slowly, she slid upward to the tip, keeping the pressure on, then down again. Fucking him with her mouth. Driving him insane.

Rivulets of sweat trickled down his cheeks. His eyes were closed, his chest heaving with the effort to stave off an orgasm. Releasing the turgid erection, she stroked the length of him with her fingers, then kneaded his balls.

"Look at me, slave," she ordered, her voice warm and husky.

His eyes opened, their golden depths no longer defiant, but glazed and desperate with lust. Pleading in silence as he stared at her.

One slender finger traced the vulnerable skin of his groin at the base of his cock. "Do you know what I'm going to do, just here?"

Johan started to shake his head, then stopped, eyes rounding in comprehension. His lips opened. Closed.

"Shh, love. My earlier taste of your friend only served to whet my appetite. Quiet, and do not come or the penalty will be quite severe."

Okay, she'd embellished the part about a penalty, but from the anguished look on his handsome face, he believed her. She shook off an unwelcome stab of sympathy and smiled, giving her blood slave the full effect of sharp, hungry fangs.

Licked the throbbing artery, anticipated the blood urging her to satisfy the gnawing in her stomach.

And sank her canines to the hilt.

Johan stiffened as though shot, panting. Hot, sweet liquid flowed over her tongue. Flooded her mouth, her senses. She pulled, sucking harder. Taking more and more.

Mine.

Lost in ecstasy, she drank until sated, renewed. Withdrawing, she glanced at his face, and recoiled in fear.

His cheeks were parchment white under the dark stubble of his beard, and his head lolled to one side, eyes wide.

"Johan!" Wheezing breaths rattled from his chest, and he appeared about two seconds from a stroke. *Oh, gods!* She scrambled to his side and grabbed his face in both hands, forcing him to look at her. "Johan?"

Quickly, she tore her wrist with one fang and placed it to his lips. It was too soon for his nightly blood reward, but a few drops would help restore him from her stupidity. How could she have been so selfish to take blood from an already weakened human?

After a few sips, Johan turned his face away, refusing more. His expression belied misery, and no little contempt. For her, or himself?

"Are you all right?"

Staring at the far wall, he hesitated, then nodded.

"How long since you've eaten? And do not think to lie to me," she demanded.

"Three days," he croaked. "Before that, I'm not sure."

Shame suffused her, unfamiliar, bitter to the taste. This man had been through hell these past weeks, and she'd almost killed him for his trouble.

"Can you manage a shower, or shall I fetch Alexi?"

"I don't need anyone's help."

The spark of anger returned, and she could've wept with relief. "Fine. Shower, put on your uniform, then go to the kitchen and Hope will have a meal waiting for you. Zane's there now. After you've eaten, you'll both see me back here."

"As you wish, my *lady*." A hint of sarcasm. He waved a hand at his rampant cock. "And this?"

Fingers trembling, she licked the wound on her wrist to seal it, and dabbed his blood from her lips. "Your erection is bespelled to remain intact until I decide you've earned release. Next time you use that gorgeous cock, you'll do so at my leave. And you'll be *awake* to know who's on the receiving end. Got that?"

Sitting up, he leveled her with that blazing stare. Oh, he was pissed.

Oppose me, damn you!

"You betcha…Highness."

With a last, scathing look, he left the bed and headed for the bathroom. She expected a loud slam, but he surprised her again by closing the door behind him with a soft click.

The thrill of power she'd expected from besting him didn't materialize. Dammit to hell and back, she was *disappointed* that Johan had submitted to her will, and passed her test. *How screwed up is that? What's wrong with me?*

The truth hit her like a bolt from the heavens, driving the air from her lungs.

Johan had been a Warrior of Exodus. A skilled, respected champion touted for his iron control in any situation. *Johan*, not her, won the battle between them just now by drawing on his expertise to beat her at her own game.

Johan Stone was a stubborn man willing to do anything, even die, to match her every demand. To prove his mistress could ask nothing he wasn't capable of handling.

To prove he would not be broken, just as she'd witnessed when he'd glared in bold defiance over the crowd at Lash.

Because somehow he knew, damn him to Hades, that his Queen longed to bring him to his knees.

Yes, the sexy slave had one up on his master.

Again.

Chapter Five

∞

"Infuriating, bloodsucking bitch!"

Johan stalked into the shower and slammed the glass door, wrenching on the faucet. She could probably hear every word, but he didn't give a goddamn.

Not even the nastiest demon had ever spoken to him— *treated* him—like a junkyard dog and lived to regret it, much less a high-and-mighty, arrogant slip of a female vampire.

"You'll be *awake* to know who you're fucking," he mocked in a falsetto voice, grabbing the shampoo.

It had taken all of the control he possessed in every molecule of his body not to snatch the evil seductress, throw her onto her back and pound his cock into her sweet pussy until she screamed his name.

And afterward, she would've executed him.

By the gods, the pleasure would've been worth the price.

He'd vowed to remain strong. Unmoved by her manipulations. How long could he last? In all honesty, he doubted his ability to endure this sort of mind game for one more day, much less another century or so.

As he soaped and rinsed, the red rage quieted to helpless anger, giving him a measure of relief. Room to breathe. But not much.

Be fair, Johan. He and Zane would be living in hell as Drakkon's sex slaves right now, if not for Raina. The Demon King would've taken great joy in healing Zane's sickness for the depraved purpose of killing him slowly. Raping not just his friend's body, but his mind.

Drakkon eventually killed all his sex slaves, without exception. For his part, Johan didn't much care. Death was freedom from bondage...even the kind that came with prettier trappings.

To see Zane happy, however, he'd endure anything. If he gave up, his best friend would be left alone in a strange place, in a difficult new existence. He'd probably blame himself, and that was unacceptable. Nor had Johan once taken the coward's way out in the face of battle.

Which left him enslaved, sorely pissed and beset with a raging erection. Damned insufferable witch! No telling how many handy little parlor tricks an Ancient like Raina had in her collection.

He turned off the shower and stepped out, using a fluffy towel from the nearby rack to dry himself. Scowling down at his poor cock, he considered taking the matter in hand and attempting to thwart Raina's spell. No, he'd only succeed in making the problem worse. She'd probably bespelled it to fall off.

Tossing the towel aside, he strode into his bedroom and headed for the dresser. A quick investigation of the lower drawers revealed a supply of new jeans and shirts, silk boxers and socks. The sight of something as mundane as clothing from his old life tightened his throat with gratitude, although he supposed he was only allowed to wear them with Raina's permission. Next to the dresser, a pair of supple, black leather boots awaited his next outing. Whenever the hell that might be.

With a sigh of resignation, he yanked open the top drawer and picked out one of the black g-strings. He lifted the wretched thing with one finger, regarding it like a poisonous snake. Might as well get it over with. Defying her by wearing the jeans crossed his mind, but she was probably dying for him to give her an excuse to extend his punishment.

Wrestling the elastic, he positioned the thin string in the back, crotch in the front. Slid them on. The string burrowed up his ass, digging in like a crazed piranha. He'd heard women refer to thongs as *butt floss*. Now he knew why.

Turning, he faced the dresser mirror.

"Son of a *bitch*."

He looked abso-fucking-lutely ridiculous.

The tiny, filmy triangle did nothing to hide his crotch. The head of his stiff cock peeked over the top a good three inches, and every detail of his package was clearly visible through the material. Even if he weren't erect, the household would see all.

He reached to rip off the offending garment.

His hand stayed on the elastic band at his waist. Sure as he breathed, he knew Raina wanted him to defy her. He didn't know why, but he sensed this. Damned if he'd give her the satisfaction.

Yes, he'd wear the hideous thing, and not give a fuck what anyone thought. Let them stare.

Shoulders squared, head high, he went in search of the kitchen. Several twists and turns later, he located a staircase. Descending, he found himself standing in a spacious, and thankfully deserted, tiled foyer.

A large living room to his left boasted fat divans and palatial marble columns. Beyond that, he glimpsed what might be an office or parlor.

A huge dining room lay to his right, resplendent with a mahogany table long enough to seat an army. Of little use to Raina or Alexi and their brethren, but he supposed royalty like her had plenty of guests to entertain.

Guessing the kitchen must be in that direction, he headed through the dining room. His stomach rumbled in loud, angry protest at being denied nourishment for so long. In truth, he'd become weaker than he'd let on, so hungry that if he didn't eat soon, he'd either be sick or faint like a rookie warrior who'd just decapitated his first enemy in battle.

He found the kitchen easily, and paused inside. The modern setup gleamed with stainless steel appliances. Copper-bottomed pots and pans hung suspended over the cooktop island.

A slim, plain woman dressed in jeans and a serviceable blouse stood at the counter by the sink. Unaware of his presence, she added a mound of potato chips to a plate of sandwiches.

Johan cleared his throat. "Excuse me."

The woman looked at him and merely arched a brow at his lack of dress. Unruffled, she wiped her hands on the apron tied around her waist, then pushed a strand of dark brown hair out of her face. To his surprise, she gave him a friendly smile.

"Hello there, I'm Hope. You must be Johan."

She wasn't plain at all, he thought. The wide smile lit a face perhaps a few years older than himself. A fresh, earthy countenance unadorned by makeup.

"Yes, I'm her Majesty's new..." He choked on the word. Shamed, he looked away, and crossed his hands over his crotch in a futile effort to hide the rampant erection.

"Don't worry," she said kindly. "I've worked for Raina many years. Nothing that goes on around here surprises me anymore, especially when she's bored. Saints preserve us."

"You're not a vampire," he observed, glancing at her eyeteeth. Her frankness and lack of censure helped to ease the sting of his situation a little.

"Nope. Just a human who needs a good job, and this one is far better than most."

"You *enjoy* working for her?" And in what capacity? More than just a cook and housekeeper?

Hope's face closed a bit, her tone sharpening to evidence loyalty. "The Queen is good as gold to those within her circle, friends, lovers and employees. She'd do anything for her loved ones. You won't find a creature anywhere who'll dispute that."

Tread carefully. This woman might make an ally. He nodded. "Good to know."

She waved a hand to a small table in a nook by the window that he hadn't noticed. "Sit over there with your friend and eat. You're looking a bit peaked."

"Zane?" His heart leapt with joy as his friend glanced up from his own plate and smiled, looking none the worse for wear. Johan started forward. "Saints, it's good to see you."

"Alive and well, if a little underdressed. Sweet Virgin, you look as ridiculous as I do." His brows lifted at the sight of Johan's erection. "Damnation, are you in pain?"

Johan's lips curved into a genuine smile for the first time in days as he lunged for Zane. His friend pushed to his feet and they wrapped one another in a bear hug, slapping each other on the back. Johan released him and pulled away with a good-natured grimace.

"The spiteful little she-devil bespelled my cock. Gods, given what we're almost wearing, I can only imagine how that hug might've looked to someone watching."

"Who cares?" Zane grinned. "It's great to see your ugly ass too, old friend."

His smile faded, some of the joy dimming with guilt. "You're certain about that? I sold us into slavery, Zane. My idea, and you were too sick to argue."

"No. I knew what we were doing, and I'm grateful you stuck by me. You would've survived just fine on the streets by yourself, without me dragging you down. If it hadn't been for my illness—"

"Never suggest that again," he said with vehemence. "You're as much a part of me as my blade hand, and you damned well know it. All our lives, I've never abandoned you. *Nothing* could make me."

Overcome by his fierce declaration, Zane glanced away, clearing his throat. "Well, same goes. Hey, we'll make the best of it."

Johan couldn't stop himself from asking. "Have you seen Raina?"

"Oh, *yeah*." The grin returned. "Baby, light my fire. *Ooww!*"

He shook his head at his friend's enthusiasm, amused in spite of himself. "She sank her fangs into you too, I see. You're incorrigible, you know that? We're slaves, pal. We have no rights."

"Your point?" Zane waggled his brows. "Sweet thing can enslave me anytime her little heart desires."

"Can't you ever be serious?"

"Sure, but it doesn't mean I have to walk around like Mr. Gloom and Doom. You might try using an ounce of charm sometime."

"I'm not that bad, am I?" He frowned.

"Worse," Zane assured him. "Sit down before you fall over."

Johan pulled out a chair and sat across from Zane, cringing at the odd feeling of cold wood against his bare ass. Chilled, he glanced out the window at the moonlit night. How strange to rise in darkness to take his first meal of the day, living his pathetic existence for creatures of the night. For their sport.

A plate appeared in front of him, loaded with two sandwiches on hoagie rolls and chips. Each was laden with a pile of roast beef, the sight so welcome and aroma so tantalizing his head swam. Hope placed a glass of wine next to the plate and smiled.

"There, enjoy. Eat, drink your wine and try to cheer up. Everything will be fine, you'll see."

He doubted that, but he took Zane's advice, smiling back at the woman to show his gratitude. "Thank you."

"You're welcome." She patted him on his bare shoulder, like a sister would. "I have some errands to run. See you two."

The housekeeper untied the apron, tossed it on the counter and breezed out. Johan barely hesitated a beat before grabbing the first sandwich. Ravenous, he attacked the food and wine, finishing in minutes.

Studying Zane closely, he posed a question that had been niggling at his mind. "What do you suppose Raina will expect of us? Sexually, I mean."

His friend shrugged. "Whatever she wants. You and I have never shared a woman, but we've fantasized about it. You have to admit the idea is wicked fun."

"Yes, but what if she expects more?" His face reddened. "What if she wants you and me to..."

"Become involved?"

"Gods," he whispered. What a time for Zane's expression to drain of his trademark humor. "I'm assuming she didn't purchase two slaves so she'd have one to play gin rummy with."

Zane's reply was pensive as his jade eyes bored into Johan. "You're a part of me, old friend. Same as my heart and lungs. That's why you couldn't leave me to die any more than I'd leave you. No matter what happens between us, remember the physical is merely an expression of what words can't do justice."

Oh, that observation hit just a bit too close to the mark. Staring at Zane's honest face, shaggy sun-streaked hair falling into dancing green eyes, Johan's throat tightened with an emotion he'd never had the courage to speak aloud between them.

"Raina doesn't love us." That treaded as near to speaking his mind as he dared.

"We could persuade her, I'll bet." One corner of Zane's mouth kicked up. "Be truthful. We've been at war with the monsters of society for years. I'm tired of battle, aren't you? Hasn't something been missing from our lives? We're bound to her and each other for eternity. Why not make the most of it?"

Indeed. He pictured Raina, proud and unbending. Bravely taking on a vile predator such as Drakkon to rescue the two of them from a worse fate. An admirable thing, if her motivation was pure. Then again, she'd come to the auction for the purpose of purchasing a slave or two. Maybe the Queen just didn't relish being thwarted in her goal.

"Perhaps," he conceded. Though he had no clue how to reconcile the slave with the free man he'd once been.

"We'd better go. She's expecting us."

* * * * *

Johan traipsed up the stairs and down the long corridor to Raina's chambers, Zane on his heels. Ornate wall sconces spaced at even intervals sported dim bulbs rather than candles or oil lamps, and cast an eerie glow interrupted by shadowy recesses along their path.

Nervous, Zane hissed a loud whisper at his back. "Creepy, huh? I feel so damned naked without my weapons. How in the hell would we protect Raina if that crazy demon bastard decided to make a house call? Plus, we look stupid."

Johan stopped, a grim smile hovering on his lips. "We could take him, even dressed like beefcake calendar rejects. Besides, you're a *slave* now. Everyone *expects* you to be naked. Embrace our destiny, remember?"

"Yeah, but having to wear this cheesy contraption in front of Hope and the staff? And guests!" He slapped a hand on his forehead. "What if she has visitors? I'd die if anybody saw me like this! It's worse than wearing nothing at all."

"Relax, Zane." Raina appeared in her doorway, cocking her head, expression unreadable. "You won't be required to entertain guests until the party next Saturday night. Come into my chambers, gentlemen."

Johan blinked. "Whoa, back up. A party? Who are we entertaining, and how?" Did he really want the answer?

"Goodness, you two ask a lot of questions." Waving a hand in dismissal of the subject, Raina turned, leaving them to follow. "Don't worry about the details yet. Trust me, our private gatherings are evenings to remember."

A note of fondness colored the vampire's low voice. Somehow, Johan wasn't comforted in the least.

By the time they reached the end of the hallway, his hands were shaking in anxiety. And yes, excitement. Damnation, he wasn't supposed to be intrigued by his surroundings. By Raina.

The gentle sway of her slim hips and curve of her rear hugged by the silk made his fingers itch to touch. To explore. Not more than an hour ago, he'd been seated between those creamy thighs, poised and ready to take her.

By the gods, he'd come so close to having her. For a moment, she'd been as lost to desire as he. She'd longed for him to take control like a man, not a scrawny wimp. Then her shields slid up and *bam*, the pissed-off she-devil was punishing him and leaving his raging body unsatisfied.

This, he suspected, was why he'd never mated.

"Zane? Johan?" Raina stood inside her chamber, awaiting their entry.

Heaving a steadying breath, Johan went inside, jumping a bit as the door shut behind him and Zane. Here, in this decadent place, he didn't know himself and the void filled his heart with…not fear, exactly. More like the adrenaline rush of a thrill-seeker. Like a man about to be shoved from a jet. Free-falling.

"This way." Raina crossed the vast bedroom, a tasteful space arranged with the light furniture and breezy tapestries of pale blue and gold he recalled from the night before.

Designed to complement her, Johan realized. The décor worked all too well, deepening the vamp's blue eyes and accenting her burnished locks. Padding across the plush carpet after his mistress, a shiver zinged down his spine.

The huge bathroom sported a similar theme. Gold spigots adorned a long countertop and a bathtub so big the thing could hold ten people, all done in marble so pale a blue the surface appeared almost white.

"What does 'chosen' mean?" Zane blurted into the awkward silence.

Raina studied him, expression thoughtful. "Simple. 'Chosen' means I've selected you to satisfy my thirst each night, usually when we arise, as I did earlier. Johan is Chosen, too. From now on, I'll feed from you both and no others, taking turns so that you aren't harmed. You give me life, and I'll protect you with mine."

"Oh," Zane said, eyes round. "Cool. We'd do that too, wouldn't we, buddy? Protect her with our lives? We owe Raina, big time."

He caught Zane's intense look, and cleared his throat, unreasonably annoyed that he hadn't said it first. "Of course. I gave my oath of loyalty, and I never go back on my word."

Raina would protect them. With *her life*.

The significance of her statement caused strange warmth in his chest. The wonderful heat bled to his limbs, fingers and toes, between his legs. The husky promise in her voice, the permanence of that sort of commitment, made him long for...what? He didn't dare guess.

"Thank you, gentlemen. You don't know how much that means to me. I haven't enjoyed the luxury of a protector in more than a thousand years," she said softly.

The pain that flashed across her face was so profound, Johan felt her loss stab through his gut. "Who was he?"

"Ancient history." Recovering, she flicked a hand toward the tub. "Fill that and let's have our bath, shall we?"

The reminder that Raina had once been human, a mortal who'd loved and lost like any other, gave him pause. He glanced at Zane, and the slight nod his friend gave said they were on the same wavelength.

She might be a royal immortal, but buried underneath the façade of ice beat the heart of a woman, with a woman's hurts and unfulfilled dreams.

Perhaps he and Zane might be able to soothe the ache of a lady left lonely and wanting. Suddenly, he wanted very much to try.

Aware of the stunning creature lounging with one shoulder against the wall, watching with those intense pale eyes, Johan resisted staring back. Zane turned on the faucet and plugged the drain while he checked the temperature of the water, keeping his gaze fixed on the steam rising as the big tub began to fill. What did the lady have in store for them? The wait proved brief.

"Johan, leave that for a few moments. In my top dresser drawer, there's a black velvet bag and a bottle of oil. Go get them, and bring them here."

Oil? *Don't think, just do it.* Retrieving both, he tried not to gape at the vast array of toys and lotions stuffed in the drawer, some colorful, some plain. All promising an assortment of sensual delights. *And she's had a thousand years of practice perfecting the art of lovemaking.* Slamming it shut, he returned to stand before Raina, items in hand.

"Good. Place the oil on the ledge of the tub." She waited while Johan set the small glass bottle down. "Next, take the items from the bag and spread them near the bottle."

Fumbling, clumsy, Johan loosened the drawstring and emptied the contents onto the slick, wide marble. His heartbeat kicked up a notch, and he couldn't have kept the stupefied expression off his face to save his soul. Standing beside the filling tub, even Zane goggled.

Neither of them considered themselves sexual innocents, and had never lacked for female company to share an otherwise dismal evening. Dinner, a few laughs and sex. A giant scoop of vanilla in a missionary waffle cone. To his thinking, that fact equated sufficient experience.

What an idiot he'd been.

Pushing to his feet, he stared at the implements. He had no idea what half of this stuff was, or how to use them. The few items he did recognize made his cheeks burn in embarrassment like a horny, untried virgin.

"Wow," Zane breathed.

A string of nickel-sized beads, leather straps, padded cuffs, a butt plug, some sort of rubbery gel thing with ball bearings inside and a huge marble phallus identical to the one Alexi had given him. The rest, he couldn't guess.

A gentle hand came to rest on his shoulder. "Those toys are a mere introduction, an appetizer for two relative beginners," the vampire teased. "And I suspect, only the tip of the iceberg for the true, dark desires you've kept hidden from yourselves. Tell me I'm wrong."

Oh, gods. His rock-hard cock twitched, betraying the lie hovering on his lips.

"You're not wrong," he murmured.

Raina turned him around, so close their bodies brushed together. "Both of you, undress me."

Zane took a deep breath and stepped forward. Hands surprisingly steady, he reached for the belt of the blue robe at the vampire's trim waist. Freeing the material, he let it fall, then hesitated, uncertain.

"Go ahead, touch me," she whispered.

Johan placed his palms flat on the vampire's shoulders and slid his hands underneath the cool silk.

Her warm, supple skin met his fingers as Zane's arm brushed his. An unexpected thrill bolted through him. A connection between three hungry souls, smoldering with promise.

Parting the robe, he slid it off his lady's shoulders, and the silk drifted to the floor in a shiny puddle.

Damn me, she's beautiful. Long, lean and graceful. Full, high breasts, rosy tips taut as pebbles, begging to be suckled. Long, toned arms and thighs, the fiery patch between her legs beckoning. The cherry atop the cream. An ethereal flame-haired goddess of a creature.

Cupping her breasts in his big palms, he tested their fullness, loving the way they fit his hands. Taking her nipples between his thumb and forefingers, he pinched. Hard enough to elicit a gasp of pleasure, but not to hurt.

Zane's hands skimmed her flat tummy, fingers combing her curls. He hesitated, looking at her in question.

Johan's gaze strayed to the rod jutting proudly from the apex of Zane's thighs. They'd seen one another naked a few times over the years. They'd been roommates, for pity's sake. But looking wasn't the same as *noticing.*

Zane's cock was long and almost thick as his own, balls perfectly formed, the area recently shorn smooth. He'd heard bare skin increased sensual pleasure, and he shuddered, not knowing what to think of these strange new feelings.

"Boys, turn off the faucet and climb in."

Zane complied, careful not to slip, and moved over to make room. Not that there wasn't plenty. "You could fit an entire starting lineup in this thing."

She stepped in and sank into the steamy water next to Zane with a content sigh. "Yes, you certainly can." She grinned, as though enjoying a fond memory.

The idea wasn't at all amusing, and Johan frowned as he followed, easing into the water on her other side.

Raina arched a slim brow, resting her elbows on the ledge on either side of her. "Goodness, I was joking. Get rid of the scowl and grab that washcloth from the rack behind you."

Snatching the cloth from the bar on the wall above the tub, he wondered whether he could handle being ordered around for the rest of his mortal life.

Not that his traitorous body was having any problems with these particular orders.

She smiled, expression gentle. "Now, use the cloth to wash me. Shower gel is on the ledge, close to the oil."

He wet the rag, squeezed some gel into the center and soaped it. "Do you always bathe rather than shower?"

"Showers are for people who are in a hurry. What purpose would it serve an immortal to rush? Time isn't exactly going to get away from me."

"True."

So much for talking to calm his frayed nerves. Wouldn't help anyway, he decided. Not with the she-devil reclining before them, resplendent, luxuriant red hair floating in the water lapping at her hips.

Moving to sit in front of Raina, he began to soap the vampire's chest, admiring the sleek planes of her body. Bubbles danced around her nipples, slid to her tight stomach.

Taking a spare cloth from the rack, Zane quickly took the initiative to help. He bathed her midsection. Lifted her dainty feet, tending to one leg, then the other. Taking his time, he had the vampire turn and move her hair so he could reach her back as well.

Raina settled back again, raising her hips, pinning Johan with a stare hot with blue fire. The look sent a jolt to his groin. He wanted to touch his lady without the cloth, but didn't dare unless given permission.

So he dipped the cloth, caressing, rinsing the soap with care. At last, he drew back. "Was your bath sufficient?"

"Well done," she praised, voice thick. "Now wash yourselves."

They'd already showered, but neither argued. The decadent intimacy of sharing their bath was relaxing. Hypnotic. She'd done this to break the ice between them, he realized. To allow them to familiarize themselves with one another.

Her method worked. Sitting back against the tub, legs spread, they bathed. Soaped their chests, stomachs. Lathered cocks and balls. The nubby cloth tortured Johan's sensitized, throbbing shaft as he stroked, palm curled around it.

Neither hurried while she watched, eyes glazed with mounting desire. A thrill shot to his toes. This foreplay heated his blood, drove him mad. He knew the exact moment he capitulated to her wishes. Had she bespelled his mind as well as his cock? He didn't know. Only knew that he loved being spread for her, longed to do whatever she desired.

Done, they wrung out the cloths, laid them aside and waited. Raina opened her arms in welcome. "Come here, darlings."

They needed no further incentive. Zane moved to her side, bent and licked one pert nipple. Wrapping an arm around him, she buried her fingers in his brown-gold hair, arching her back. He took the pebble in his mouth, suckling. Her breaths quickened. The sight of the entangled pair unraveled the last of Johan's restraint. Positioning himself between her legs, he knelt, hooking her thighs over his forearms to lift her bottom clear out of the water. The slick folds of her sex, glistening with streaming droplets, tantalized him. The pink bud of her clit peeking from its cozy nest tempted him beyond reason.

Johan looked into her cobalt eyes over the top of his friend's bobbing head. His lips turned up.

"What do you wish, my lady?"

"Your tongue," she said, a hint of pleading in her voice.

Lifting her, he gave the sweet nub the lightest flick. "Beg me," he purred, low and dangerous.

"Johan, *please*," she panted.

Ah, yes. The Queen spread for the warrior. Pleading for his tongue.

Groaning his triumph, Johan fastened his mouth to her sex.

Chapter Six

ဆ

Raina heard herself begging for Johan's mouth from far away. The husky voice, pleading like a common woman rather than royalty, must belong to someone else.

No, her body was ablaze, burning with an inferno she hadn't experienced in centuries, not even with Alexi. Not since—

Don't think of Marcus. No room for sadness here, of irrevocable losses. At last, the frozen pond of her soul had begun to thaw, leaving her raw and new.

She gripped Zane's hair as he feasted on her breasts like a starving man. Scraped the tips with his teeth. Johan's powerful biceps bulged with the effort of holding her up, face lowered to her sex, torturing her. She hardly knew the urgent plea that sprung from her lips.

"Johan, *please.*"

With a low groan of pure male satisfaction, he took her in his mouth. He wasn't gentle. His actions were hard and sure, like the man himself. He took what he wanted.

Ravaged. That was the sole word for her body opening to him. Feasting on her sex, the devil sucked and laved the smooth folds, avoiding the tiny magic button desperately craving his attentions. Next, his tongue thrust into her vagina, stroked in and out with relentless precision, driving her mad.

"Oh, yes. More, please!"

Making a noise suspiciously close to a laugh, he drove his tongue deeper, tasting. Oh, this was almost Nirvana, being at his mercy. Almost, but not quite. As he continued to tongue-fuck her, she pulled on Zane's hair.

Immediately, his sparkling green eyes were smiling into hers. "Yes, my lady?"

"Your cock," she gasped as another wave of electricity tingled through every nerve ending. "Straddle my face."

"Not a problem, sweetheart," the rogue grinned.

Sweetheart? Had any male ever dared such? Yet the cheerful endearment warmed the rapidly melting cold spot in her center even more.

Johan began to lick her pussy in long strokes, back to front. Laved every inch of skin from the crack of her ass, along her slit, to the nub. She wriggled, moaning, as Zane planted his feet on either side of her upper body and braced one knee on the tub by her head.

Like his friend, Zane's physique was a study in male beauty. Bronzed skin over taut muscles, slick and shiny as a seal, not an ounce of hair to interfere with sensation.

His cock and balls hung in front of her face, ripe as fruit for the picking, graced by the gold ring gathering and lifting them forward. Reaching out, she kneaded his heavy testicles in her fingers, smiling at his tortured groan and the instinctive swivel of his hips toward her.

With her other hand, she gripped the blue-veined rod and lowered it to her lips. Gave the broad, purple head an experimental swipe with her tongue, then kissed and licked away all the little water droplets clinging to his cock and balls.

Only then did she become aware that Johan had paused in his attentions. Angling her head, she peered around Zane's hip to find Johan staring up at them, golden eyes dark with lust, long black hair falling around his brawny shoulders. A shiver of anticipation ran down her spine, a thrill of power. The warrior couldn't hide his arousal if he tried. He was as turned on as his companions by this sharing of bodies and souls.

Deciding his friend was angled enough to provide Johan with a nice view, she returned to Zane's cock. Pulling the head down, she took it between her lips. Slowly, careful of her fangs, she slid the velvety length down her throat and sucked him like a piece of stick candy.

"Ahh, yeah," Zane rasped, cupping the back of her head. Burying a big hand in her hair, he pumped his hips, leisurely at first. Then faster, harder. Fucking her mouth, taking control.

"Do her," Johan encouraged, voice smoky with desire. "Shoot down her throat. I want our lady to drink you up while she creams all over my tongue."

Beyond words, Zane drove into her mouth with long, forceful thrusts. So deep she swallowed his cock whole, his balls slapping her face in rapid tempo. At the same time, Johan fastened his mouth tight around her sex, sucking hard at the throbbing, hot clit. Ruthless, spiraling her higher.

Oh, gods. Delicious!

At that moment, Raina couldn't have said who was the master. The two slaves, perfect specimens of maleness and raw strength, giving and taking, sucking and fucking her willing body? Or the woman disintegrating into a ball of flame, given over to their control?

Rational thought fled. As Johan sucked her pussy, she began to unravel. The wonderful sparks vibrating her clit became tremors that engulfed her sex, radiated from her womb to her limbs.

She came undone, gave herself to them. The tremors exploded with her release and she bucked wildly against Johan's relentless mouth. Zane gave a last lunge and stiffened, grinding her face into his groin. His sac tightened and he cried out, cock pulsing. She grabbed his ass cheeks, holding him deep as thick, warm semen jetted down her throat. Swallowing greedily, she drank as spasms shook him, on and on. In perfect tandem, Johan ate his fill of her honey, lavishing sweet words of praise between licks as she floated.

Never anything like this. So wicked and wondrous. Special.

A thread wound a path between the trio, fragile and new. Quickly the filament strengthened, pulsing and glowing with life. While they drifted back to earth, she marveled at the intensity of the bright light, the way the thread seemed to hum with joy as though it lived and breathed.

Zane stepped back, slipping his cock free, and ran a hand through his hair. "Did you guys feel that?" he whispered.

Johan lowered her gently into the water and scooted back, splashing his face. "Yeah. Some sort of weird connection. What was it?"

"The blood bond," Raina said in awe. "Being together sexually must excite the link, in a good way. Even make it stronger and...happy."

"Smart bond. Sure as hell made *me* happy." Zane grinned, washing off his half-erect shaft.

"Glad to hear it," Johan muttered, frowning at his unsatisfied erection. He sighed, looking at Raina in question. "You sound surprised. Didn't you know the bond took on a life of its own, so to speak?"

She shook her head. "No, just the basics, like both of you must receive the blood reward each night and so forth. I've never blood bonded with anyone before, not even when I turned Alexi. I've been told the connection between the participants can be very stimulating and that a high level of illumination along the thread can be in indication of — "

Raina choked off the end of the sentence, eyes gone wide. No. They were her slaves. Humans. That wasn't possible, nor would such a revelation be accepted among the royals even if it were.

"An indication of what?" Zane prodded.

"Of...an excellent match," she hedged. "An immaculate bond will continue to grow, drawing the ma — um — subjects together more often and with greater power each time, until they are as one." That was the truth, as close as she dared tread.

"Wow. Sounds orgasmic."

"Since my cock is still bespelled, I wouldn't know," Johan grouched.

Raina stood, eager to divert the topic. "Goodness, you poor man! You're absolutely right. Why don't we dry off, retire to my bed and see what we—"

A firm knock on the bathroom door interrupted what had promised to be a titillating adventure for all three of them. Blazing Hades!

"Yes, what is it?"

"Raina, you have a guest," Alexi called, staying discreetly out of view. "You're late for your planning session for the party, and I've exhausted my charm with the little witch."

Who on earth? "Planning session?"

"Yes, love. Delilah's here." A hesitation. "And she's demanding to see, quote, the 'hot new birthday presents' you purchased last night."

Shit, shit. "I'd completely forgotten. Tell her I'll be along shortly."

"Let me guess," Johan surmised, tone bleak. "Zane and I are expected to dance in attendance to your visitors, provide the eye candy for your jet-setting friends. And more."

"I'm afraid so." Stepping out of the tub, she took a towel Zane handed her and began drying off. The men did the same. "Slaves entertain royal guests. That's what is done between the two classes, and what's expected. The law has been thus for centuries. You know this."

His face closed up. "Doesn't mean I have to like it."

Zane's humor had faded as well. He glanced between them, looking uncertain and lost. "Me, too."

Funny, but suddenly she felt more than a little sad and lost, too. When they'd been together, she'd forgotten their relationship should remain one of royal mistress and slave. But down that path awaited heartbreak. Society demanded what it expected, and history was littered with the bodies of those who strayed from the edicts designed to protect the high class.

Marcus's dark, handsome image rose unbidden.

Yes, punishment for crossing the barrier was often swift and cruel, inviting horrible tragedy. Her shoulders would never be able to bear the weight a second time, not when the first had almost destroyed her.

Steeling herself, she drew the mantle of responsibility around her, painfully aware that it rested colder and heavier than before. Johan and Zane were slaves, and her duty entailed training them properly.

The men eyed her, wary, sensing her change in mood. "Put on your uniforms. After I dress, you'll accompany me to the parlor."

Johan glowered back, blistering her with the heat of his glare. "Yes, *Highness*." He snarled the title as though ridding his mouth of a hairball.

His contempt and Zane's glum silence flustered her. Confused and struggling to hide her discomfort, she took an action most unworthy of the Queen.

She turned and fled their accusing stares.

* * * * *

A small smile curved Zane's lips. "Just remember, we signed up for this, as they say."

"So we did," Johan gritted. And if he had the episode to do over again, nothing would change. He and Zane were outcast, and he couldn't have let his best friend die in the streets. No matter what anyone thought, he wasn't as cold and heartless a bastard as he seemed.

The sacrifice of their freedom would not be in vain, either. Before he drew his last breath, he'd learn what animal had butchered five young women and set up Zoltan to take the blame. This time, he'd take care to find proof of Drakkon's involvement before approaching the Council.

How to get close to the slimy Demon King in his current position?

The obvious solution to that problem made him want to vomit.

That predicament gave way to the one at hand as they followed Raina into the room he'd glimpsed through the living area earlier. Several fat candles perched on the fireplace mantle and resting on a table beside the nearby chaise lounge cast a glow around the generous space, not quite reaching into the shadowy corners.

Large pillows covered the floor in front of the empty lounge and fireplace, and a massive four-poster bed loomed in one corner, outfitted with every imaginable device capable of restraining a willing—or perhaps not-so-willing—participant.

Raina closed the door behind them. "This parlor is for entertaining visitors who require a bit more privacy. I suspect it will be put to good use during the party next Saturday night, though some are more adventurous and don't mind crowds."

Damnation. A headache bored into his temples, but his eager, traitorous cock failed to understand the dilemma. "Should be interesting, my lady."

She laughed, low and husky, the sound pouring over his skin like a caress. "My, such worry. Don't trouble yourself, warrior. You and Zane will be my shining stars, the toast of the evening."

"Raina, I don't—"

"Our guest is here," she said smoothly, the warning in her casual tone unmistakable. "Meet my friend, Delilah Vane."

The woman emerged from the shadows quietly, like a wraith. Small and petite, she stood several inches shorter than Raina, even in black high-heeled boots. Dark, straight hair fell to her slim hips and framed an exotic face with sensual lips and onyx cat-eyes, tilted at the corners. Given her features and bronzed skin, he placed her as hailing from Arabia, or maybe India.

"Johan, Zane, greet Delilah properly." She waved a hand to indicate the floor.

Mortified at having to abase himself, he dropped to his knees, Zane following suit, and took the lady's slender hand. "My pleasure," Johan lied.

"Blazing Hades, Raina! *These* are your acquisitions from Lash? Now I'm doubly sorry I missed your birthday."

"Indeed. Well, what do you think?"

"You always did have the devil's own luck, you bitch," she purred. Cupping a hand under Johan's chin, she forced him to look up at her.

Irritation at having the two females discuss them as though he and Zane were deaf and dumb blew to dust. His nose was almost even with the dark thatch underneath the miniscule skirt just covering the globes of her ass. The spicy scent of her arousal teased his senses, twisting his groin in a vise. If he'd been allowed to achieve completion earlier, no doubt his physical reaction could've been controlled. Damn, he was in trouble.

Delilah smiled, fangs sharp, gaze predatory. "I think our plans for the party can wait, Raina dear. I'm in the mood for an appetizer first. I choose this one. Johan, isn't it?"

Johan glanced at Raina, amazed to see her face tighten. A flash of emotion darkened her eyes, and disappeared so fast he might've imagined it. Jealousy? Possessiveness? No, those volatile emotions were too much to hope for.

"Their training is not complete, love," she demurred. "Since you were curious, I merely brought them to meet you. I couldn't think of unleashing them on guests before their skills are honed."

At that, he and Zane exchanged a quick look. Zane's eyebrows rose, the droll expression on his face communicating *my skills do not need fucking honing.*

Delilah waved a hand in impatience. "Bullshit. This is me, *hell-o*. You've never made up excuses not to share with your dearest friend before. Don't be stingy."

Too much information. How goddamned many lovers had these two passed around? For a millennium-old vampire, the number might equal the national debt. And what a nice ego booster *that* was. For a few blissful minutes in the bath, he'd allowed himself to believe that crap about some sort of special connection between him, Zane and Raina. Yeah, right.

"It's not a good time, sweetness. I only carved enough time out of the day to plan the party with you then we really must—"

"What's going on here?" the little vamp demanded, frowning at her friend. "Is Queen Ice going soft over a couple slaves?"

"Honestly," she laughed, the sound forced. "Let me send Johan to fetch you some wine while we get started."

"Raina, are you refusing the use of a slave to a royal?"

Damn. Her so-called friend had put her between a rock and a hard place. If Raina said yes, she'd deliver a direct cut to a peer of her class and break the law as well.

"Of course not," she said coolly. "I'm saying I won't force my men to service guests before they are ready. This adjustment is extremely difficult for a former Exodus warrior."

Raina, defending them? *My men*? She hadn't said *slaves*. Surely his ears deceived him.

"How kindhearted of you," Delilah purred, slanting her a calculating look. "I'm glad to hear you're not stupid enough to risk the Superior's wrath again. You got off easy after that whole nasty business of hiding Alexi—a mere slave—from Drakkon, then turning him, for pity's sake. I wager you'd lose more than a Council seat this time around."

Johan and Zane stared at Raina in surprise. Alexi told him that the Queen had turned him fifty years before, but now something the young vamp said last night made perfect sense.

80

What makes her so different from Drakkon?

Pray you never learn the answer to that question.

Raina was trying to shield him and Zane from unwanted attention, and Johan knew a veiled threat when he heard one. Why did Raina count this unsavory creature as a friend?

Their mistress crossed her arms, pushing the swell of her full breasts over the top of her skimpy black sleeveless shirt. "You know better than anyone that I don't give a fuck what the Council thinks."

"You should. If you aren't careful, word will leak back to the old farts. You might be the Queen, but they are the ruling body of all the species and classes. You could end up losing custody of these two to another owner," Delilah pointed out.

"This is about to get nasty," Zane whispered in his ear. "What should we do?"

His spirits sank. Raina had placed herself in an impossible position. For them. "I'll handle this."

"The Council can go masturbate on a—"

"My lady," Johan said, cutting Raina's tirade short. Squaring his shoulders, he swallowed hard. "There's no need to offend the Council or anyone else. I'm ready to assume my duties and I'd be honored if Mistress Delilah would deign to further my training."

Stunned, Raina gazed down at him, myriad emotions crossing her face in the span of two heartbeats. Trepidation, relief…and the unmistakable flare of arousal. "Johan, are you certain?"

Not trusting his voice, he nodded.

A long silence ensued while she seemed to grapple with capitulating to proper decorum.

"Very well. Zane, love, undress and go relax on the pillows for now. Should you feel compelled to touch yourself while I assist your friend, go ahead," she encouraged, more at ease. She looked to Delilah as Zane complied. "What is your pleasure?"

"Mmm. The slave will begin by licking my pussy, I think."

"Do as she says," Raina commanded softly, not unkind. She peeled off her shirt, kicked off her boots, slid off her pants.

She stood before them, naked and glorious, pale skin and long, toned limbs. Wild hair of deep red flame matching the curls between her thighs. Her expression revealed only patience, secrets in her cobalt eyes that she'd reveal to him in due course. Knowledge that frightened him for the revelations she seemed certain he'd make about himself.

His gaze locked with Zane's. His friend was sprawled on the pillows next to the fireplace, resting on his elbows, legs spread, one knee bent. Idly, he palmed the erection resting against one muscled thigh and began to stroke, green eyes burning with lust.

Zane and Raina plan to enjoy this. Now that he'd committed himself to his role, they were turned on.

The idea heated Johan's body like a torch. He laid his palms on Delilah's slim thighs. Skimming upward, he pushed the skirt to her waist, exposing the soft curls begging for his touch. Bracing a hand on his shoulder, she spread her legs, the pink bud of her clit inviting him to taste.

With two fingers, he rubbed the folds of her slit, already hot and wet for him. He stroked, swirling the dewy moisture, teasing the hard little nub until she moaned, nails digging into his flesh. Swiveling her hips, she pulled him in, making her desire clear.

Nuzzling her mound, he cupped her ass and flicked the little clit with his tongue. Quick, darting in and out. Driving her higher with the promise of the lovely things he'd do to her body.

Raina came to stand behind him, so close he felt her heat, smelled the potent almond musk of her excitement. She touched his hair, almost in a loving gesture of approval.

"Yes, darling, very good," she whispered. All trace of hesitation or jealousy had surrendered to the decadence of the moment. "That's right, eat her. You want this, your body needs this. Why suffer?"

Why, indeed? Saints help him, he was just a man. One tortured, sexually tormented man at the mercy of two beautiful females. Honor bound to bring them both erotic delight.

And to his great shame, he *wanted* to pleasure them, to be...enslaved.

Burying his face in her, he fastened his mouth to her sex. Suckled and laved, eating her cream. Dripping for him. So sweet, nothing finer than a woman's honey on his tongue, sliding down his throat. Sheathing his cock.

"Yes, oh, yes," Delilah hissed, fisting her hands in his hair.

He sucked until the little vamp's juices coated his face, until she pushed at his shoulders and stepped back, detaching him.

"On the pillows, now," she panted, gaze feral. "Lie on your back and take off that sorry excuse for underwear."

Glad to be rid of the itchy material, he lay next to Zane, flinging the scrap aside. Hopelessly aroused, his friend continued to work his cock, his attention riveted on the scene.

Settling back, Johan watched Delilah crawl on all fours between his legs. Gave the steel rod of his erection a long, luxurious lick. He couldn't stop the low moan in his chest.

"Yum. Love the cock ring, too. You want to fuck me, don't you, slave?" Another lick.

"No."

Anger flashed across her face. "Raina, what is the penalty when your slave lies?"

His mistress sat by his side, near his head, and reached for the ring adorning his left nipple. "Then I encourage him to tell the truth."

Grabbing the ring, Raina twisted. Johan gasped, pain knifing through him, radiating outward. She kept turning, increasing the pressure. Tears stung his eyes and he gripped the pillows at his sides. Strangely, the torture only ramped up his blinding need to come. If his cock weren't bespelled, he'd have shot through the roof.

"Now, tell our guest the truth," she said. "You want your cock inside her pretty pussy, don't you?"

"Y-yes," he rasped. Gods, it was true.

"You want to give yourself to our wishes, let us do whatever we want, isn't that right?"

"Yes, *yes*."

He was lost.

Raina released the nipple and Delilah straddled his lap. Positioning her opening over the broad head of his cock, she guided the tip into her entrance and sank down, burying him deep.

He cried out, thrusting his hips upward. Seeking sanctuary in her velvet heat. Eyes closed, dark head tilted back, she slid up and down, pumping his shaft. Squeezing, delicious.

"Ahh, yeah, fuck me."

Did that pleading, far-off voice belong to him?

When Raina turned her attentions to Zane, bent and sucked his nipple ring into her mouth, Johan was shattered. No more control, no will to fight. Raina laved the flat brown nub, sucked the ring so hard Zane hissed in a breath. Then she released it and drew his friend in for a deep kiss. Tongues dancing, hungry mouths exploring.

Suddenly, the thread between the three of them flared to life. Began to glow and hum with joy as it had earlier. Johan *felt* Raina's and Zane's heat spiraling higher. Through the bond, he read their emotions, knew that watching him fuck Delilah, sharing his dark desires, had fueled their own.

They approved of this sharing and wanted more. This wasn't about Delilah anymore, but what pleasured his mistress and best friend. They wanted to see his powerful body inside hers, taking, giving. That totally did it for him. Flipped the switch. He was theirs and didn't care.

He pumped harder, eliciting a glad cry from his tormentor. A few more thrusts and Delilah climbed off, leaving his poor, aching dick pointed at the ceiling. But only temporarily.

Crouching on her knees and elbows, she poked her ass in the air. "Johan, darling, prepare me."

A look passed between Raina and Zane, filled with lust. Straddling his hips, she sank onto his friend's cock. Began to slide up and down his pole, her hungry eyes fixed on him and Delilah.

Johan knelt behind the little vamp, parted the perfect bronze cheeks, exposing her anus. Poked his tongue in the puckered entrance, swirled, making it nice and wet. Licking a finger, he worked it into the channel, slicking the passage. She moaned, backing into the even strokes, communicating her readiness.

"Take her," Raina urged, impaling herself on Zane's shaft with slow precision. His friend moaned, fisting the pillows in his hands. "Pretty, isn't she? You want to fuck her there, don't you?"

"Yes," he admitted hoarsely.

"Do it, love. Let us see you take her in the ass. Let us *feel* you."

Like a stranger in someone else's body, he obeyed. Eagerly. He removed his finger from Delilah's hole, tracing the opening. New desires crashed through him along their bond. Unfamiliar, terrifying.

He steadied himself with one big hand on Delilah's flank. With the other, he brought the head of his engorged shaft to the tiny rosette. Worked in a couple of inches, spanned his hands around her hips.

And sank, deeply, fully inside.

"Ahhh, yes!" His hoarse shout echoed, so loud the entire household must've heard. Let them hear.

Control in shreds, he pounded into the vampire's sweet ass. Lost to the wicked sensation of her channel hugging his cock, his balls slapping against her soaking-wet pussy.

"Ohh, so good…so fucking good," he growled.

"Fuck!" Zane shouted. "Fuck, yeah!" His hips pistoned upward as Raina rode him hard. Flesh slapping in rapid tempo, wicked noises.

I feel them fucking! And gods, they feel me. Johan thrust harder, faster, deeper. The female under him keened in ecstasy, arching her back, urging him on. He gave it to her. Long, powerful strokes. *Can't get enough, not nearly enough.*

Delilah screamed. "Give me your cock, fill me up!"

She began to spasm, coming, hurtling him over the edge. The load that had been boiling in his balls, driving him mad for what seemed an eternity, rocketed from his shaft at the exact moment his companions hurled skyward. He roared with the sheer force of experiencing their mind-blowing release as well as his own.

Shuddering, he filled her to overflowing, came until his pearly cream dripped down the seam of her ass. Until he slumped, breathing like a racehorse, still deep inside her.

Raina stayed draped over Zane's sweaty chest as the last of his spasms subsided. After a moment, she touched his face tenderly, then climbed off to join Johan and Delilah.

She kissed Johan's shoulder, slid a hand down his ass. Reaching between his shaking legs, she cradled his balls. Squeezed gently, and rubbed them against Delilah's sex. It felt so damned good, he shivered and groaned, coming twice more.

"Excellent," she praised, voice thick, sultry. "Stay where you are for a moment, your gorgeous cock buried inside our friend, and speak the truth this time. You enjoyed fucking her, didn't you?"

He hung his head, sweat dripping off his jaw. "Yes, I did."

"And *why* did you enjoy it, do you think? Other than the obvious, of course."

Why? Other than the fact that sex feels good? He frowned — then understanding dawned. He'd known all along, and the bond was foolproof against lies. At least when it involved sexual matters.

"You know, don't you?" she pressed. "Tell me."

He closed his eyes. "I enjoyed fucking her because it pleased you and Zane."

"And you completely lost yourself. You embraced your new role, and reveled in being my slave. Am I lying?"

Goddamned if he hadn't walked right into her silken web. Hopelessly trapped, he'd stopped attempting to break free. Misery clogged his throat anew. "No, you aren't."

She pressed a kiss to his temple. "Fighting your destiny does you no good, don't you see? Don't hurt yourself more by struggling, Johan. You may rise."

His heart broke. What had he done?

The agony spearing his chest, the grief, doubled him over. For the first time, he truly comprehended all he'd lost. His old life was gone. Finished.

Withdrawing his cock from Delilah, he stood, his heart frozen and dead in his chest. The dark-haired vampire followed suit, a satisfied smile on her lovely face.

"How much?" she demanded, facing Raina, who'd bent to retrieve her clothing.

"How much what?"

"To recoup your investment on this slave, plus interest. How much do you want? A million and a quarter?"

"No, dearest," she refused, shaking her head. "He's not for sale."

The little vamp stuck out a petulant lip. "Oh, don't be a bitch. Everyone has their price. A million and a half, then. I'll have my accountant wire—"

"I said no. Not for any price." She arched a brow, her gaze suddenly chilled to blue ice.

Johan could've sworn he caught a flicker of malice in Delilah's soulless eyes, but the impression was so fleeting, he must've been mistaken.

"Oh, very well," she sighed, brightening again. "I have to run. Can we discuss the party later, perhaps tomorrow?"

"Sure."

The women dressed quickly. Recovered, Zane pushed to his feet and caught his arm. "You okay, pal?"

Nodding, Johan shook him off and retrieved the pitiful scrap that was his uniform, but didn't put it on. Why bother? Besides, he desperately wanted a shower. And to get the hell out of this house, even for an hour or two.

After Delilah left, Johan addressed his mistress. "May we please get dressed and go into the city for a while?"

She hesitated, the tip of one fang biting her lower lip as she considered the request. "I'm sorry, not tonight."

Frustrated anger surged, hot and bitter. He couldn't keep it out of his voice if he tried. "Why the hell not? I've done what's expected of me so far. I even bailed your ass out with that bitch who calls herself your friend."

"No, it's too soon. I'm sor—"

"The fuck you are!" He took a step toward her, risking retribution when he didn't yet know the full scope of her powers. But he'd gone beyond caring. "We're prisoners now? Alexi said we'd be able to leave the house, and we have unfinished business to attend."

"No."

"It's about Zoltan, and our case! Don't you give a flying rat's ass about your ruling counterpart? They're going to *execute* an innocent vampire, do you get that?"

"Step back from me," she ordered. Cool fire surged in her blue eyes, glowing. Powerful.

Seething, he took a step backward as she continued.

"I've got some ideas on how to proceed with getting Zoltan out of this mess. That is not the issue here, at this moment. You've made progress today, but you haven't yet earned such freedoms as leaving the grounds, and this outburst proves my point."

He *had* to get out of here, or he'd go insane. "Raina, please," he entreated, holding out his hands.

"This discussion is over. Leave me and get cleaned up."

Deep breath. Calm down.

"Yes, mistress." The words emerged as a choked whisper.

Spinning on his heel, he walked away from her and Zane with as much dignity as he could muster. As soon as he reached the solitude of his chambers, he closed the door and leaned against it, unable to move.

The enormity of what had transpired in the parlor crashed in on him. She was right. He'd given in to the darkness, had gone willingly into its embrace.

I can't live like this forever.

The moment he and Zane proved Zoltan's innocence, he'd leave. Zane could go, or stay if he wished to lead this sort of existence. Johan would have no choice but to respect his decision.

And if tearing the blood bond killed him, as Alexi had warned? A mere technicality.

Johan Stone was already dead.

Chapter Seven

ʁᴏ

Vampires don't dream.

Raina's dayrest hadn't been plagued in fifty years, since she'd discovered a brutalized, half-dead exiled prince and swept him under her protective wing.

Prince Alexi of North Umbra had been grateful to awaken healed, immortal and safe from Drakkon's clutches. Her intervention had been the beginning of a warm, lasting friendship. Despite losing her seat on the Council and catching ten kinds of hell, Alexi was worth it.

Johan Stone was far from grateful for his "rescue". Then again, the man knew nothing of hell. Betrayal and wounded pride, yes. Johan once worked under the Council, and he knew Drakkon better than most. Didn't he realize how lucky he'd been to avoid a much crueler fate?

His golden eyes haunted her. Following Delilah's departure, he'd been so cold. Hollow. Then she'd refused his humble request for leave, and the brief, unguarded flash of devastation she'd glimpsed cleaved her breast like a knife. She understood what it cost such a proud man to walk out with his shoulders back, head high.

But Johan was only a human slave, and the sooner he adapted to his new circumstances, the happier for everyone. Right?

The devil take it. She'd get no rest, so she might as well rise and dress. A hot shower eased some of the tension from her shoulders and neck, and by the time she donned black pants and a loose white blouse, she felt much improved. Ready to tackle even the stubborn, sexy Johan.

First, she sought Zane in his chambers and found him awake, brooding over his friend's unhappiness. He lay on his back, over six feet of gorgeous, naked perfection, ankles crossed, hands clasped behind his head.

"Hey, beautiful," he said without an ounce of guile.

He looked so natural, so darned fetching, she didn't bother to remind him about kneeling. "How are you, Zane?" Crossing the room, she sat on the bed next to him.

"Good. Just worried about Johan."

"He'll come around, you'll see."

"I don't know. He's proud, Raina. For Johan, the world is painted in black and white. Good and bad. He doesn't know how to let go and embrace new ideas. Never has."

"Like opening his sexuality to more experiences? Making himself vulnerable?" Needing to touch him, she laid a palm in the center of his chest.

"Yeah, exactly. Yesterday seriously shook his foundations. Through our bond, I know that he loved the hell out the three of us being together, the emotion of that sort of commitment as well as the sex. The question is whether he'll ever *admit* it."

"What about *your* feelings? Did you enjoy being with us?"

"You know I did, and so does Johan." He fell into a troubled silence.

"You love him, don't you?" she guessed.

He sighed, closing a hand over hers. "We've never explored a sexual relationship before. To be honest, I don't think it's ever occurred to either of us. But he's always been there, my best friend. My rock. He leads, I follow. When I fall behind, or flat-out fall down, he picks me up. What we have goes deeper than friendship, and now that we're bonded to you..."

"You'd like to take that relationship further," she said gently, smiling a bit. "With our bond erasing the barriers, that's expected. Normal."

"I'm not sure if it's because I want to be with him, or that I *have* to." Taking her hand, he brought her fingers to his lips. "All I know is I need you both so much I can't breathe. I want to do whatever pleases you, and the desire has nothing to do with being your slave. I get that, even if Johan doesn't yet."

"Oh, my." Unexpected tears burned in her throat. "That's the nicest thing anyone's said to me in ages. Thank you."

He grinned. "Hey, don't get all weepy on me. I'm allergic."

"Oh, you!" She tried to shake her hand free, but he wouldn't let go. "Here I thought you were sweet and charming, and you're just a typical male."

"Hmm. Not all that typical," he said, sobering. "Can you keep a secret?"

"Depends. Tell me and we'll see."

"Naw, forget it."

"What?" He clamped his lips together, and she laughed. "Oh, all right. You can trust me not to tell."

He considered her for a long moment. "I think—I mean I'm pretty sure I'm..." Heaving a deep breath, he blurted. "A submissive."

"Good grief. I thought you had a fatal disease." Exhaling in relief, she squeezed his hand. "I'm not surprised."

"Why not?"

"A couple of big clues. I'd sensed your desire to be dominated from the first time I fed from you, and from the bond since then. You're taking to the slave role too well to be anything but a sub. And you just told me you've followed Johan all your lives. He's the dominant male, which is why he's having such difficulty."

"Do you think I could…" Unable to finish, he flushed to the roots of his hair.

"You wish to try your hand as a submissive to me and Johan?"

He nodded. Raina's sex heated. Oh, yes. The idea held delicious promise.

"Very well. From now on, your sexual satisfaction will be achieved by pleasing us. You will undergo a formal initiation and afterward you'll submit to whatever we wish to do to you, no questions, no matter how rough your treatment. Understood?"

Zane's cock answered before he did, waking from repose to lengthen and arch toward his flat belly. "Yes," he croaked.

Yum. She couldn't wait to explore this new horizon. "A word of fair warning, however. If you're as accomplished at being a sub as I suspect, you'll be much in demand. A blood slave who's a true sub, or thrall, couldn't hide that fact if he or she wanted to, especially in a room full of immortals. Your sensuality as a beta male is innate, and will call to others."

His eyes widened as he surmised the full import. "So when we have visitors and a particular guest wishes to have me, I must submit completely?"

"Yes. Do you have issues with that? Make certain. Slave laws are strict, and though I'd fight the Council on your behalf, I'd just as soon avoid the attention."

Glancing down at his iron-hard cock, he smiled ruefully. "I suppose not, as long as none of your guests are homicidal. We do have a killer running loose," he reminded her.

"I don't invite dangerous guests into my home," she assured him. "Delilah is the most challenging. I keep her close to me because she's a wild card, neither wholly good nor bad. And she knows *everyone*. She's selfish and pushy, but not malicious. Deal with her, and the rest are easy. You'll like my friends, I think."

"I'm sure I will. Are you going to see Johan now?"

"Yes, but I'll begin my nightly feedings with you first. I'm hungry, and I doubt Johan will be very receptive tonight. Be a dear and sit up for me."

He did, bracing his arms behind him and letting his head fall back. Wasting no time, Raina accepted the scrumptious invitation. Placing one hand over his heart and cupping his head with the other, sank her fangs into his throat. He cried out, stiffened, then relaxed in complete trust, closing his eyes.

She drank, loving his moans and sighs of ecstasy. His happy cock bobbed and strained, but she didn't allow him to achieve release. His training as a sub would begin now, and he must be left aroused and eager for their sessions to begin on the right foot.

After she'd taken enough to satisfy the gnawing in her stomach, but not a significant amount to weaken him, she withdrew and wiped her lips.

"Wow," Zane drawled, expression dreamy. "Can we do that again?"

"Not so fast, superstud. It'll be your turn again evening after tomorrow. Oh, I almost forgot! Your blood reward."

Tearing open her wrist, she held it to his lips. He suckled greedily, and she couldn't help but smile at his unabashed enthusiasm. "Okay, that's enough."

Ignoring his protest, she pulled her wrist away and licked the wound to seal it.

"What's on the agenda tonight?" he asked, reaching out to wind a strand of curly red hair around his index finger.

"Get showered, dress in jeans and a T-shirt, and get a bite to eat. Then meet Johan, Alexi and me in the parlor. You'll see."

"You're killing me, sweetheart. Such abuse." He waggled his brows, teasing.

She rose from the bed and gave him a seductive smile. "Ohh, you haven't seen abuse yet, *sub*."

"Ooww!" Grabbing his chest as if he'd been shot, he flopped onto his back, twitching.

Raina shook her head, laughing aloud at his antics as she left. Gods, what a man. Sexy, sweet, funny.

She had a feeling her talk with Johan wouldn't be such a riot.

Raina returned to her own chambers and paused at the door connecting Johan's room to hers. Cocked her head and listened.

No human could've detected the muffled, throaty sound of misery drifting from within. Her lips parted in dismay.

The warrior was weeping.

Oh, sweet Virgin. What to do?

She was rusty in demonstrating compassion and understanding. The past half-century of Alexi's companionship had been peaceful, her nurturing skills dormant. Even so, one thousand years of walking the earth didn't change the fact that a grieving male destroyed her. Especially one who'd rather die than bear for her to witness his loss of control.

She hesitated. No royal deigned to ask permission to enter from a mere slave.

Raising a fist, she knocked anyway. Immediately the noise ceased, all gone quiet inside. Composing himself, she guessed, and wondered whether he'd figure out she'd heard and had purposefully given him time to do so. She hoped not. A puzzled frown pulled at the corners of her mouth. Why should she care about sparing his pride?

More to the point, why did she have this overwhelming desire to barge in, take him into her arms, hold him while he cried? To know this man was in emotional pain cut her to the quick and she couldn't fathom her reaction. This plunged deeper than empathy for another creature, more profound than their bond, which wailed in sadness. Confused, she rubbed her chest to ease the ache there, but it didn't help.

A full thirty seconds ticked by before his masculine voice called out, wary.

"Come in."

Deciding not to waste energy by zone surfing such a short distance, she opened the door and stepped inside.

The room was bathed in darkness, a pool of moonlight spilling across the carpet. Next to a chair by the wide window, Johan knelt on the floor clad in a pair of the silk boxers, knees spread, hands at his sides. Caught by moonbeams, silver-gilt hair enveloped his downturned face.

She walked over to stand before him. "You anticipated me. Excellent. You're a quick study, Johan." She winced at how cold and unfeeling that sounded to her own ears. Why was it so easy to be with Zane, yet difficult to relate to Johan?

No response from him. Biting her lip in indecision, she paused only a moment, then knelt and cupped his chin in her hand. He'd wiped away his tears, but the telltale moisture lingered on his skin. Once more, her heart gave an unpleasant wrench.

"Are you well?"

"I am, my lady," he said quietly.

"Raina, when we're alone."

"As you wish."

He peered at her from the gloom, beautiful and mistrustful as a trapped wolf. Withdrawn, his pain gathered in a hard, tight ball inside him, protected from those who'd use the weakness to hurt him more.

Like me. The band around her chest gave a ruthless squeeze. Shaking off the strange response, she pushed to her feet. "You may rise." She eyed the way his muscles bunched as he stood. The power of his shoulders and arms, his flat stomach.

In particular, she perused how the boxers hung low on his hips, accented his thighs. The dark blue silk whispered against his skin, a slight bulge in front hinting at his huge sex without revealing the prize underneath. Like a lovely, gift-wrapped present waiting to be opened in delight.

The idea of his cock and balls hanging free and heavy under the pretty material, so accessible, moistened her pussy. To her surprise, she found this look much, much sexier on a male than the tiny g-string. More enticing, more manly...more everything.

Stepping back, she crossed her arms over her breasts and studied him thoughtfully. "Tell me, do you enjoy wearing the g-strings?"

His guarded expression cleared a bit, and he blinked at her. "They're hideous," he replied honestly. "They itch, and make me look like a gay gigolo. I look like a fucking idiot in them, and to tell you the truth, I've always believed a little mystery is usually sexier than revealing too much."

"Good point." Some of the wariness crept back into his face as she tapped one blood-red fingernail on her arm. She could not deny the truth of his words. "By the gods, you're right! I'll have Hope throw them out at once. Hmm, let's add a matching knee-length silk robe for each pair to wear over them around the palace. Will that suit you and Zane?"

"I—yeah, I'd say that's a vast improvement. I appreciate the compromise. Thank you, Raina," he murmured.

His sincerity and relief was palpable, and she smiled. "See, I'm not always unreasonable. As further proof, I've reconsidered allowing you and Zane to go into the city. You have the first few hours off, but I expect you both to return by midnight."

He nodded. "This isn't just for me. Every hour we spend searching for the murderer of those women brings us closer to freeing Zoltan. We were so damned close, and then I fucked up by bringing circumstantial evidence of Drakkon's involvement to the Council."

"And the demon promptly screwed you both over."

"Oh, yeah. I underestimated his hold over each of the Superiors, and we paid, big time." Johan raked a hand through his hair. "Care to share your ideas on how fry Drakkon's ass?"

Raina thought of Alexi, and the debt of vengeance she'd never had the opportunity to repay Drakkon, the demon bastard. Not to mention the blow he'd dealt two honorable men, and repeatedly getting away with murder for centuries.

"I've already planned a meeting to discuss the matter. Come to the parlor after your meal with Zane, and we'll discuss strategy before you go. In this, at least, we are allies, Johan."

A corner of his mouth kicked up, and the effect was devastating. "Nice to know."

There. That odd, aching sensation squeezed her heart again. Flustered, she turned to go, but steely fingers wrapped around her upper arm, halting her progress.

"Wait. Don't you need to feed from me?"

"I fed from Zane tonight," she managed. "Besides, you'll need to be at full strength if you're going to go about battling monsters."

Hurrying out, she didn't look back at Johan. But his sad whisper, not meant for her ears, floated on her retreating heels. Shoved the blade a little deeper.

"Which ones, Raina?"

* * * * *

Forty-five minutes later, fully dressed for the first time in days, Johan stood in the parlor, shifting uneasily. He understood why Raina had decided to meet here—this was a private room, closest to the front door of the palace—but his gaze kept drifting toward the pillows on the floor. The place where Raina's hot little friend had taken him down like an elk in season.

Shit, why was it so goddamned stuffy in here?

In spite of the thick, delicious steaks Hope fed him and Zane, his stomach roiled. His skin itched and burned, and he worked hard to resist clawing at his arms and chest.

He glanced at Zane standing beside him, dressed in jeans, a dark T-shirt and a chocolate-colored leather jacket. His friend seemed pretty flipping cheerful. Zane hadn't stopped grinning since they'd embraced in the kitchen earlier. Over the top, even for his normal, happy charm.

He knew Zane as well as he knew himself, and his friend's joy was genuine. Something dark and mischievous lurked in his green eyes, adding a troubling glow to his usual radiance. The second they left, Johan intended to find out why.

Alexi, he noted, hadn't taken his attention off Zane since they'd walked in to find the two vampires waiting for them. The vamp leaned casually with one elbow propped on the fireplace mantle, looking chic in black pants and a snug, ribbed T-shirt that showed off his lean, graceful frame. His long, white-blond hair was pulled back from his striking face and secured in a ponytail.

If the handsome vamp touched Zane, Johan would fucking disembowel him.

Satisfied with that plan, he focused his attention on Raina. The she-devil sat perched on the chaise lounge, mile-long legs crossed, swinging one booted foot. Recalling her gentle kindness earlier, her delicate fingers touching his face as she asked whether he was okay, he shook his head to himself. He had no clue how to reconcile the tender woman with his mistress. Yet his body and soul responded to both.

Gods, he wanted to bury his hands in that glorious red hair and fuck her in every conceivable position. Hard and nasty. Slow and—

"Johan?" Raina said.

"I'm sorry, what?"

"You don't look well," she commented. "Perhaps you should rest and go out tomorrow night."

"No!" All three jumped at his outburst, and he flushed. Shut up one more night, and he'd go stark raving mad. "My apologies. I'm fine, really. It's just so damned hot in here, but I'll feel better once I'm outside."

"You're wearing a denim jacket, moron," Zane teased. "Take it off."

The jacket wasn't the problem. The awful, itchy heat blazed from the inside out, like a stoked furnace. Rather than try to explain, he shrugged. "We're leaving in a few minutes anyway. Mistress, you were saying?"

She sighed, as though dealing with an unruly boy. "Very well, let's get to the heart of the matter. Tell Alexi and me why you and Zane focused on Drakkon as the main suspect in your murder investigation."

"Not that we have any doubts that the bastard is involved," Alexi added with vehemence.

Johan wondered at the young vamp's story with the demon, and bet it was a helluva sad one. "It was quite simple, actually. Or so we believed. Each of the five murdered working-class women bore identical markings on their corpses, fang and claw wounds consistent with a demon's kill. The creature's upper and lower jaw bite measured much too wide to belong to a vampire, plus the bone was crushed and flesh torn in a demon's feeding pattern."

Alexi glanced away and lowered his head, but not before Johan saw the flash of pain in his pale eyes. *He knows exactly what I'm talking about. He's seen the horror before.*

"Couldn't the killer have been a shapeshifter?" Raina suggested, casting a sympathetic look at her old companion.

"No," Zane put in. "Tests on the creature's saliva left on the wounds ruled out a shifter. Remember, shifters are human in their genetic makeup, combined with altered animal genes. No human or shifter DNA was present on the women. Instead, the lab people found a big load of *ardin*. Our killer used his tongue barb—how gross is *that*—to inject the victims with his brand of joy juice."

Johan studied Raina. "I'm sure you know this, but the injection of the *ardin* works very much like a spider stinging and numbing his prey. The victim is physically helpless, suspended in a state of sexual ecstasy for hours. If the person somehow survives the attack, the *ardin's* properties eventually bond with their DNA. The merging is quite agonizing, but the victim is left with a highly enhanced sex drive for life."

"Most don't make it that far," Alexi said quietly. "The demon usually devours them alive long before then."

"True," Zane nodded. "In this case, instead of killing them right away, the demon probably kept the girls captive a while, playing with his sex toys, then brutally murdered them and dumped their bodies near the river when he'd tired of them."

"Sweet Virgin, that's horrendous," Raina breathed, hand going to her throat. "And you suspected the killer was Drakkon."

Johan's gut clenched. "We were positive. A demon's *ardin* secreted from his tongue barb is as distinctive as a human fingerprint, carrying the specific demon's DNA. So we put the pressure on Drakkon to give a sample, and he went without too much of a fuss."

"Our first clue we'd fucked ourselves up the ass," Zane grumbled.

Raina leaned forward in her seat. "Why did you focus on him to start, rather than one of his sentinels, for example?"

"Easier to work from the top down," Johan shrugged. "Nothing gets by Drakkon, and he'd never tolerate a male demon more dominant than himself carousing the city. We figured if he didn't commit the murders, he knew who did. Maybe he'd give up the rogue to save face with the Council."

"So the test came back negative, and you'd pissed him off," Raina guessed.

A bitter laugh erupted from Johan's chest. "Close. The test

came back as a ninety-six point eight percent possibility the *ardin* belonged to Drakkon, *then* we pissed him off. The stupid fucking little three point two percent was a problem for the Council. After all, the DNA could've belonged to a close relative, like a sibling or his progeny, though Drakkon claimed to have no family. The Demon King grabbed the Superiors by the balls and twisted, and Zoltan ended up under arrest."

Alexi held up a hand. "Wait, given the evidence, how does Zoltan figure in this at all?"

"That's what Zane and I wanted to know, believe me. The Council whipped out a tape of the Vampire King meeting outside his palace with an unidentified demon in secret. Conveniently, they don't know who made the tape, and it's garbled just enough to make out Zoltan spouting damning words like 'kill her' and 'no one must know'. The demon, who is unidentifiable but Drakkon swears could not be part of his clan, defers to Zoltan as 'master' and says stuff like 'where shall I do it' and 'as you wish'."

"After they placed Zoltan under arrest, Johan and I were ordered to drop the whole thing. The murders had stopped, hadn't they? We refused, and became a problem the Council couldn't afford any longer and keep Drakkon from devouring their livers," Zane said grimly. "And here we are."

Alexi shoved away from the fireplace, fisting his hands. "That evil son of a bitch is involved, I *know* it. If he's not the killer, he's protecting the culprit. The question is why, and how do we draw them both out?"

Raina stood. "By employing the oldest rule in the book. Keep your friends close, your enemies closer."

"I'm almost afraid to ask." Johan arched a brow. "How?"

"By burying the hatchet, of course."

"In his black heart?" Alexi suggested helpfully.

"In due course." She glanced from Zane to Johan. "In the meantime, brace yourselves for the most difficult assignment you'll ever face."

Oh, he didn't like the sound of this. "Mistress—"

"We've expanded our guest list, gentlemen," she announced. "Alexi, send out one more invitation for the party next Saturday night."

Johan closed his eyes, heart sinking in dread.

"And an invite for drinks at Lash two evenings from tonight, Drakkon's choice of a date."

Ah, shit.

Chapter Eight

ဢ

"He's escaped again, Your Magnificence, I'm sorry. There isn't a restraint in all of the Continent capable of—"

"I don't want to hear your pathetic excuses, Charon," came the low reply, deceptively affable. "I want to see assholes and elbows flying until you find him, or someone will pay. That someone will not be me, is that clear?"

"Yes, Your Mag—"

"Get out before I get hungry."

Delilah Vane flattened herself against the wall outside Lord Drakkon's private chambers as the Demon King's top sentinel hurried past in a flurry of robes, not bothering to spare her a glance. Hovering in the gloomy corridor, she wondered what slave had been clever or strong enough to escape this little slice of Hades below the earth. Secretly, she hoped the poor soul managed to find his way out of the intricate labyrinth of the cave system Drakkon called home to his empire...and envied the man his chance at flight. For one insane moment, she considered following on Charon's heels, never to return.

The Demon King would find her, of course, and the punishment would far outweigh the slight. No, she didn't dare. Ever since she'd moved to St. Louis a decade ago, Drakkon had taken a fancy to her. She provided an itch he liked to scratch every now and again. The reason eluded her. In the beginning, before she knew the depths of Drakkon's rotted soul, she thought he used her to get closer to Raina. Foolish.

The Demon King wasn't so complicated. He took what he desired, when he desired it. Period. If he sent for her, he'd make his intentions clear. If she resisted…

Delilah shuddered, thinking of his dulcet baritone voice while speaking to Charon. That was his most dangerous tone of all, the seductive, eloquent modulation that heralded his most evil of moods. The calm before the bloodbath.

She lifted her chin, steeling her backbone to enter his private chambers. To carry on this uneasy alliance for survival, if nothing else. And she was a survivor, no question.

Straightening her skirt, she exhaled and stepped inside, shutting the door softly behind her. "You summoned?"

He turned, and she sucked in an involuntary breath. For their meeting, he'd chosen the more human version of his true demon form, the one used to charm and otherwise blackmail his peers.

Raven hair spilled unbound down his back in a silken waterfall, offsetting a cruelly handsome face of sharp planes and angles, though not as pronounced as his demon. His ripped torso was bare, displaying awesome musculature, unequalled in raw strength. He wore jeans that cupped his huge sex like a glove and encased powerful legs supporting his six-foot, six-inch height. In true form, he grew to seven feet.

"I did indeed," he rumbled, crossing the distance between them to tower over her. "To show you these."

Instead of ravishing her on the spot, he pulled two identical envelopes from his back jeans pocket and handed them to her. Not certain whether to be relieved, she took them and read the outside of the envelopes aloud. "Lord Drakkon, Demon King." She turned her face up to his in question.

"Go on, read them." He sounded amused and curious.

Intrigued, she pulled the first beige card from the small envelope and began to read. Her mouth dropped open in astonishment. "An invitation from Raina! To her party next Saturday night. Why, this is unbelievable."

He gave a wicked, toothy smile. "I could be offended, sweet."

"Sorry, I just—"

"Well, you're her best friend, what do you think?" he demanded, waving a hand at the missive. "What is her game?"

She shook her head, at a loss. "I have no idea. If she'd planned to invite you, she certainly didn't tell me."

"Read the other."

Pulling it out as well, her eyes widened. "Drinks at Lash, evening after next—with a *date*?" The idea of Drakkon on a nice, staid date was so ludicrous, she almost snorted before she could stop herself.

"You knew nothing of this?" he pressed, probing her gaze for hidden deception.

"Not an inkling."

Reading her honesty, he grunted in satisfaction. "She hates the shit out of me. I'm damned tempted to attend, just to see what she's up to." His eyes narrowed to slits.

"I'll bet she's thrown her support in with those two pitiful ex-warriors to try to get something on me. Satan's cock, she's been gunning for me ever since that unfortunate incident with my former slave. I should just eat her one evening and get it over with. Damnation, I'd hoped to at least fuck her first."

What *was* Raina thinking? *Quick, damage control!* Smiling seductively, she laid her palms on his massive chest. Stroked his supple skin, and his ego. "Lord Drakkon, I can assure you Raina has no wish to tangle with Your Magnificence. She was very angry about Alexi, but has been very careful not to cross such strength and power as yours."

"True," he grunted.

What an arrogant jerk. "Besides, I can personally attest that she views her new human males as slaves, nothing more. For an entire Millennium, no royal has been more entrenched in our caste system than Raina. Even now, she's diligently training them for a life of sexual servitude as her blood slaves. Johan is coming along nicely, if I must say. Saints, he was so delectable I tried to purchase him, but the bitch refused."

That was the truth as she'd witnessed and experienced it, and Drakkon heard this as well. His shaft responded to the happy news with enthusiasm, making an impressive pole behind his zipper.

"Raina knows how dreadfully enraged you were when she outbid you," she went on. "I daresay she's eager to show her boys off, and collect you as an ally by sharing them. And the Queen would be an extremely useful ally for Your Magnificence to have, don't you think?"

Whether her speculation of her friend's motivations for courting Drakkon was on the money or not, the demon bought her take on the matter. The lust etched on his face was frightening, and exciting, as much as she hated to admit it. She'd forever held a love of naughty mischief and danger. At the end of the day, she was a mercenary at heart.

Catching the front of her blouse with one sharp claw, he neatly sliced it down the front, all the way to her belly button. A thrill shot to her sex as he parted the torn material, baring her naked breasts. Her nipples puckered into hardened pebbles under his hot gaze.

"You, Delilah dearest, will be my date two nights from now, and at the party. You will use your close friendship with Raina to help smooth the way for this alliance between us. Do you understand, pet?"

She understood that if she refused, he'd kill her. Still, she kept her voice surprisingly steady. "She's going to be shocked at our, um, relationship. How do we get around the fact that we've been sometime lovers on the side? She'll see it as a betrayal, considering how many times I've listened to her rail about your treatment of Alexi."

"Let me handle her. I'll explain that being a beast at heart, I did not leave you a choice because I love you madly and feared your rejection, as you feared hers. We wish to come clean with our love, boohoo and so forth. I'll say that bringing you as my date and my honesty in the matter shows my willingness to heal old wounds. Raina adores you, and has forgiven your selfish nature all these years. She'll be completely fooled. How's that?"

"Clever," she praised. "Just enough shades of the truth."

His fingers pinched her nipples, sending little jolts through the taut peaks. "I'm in a generous mood. When we succeed in this new friendship with Raina, I think I shall grant you a prize. What will you have, sweet?"

He lowered his head, sucking a nipple into his mouth.

Delilah spared not one moment's thought on the question. The benediction had hovered upon her lips ever since his enormous cock plunged into her ass.

"Johan Stone."

* * * * *

"Damn, it feels good out here." Johan sucked in the crisp night air of downtown St. Louis. Let the pungent smell of the Mississippi River fill his lungs, soothe his battered pride, if not the fever scorching his skin and deep-frying his eyeballs.

"I agree with Raina. You don't look so good, pal."

Beside him, Zane kept a watchful eye on the street and gloomy alleyways they passed on foot. They'd left the relative safety of George and the limo waiting several blocks behind them. This close to the river after dark, especially with the floating casinos nearby, all sorts of unsavory characters would be out looking for good, old-fashioned trouble. Or lurking in the shadows to pounce on a succulent, unsuspecting meal.

"Probably the start of a cold or something," he muttered, glancing behind them at a scraping noise. Just a discarded candy wrapper skittering across the sidewalk. *Gods.* With an effort, he willed his jumping nerves to calm.

"We can't get sick, remember? The blood bond — wait!" His friend grabbed him by the arm and pulled him to a stop. "When's the last time Raina gave you the blood reward?"

"Damn," he muttered. "Yesterday, when I first awoke. No wonder I feel like crap. We weren't exactly speaking last night, so I guess we both forgot. No big deal."

"Except for the dying in agony part," Zane snorted. "You need to go back?"

"No, I can deal with the discomfort for a few hours. If I have to spend all night inside I'll lose what's left of my mind."

"I hear you. But if you get worse, we're heading back to the limo, and that's final." Hunching his shoulders against the chill in the air, Zane pointed to an adjacent street leading away from the river.

"I've always wondered why our suspect killed the last two women in the same area, around the corner from each other."

"Convenient, deserted location? Taunting the Exodus crime operatives? Who knows? Let's check out the scenes again, see if we can find anything new or pick up a vibe."

"Sure."

They walked a while in companionable silence. Not for the first time, Johan wondered why anyone, especially a lone female, would walk alone in this desolate area late at night.

The back of his neck prickled, and he checked the laser blaster tucked into his waistband under the jacket. Zane carried an identical weapon, illegal as hell now that they were slaves. He didn't give a goddamn, considering. He'd give just about anything for his hand blades — beheading a demon was the only way to kill it — but Raina argued the wicked, knifelike appendages were too visible. None but Exodus warriors were permitted to carry them, and that privilege was lost along with the rest.

"*We're* here walking late at night," Zane pointed out.

"But not alone. Keep *The Probe* out of my head, brat."

Zane just laughed. Which reminded Johan of his earlier concern.

"You seem awfully cheerful, my friend, given our circumstances."

"Out alone in the dark, waiting to be eaten by monsters?" he said innocently.

"No, damn you. I'm referring to our situation with Raina. You haven't stopped smiling since we took our meal."

"Maybe I'm not as adverse to the whole slave thing as you are. There are definite benefits for both of us."

"I'll *never* be a slave," he hissed. "No matter what the law states."

"Perhaps not, but you'll always be bonded to Raina and me. You can't deny that something awesome happens when the three of us are together, can you?" Zane pressed.

Blazing Hades. An image rose unbidden, of the three of them giving and receiving untold carnal pleasure. The joy of the bond zipping through his veins, knowing that Raina and Zane belonged to *him*. That in the end, it didn't make a difference whether she was their mistress.

They're mine!

The vehement cry from his soul staggered him. He didn't understand this emotion, wasn't sure he wanted to.

"No, I can't," he admitted. Confused at these feelings, he scowled. "Let's change the subject."

"Fine."

He cleared his throat. "Have you tried *The Probe* on Raina? It might be helpful to have some insight into her motivations toward us."

"No way. She's as skilled with mind-link as I am, probably more so. Now that we're bonded, she'd catch me for sure. Besides, that's rude."

"We're slaves, buddy. We might have to be a tad rude in order to survive from now on," he said dryly.

At last they reached the street where the most recent of the women met their horrible demise. Johan and Zane had been here on several occasions, picking through garbage for evidence, boots crunching over refuse neither cared to name.

They passed a liquor store, closed for the night, burglar bars covering the windows and front entry. Kept going past deserted buildings, the former proprietors of these doomed businesses not as fortunate. The darkened windows were black eyes, the shattered windows broken teeth in a sad, gaping smile.

Broken dreams and death for sale, step right up.

Johan shivered, his gut cramping from more than just the desolate surroundings. Too late, he realized he'd been much too blasé about missing his blood reward. His legs were rubbery, his body growing weaker with every step.

He'd have to get back to Raina soon, or he'd be up the proverbial creek. The knowledge rankled.

"Here," Zane pointed, motioning toward an abandoned storefront. The crime scene tape across the door had long since been removed. "I'll go inside and make another pass over where he killed number four. Maybe I can get a vibe or a clear reading this time."

"Fine. I'll take the alley behind the store and poke around where he left number five." Johan paused, another chill of dread trailing a bony finger down his spine. "Be careful, my friend."

"Always. I'll join you in the alley when I'm done."

Johan watched until Zane disappeared, then shook his head at his own foolishness. His semi-psychic friend was the one who dabbled in all that woo-woo shit, not him.

Still, he rested his hand on the butt of his laser blaster. Never hurt to give the woo-woo shit some healthy respect.

Picking his way carefully around the corner and down the alley, Johan tugged a small pocket flashlight from his jeans. The thin beam was powerful enough to illuminate his path and keep him from tripping over piles of stinking garbage and rotted boards, but not strong enough to dissipate the murky pockets of shadows along the brick walls and rear store entries.

Damn, he hated confined, dark places. Cloud cover had blocked the moon tonight, making for lousy vision. He wished he'd brought a stronger flashlight, but there was no help for it now.

Sweeping the beam back and forth over the area for a couple of minutes, he grunted in satisfaction. The light hadn't been able to reach all of the crannies, but the prickle on the back of his neck was gone. Nothing stirred, not even the rats that would normally forage in the refuse, unconcerned about his presence.

Odd. No rats could not be a good sign. He stilled, sensed no imminent danger. Might as well get to work. Their midnight curfew would be upon them before long, and he didn't want to waste a second. Maybe when they finished here, they'd have an hour or so to grab a beer on the way back. Pretend, for just a while, that they were regular guys again, grabbing a cold one after work.

Cheered somewhat, Johan crept along the wall the remaining forty yards to the most recent murder scene. What he'd hoped to find that they hadn't already, he didn't know. The best clues had been found on the victims' bodies. The teeth and claw marks, the puzzling *ardin*, so close in genetic makeup to Drakkon's. But not quite.

Shining the beam against the lower wall and dirty pavement, he noted some of the bloodstains were visible, even after several weeks. The majority of the woman's blood had been washed away by the elements, thank the gods. The demon had, quite literally, torn her apart. Some of the stains still clung in the crevices of the brick, darkened with age.

Trailing the beam up the wall, he perused the most significant indication to date of the demon's great height. Eleven feet above, the creature had caught the side of the building with a powerful swipe of his claws. Four furrows in the brick trailed in a downward arc from right to left, leaving a five-foot scar to tell the grisly tale.

Johan imagined the poor lady huddled against the side of the building, terrified, knowing her life was over. Pictured the slavering rogue demon towering over her much smaller body, slashing with razor-sharp claws. Tearing her to pieces. A gruesome end to hours or days of captivity as his sexual plaything.

With an effort, he shoved the scene from his mind and studied the marks. In a rage, Drakkon could've made these, though the Demon King argued he wasn't quite tall enough, that even in true form, his reach didn't extend so far. Johan and Zane had pushed hard for the Council to bring him here and make him prove it.

What followed was the Exodus warriors' version of a grand, embarrassing fiasco. A smirking Drakkon, in a rare display for everyone of his true demon form, stood in this very spot, his extended claws indeed falling short of reaching the marks overhead. This embarrassment, coupled with the DNA disaster, was the last straw. He and Zane were stripped of all they held dear and out on the streets in record time.

Now what? Nothing new to be gleaned here, but he'd wanted to try. Dispirited, he wondered whether Zane was having better luck. Doubtful.

A shuffle sounded behind him. He swung the light around, keeping it low so Zane wouldn't be blinded. "You find any — "

He broke off, the words dying in his throat. Illuminated in the dim beam were a pair of muscled legs the size of tree trunks. Between those legs jutted a purple cock so huge no human could possibly house it, and balls the size of oranges. Against Johan's will, his gaze lifted, taking in the outline of a massive, naked demon at least nine feet tall, black, leathery wings outspread. Red eyes glowed from a broad face framed by a fall of dark hair.

Numb shock rooted his boots in place. In those two heartbeats between this world and the next, his horrified brain registered a couple of facts.

That's the biggest motherfucking demon I've ever seen. And then, *That's not Drakkon.*

Too late, he grabbed for the weapon at his side. His hand closed around the butt as a powerful arm swung down. Before he could free the laser blaster, the blow caught him in the side of the head, venom-tipped claws raking his face and chest.

Johan hit the ground hard and rolled, agony stealing the air from his lungs. His ears rang and his vision doubled. The flashlight...where? No time. As the creature advanced, he pushed to his knees with an effort, desperately trying to level the gun at any part of its exposed flesh.

Laughing evilly, the demon swiped his forearm in an uppercut to Johan's chest. This blow sent him flying backward like a ball shot from a cannon, slamming him into the wall with spine-crunching force. Pain exploded in the back of his head, and he slid to the ground in a crumpled heap.

His weapon fell from limp fingers. He lay stunned, unable to move, in total disbelief that his life would end this way. A disgraced warrior, torn apart and devoured by the quarry who'd eluded and outsmarted him at every turn. Perhaps he deserved this fate.

Blood rapidly saturated his shirt, pooling around his body. Gasping, every breath torture, he thought the demon must've cracked his sternum. Every bone in his body was shattered glass, screaming in pain.

The monster loomed over him, a dark shape with red eyes. Claws ripped off his clothing in shreds, leaving him exposed and vulnerable.

The creature enfolded him into a strangely gentle embrace, in confusing contrast to the violence of seconds before. His body lifted a couple of feet off the ground, the motion tearing a cry of pain from his throat. Great black wings enfolded and cradled him.

The demon lowered his head, hot, stale breath wafting against Johan's lips. "Sweet warrior."

The demon's mouth closed over his, tongue sweeping inside, tasting. Revolted, Johan used the last of his strength to push against the creature's chest, to no avail. The kiss deepened, branding him with possession.

Dimly, he was aware of a sting in the roof of his mouth, followed by a warm, languid false sense of well-being flooding his limbs. At the same time, a rush of heat speared his cock, hardening the member instantly. Desire roared through his body, demanding to be fed.

No! Gods, the thing had injected him with the *ardin*. To keep him in a pleasant haze while it played with his body, until the monster tired of the game and killed him.

Moving over Johan, the creature positioned himself between his legs. Lifted his ass. The huge rod slid over his belly, lower, seeking entry.

Terror, coupled with grave injuries and the sickness from needing his blood reward, proved too much. His brain shut down, took him away from this awful place and what was about to happen.

His vision dimmed, consciousness sliding away.

Zane! Please, let him pick up the link. *Stay away...too strong. Take my body home...to Raina.*

At last, the world and his troubles slipped into blessed darkness.

Chapter Nine

ജ

Inside the deserted store, Zane poked through the rubble, disgusted as always by the absence of evidence. What a frigging waste of time.

Personally, he was damned anxious for curfew. Grinning to himself, he tried to imagine what sorts of exercises his training as a submissive would entail. Saints, he was horny as a teenager on prom night. He longed to link with Raina and Johan again. More than that, he *needed* to connect with them. To experience the Nirvana of their bodies and souls merging with his. To feel...

Loved.

No question, he'd loved Johan forever and knew his friend felt the same, even if he had difficulty speaking of tender emotions. And Raina?

He smiled, thinking of Raina laughing and teasing with him earlier. Nothing like a cool, haughty Queen at all. Yes, he was quickly growing to love her. If Johan would come down off his high horse for an hour or two, he'd see the compassionate woman underneath the regal exterior as well. And he'd fall for her, too.

How could he get Johan to open his eyes? Maybe —

Zane! Stay away...too strong. Take my body home...to Raina.

"Oh, gods," he gasped. "Johan? *Johan!*"

Silence. Palming his blaster, Zane ran for the back of the store toward the exit, faster than he'd ever run before. He tore out the door and into the narrow alley, drawing up short.

The scene in front of him was an apparition straight from the bowels of Hades. A monstrous demon crouched over

Johan's limp, bloodied body, gigantic wings enfolding him like a lover. The wings shielded the worst from view, but Zane knew what evil the monster intended. The creature held Johan close, moving into better position, giving a low grunt of satisfaction.

A scream of grief and rage erupted from his soul, echoed off the buildings as he braced his legs. Leveled his weapon.

"*Nooo! You bastard!*"

Startled, the demon jerked its head up, eyes blazing in the darkness. Using the monster's gaze as a target, Zane opened fire, aiming for the head. He couldn't kill a demon with a blaster—might as well use a flyswatter—but a few head shots might wound the creature and drive it off.

Zane's arm jerked as he sent a volley of rounds streaking toward his nemesis. The blasts found their target.

An earsplitting screech rent the air as the demon threw his head back and spread his wings for flight. Releasing his prey, he took to the sky, howling his rage to the sleeping city. When he paused and made a shallow dive, obviously considering a counterattack, Zane sent another round his way, this time peppering the leathery wings with holes.

Another enraged screech and the demon whirled into the heavens, swallowed by the night. For a few seconds, Zane stood frozen, gun pointed skyward in case the sonofabitch decided to come back for more. Gradually, he lowered the weapon, realizing how lucky he'd been. If the demon hadn't been caught so completely by surprise, he and Johan would be dead.

"Johan?" He jogged over to the still form. His friend lay on his side, facing away from him. Kneeling, heart pounding in dread, he rolled the injured man gently to his back.

"No," Zane whispered, stricken, a sob welling in his chest. He combed Johan's long, black hair out of his ravaged face. "Oh, no, please."

Four wide, deep furrows slashed his left cheek, trailing to his neck and chest. Pieces of his shirt clung to him in tatters, but the rest of his clothing had been ripped away. From his waist up, every inch of skin and remaining material was soaked in blood, his hair matted and sticky. Even in the darkness, he saw Johan's beautiful golden eyes, half-open, unseeing. Glowing with agony, glazed with shock.

Through the bond, Zane felt the pain of every slice, each broken bone. So immense it almost felled him as well.

He stroked Johan's good cheek, hardly aware of the tears running down his own face. "Hang on, damn you. Do you hear?"

A low moan of anguish escaped Johan's lips, but he didn't stir. He struggled for each breath, an ominous, wet rattle sounding from his lungs.

Zane wanted to gather Johan into his arms, but didn't dare risk moving him. His friend's body began to shake.

"Raina," Zane sobbed. He grabbed one limp, blood-slickened hand, held it to his cheek. *Hurry, focus! Find the connection!* "Raina?"

Johan's life force was leaving his body fast, ripping a hole in Zane's middle. Tearing the bond, knifing his heart.

Zane threw back his head and screamed.

"Raina!"

* * * * *

"Which ones for the party? The hand-painted or the plain long-stemmed?" Raina held up both wineglasses for Alexi's inspection.

From his chair by the parlor fireplace, her companion gave a bored stare over the top of his newspaper. "The plain, I think. More elegant for a party."

"Good!" She sat the plain glass on the mantle and lifted the other. "The hand-painted it is."

His brows rose. Pale blue eyes fixed her with a droll look, and he snapped the paper closed. "You do that just to annoy me, don't you? Why bother asking for my opinion when you always go ahead and do the opposite?"

"Because we have opposite tastes, love," she said cheerfully. "If you choose the other, then I know I was right all along."

"Gods save me," he muttered, thoroughly vexed. "We sound like an old married couple, except I can't get old and die to escape my nuptial hell."

"Goodness, look who's in a foul mood! What's eating you?" Studying the uncharacteristic pout on Alexi's boyishly handsome face, she had an idea. "Why, you're jealous of my bond with Johan and Zane!"

"Don't be ridiculous," he grumbled, hunching his shoulders.

"Of course you are." Moved, she crossed to his chair and touched his shoulder. "You're not going to lose me, you know that. You'll always be my very best friend. When the time is right, I'll ask you to join us."

His eyes lit, and he laid a hand over hers. "Do you mean that? I'd love nothing more."

"Yes, I mean it. I've sensed you've been feeling a bit left out...and that you have an eye on Zane." She smiled.

Alexi flushed, looking away. "Yeah, maybe."

"In good time," she promised.

"You love them."

The simple phrase, spoken with such clarity and truth, stopped her. Cold chilled her bones, filled her with dread. People who loved deeply lost irrevocably. There were those who'd conspire to take her warriors away, or kill them if they guessed the depth of her developing feelings toward them.

No, the only way to protect her lovers was to remember what they were by law. Her slaves, bound to spend their mortal lives in her bed. The three of them, bringing one another pleasure until the end of their days.

And their mortal lives *would* end.

Then she'd be left heartbroken. Again.

"I can't love them the way you mean."

"Marcus is dead," Alexi said softly. "Don't you think it's centuries past time to let him rest?"

Stunned, she jerked her hand from his shoulder. "How dare you," she whispered.

"I dare more than you, dear. Stop using him as an excuse not to find your mate. Take a chance, allow yourself to be *happy.*"

Alexi was right. But admitting it meant letting go of the greatest man she'd ever known. Instead, she wrapped the memories of Marcus around her shoulders like a mantle, the one foolproof barrier between herself and the world.

"Don't presume to tell me how I should feel! Marcus was—"

Raina!

The grief-stricken scream blasted Raina in the center of her chest. She staggered and splayed a hand over her breastbone, the wineglass slipping from her hand.

Alexi bolted to his feet, grabbing her arms. "What's wrong? Raina?"

"Zane," she gasped. "Something's happened."

His gaze clouded with worry. "Can you get a fix on his location?"

"I—yes. I've got him."

"I'm coming with you." His tone left no room for argument.

She wasn't about to give him one. "Let's go."

Raising her arms, she flashed from the palace. She followed the thread of the bond, tracking Zane easily through downtown St. Louis, near the river. Fear gripped her with the realization that Johan's thread had gone cold, leaving a gaping, painful void in her middle. Very much like her guts had been ripped from her stomach.

As she and Alexi appeared in a dirty alley, fear became horror. "Oh, no. Zane?"

Bent over Johan's nude body, he sobbed brokenly. The wrenching sounds of his grief said more than words ever could.

She ran to them, fell to her knees beside Johan with a cry. "Oh, sweet Virgin! What happened? Who did this evil?" He'd been torn to ribbons, but he was alive. Barely. He was shaking, coated with sweat and blood, fighting to breathe. His eyes were half-open, unseeing.

"Zane, who did this?" she repeated, injecting command into her tone. "Talk to us."

Zane raised his tear-swollen face as though noticing her and Alexi for the first time. "D-demon."

"Drakkon?" Alexi snapped. "I'll fucking kill him—"

"N-no. Never s-saw him before. H-huge…" He choked back another sob, tried to steady himself. "Help him, please."

She closed her eyes. A demon attack. The worst of all because none, not even the largest wolf or cat shifter, could match the demon's inflicted damage for size and sheer brutality.

This is all my fault, she agonized. *I never should have let them leave the palace, much less armed with nothing more than a pitiful blaster.*

"No," Zane denied in a strangled voice. "Don't blame yourself. Just save him. Please, before it's too late."

Surprised, she opened her eyes and walled her thoughts. No time to spare mulling over how he'd read them. Looking down at Johan's face, she placed her hands on his heaving chest, knowing it might be too late already.

Blocking her own sadness, she concentrated on sending out her energy. Let the golden bond flow from her body, through her fingertips, into his. Wind around his laboring heart and lungs. In this way, she anchored him to this life while she searched his insides, surveying the damage.

All told, he shouldn't be alive. Probably wouldn't be, if not for the strength of their bond. Any other human would've been dead minutes ago. This gave her guarded hope, but the battle wasn't yet won.

"Cracked skull, vertebrae and sternum," she related. "Internal bleeding, punctured lung. Not to mention the venom from the demon's claws and the *ardin* in his system."

"He was sick, too," Zane sniffed, gaining control of himself. "He didn't get his blood reward last night."

Raina stared at Zane, wretched with the guilt flailing her from all sides. "That *is* my fault," she whispered.

Alexi laid a palm on her back. "Neither of us has ever treated a demon attack, and there's no time to summon a Healer. What should we do?"

Raina schooled herself to focus. "Johan needs blood from all of us. Yours and mine for the healing properties, mine and Zane's to keep him bound to us while his injuries knit together again."

Alexi nodded. "Sounds like as good a plan as any. I'll go first so you can keep your hands on him. When he's more stable, you can go next."

Giving her shoulder a reassuring squeeze, the younger vampire knelt by Johan's head. He slashed his wrist with a sharp fang, then slipped his index finger between the man's lips to work his mouth open. That accomplished, he placed his wrist over Johan's parted lips, allowing the healing blood to flow inside.

Except Johan wasn't swallowing. The dark crimson liquid ran from the sides of his mouth, down his neck. Anxious, Raina leaned forward. "Stroke his throat."

Taking two fingers, Alexi massaged along his windpipe, coaxing his reflex to swallow. Riveted with fear, Raina poured more energy into the bond. His heartbeat was barely more than a flutter of butterfly wings and if he didn't cooperate—

"There!" she sang out.

Johan's throat worked. He coughed twice, then began to swallow. Weak sips at first, then stronger and more deliberate drinks. At last, he latched onto the vampire's wrist and gulped, pulling hard.

"Thank the gods," Zane breathed, hanging his head.

"We're not out of the woods yet," Raina cautioned.

"But he's improving, right?"

Zane stroked his friend's hair, the simple gesture filled with such love, her heart caught.

"Oh, yes. Quite speedily, in fact, given what he's just been through. The bleeding has stopped and the bones are knitting. By the time he finishes our blood, you won't even see a scar. Then we'll take him home and put him to bed."

Zane sighed, weary. "Yeah, he's going to be pretty sick while his system adjusts to the *ardin*. Wonder how he'll deal with his libido being permanently launched into sex machine territory? There'll be no living with him after this."

Alexi winced. "He should just be glad he's alive." Seeing the pained expression flicker across Alexi's face, she brought them back to the matter at hand.

"My turn. He's strong enough for me to leave just one hand on him while he drinks."

The younger vampire moved away and closed his wrist. Raina scooted into his vacated spot. Leaving one palm over Johan's heart, she sliced her wrist and held it to his lips.

He fed well, pulling harder than before. His golden eyes lost their dull glaze, gradually brightening with returning life. He blinked as he drank, attempting to focus, perhaps organize his thoughts. His heartbeat thudded steadily in his chest, and the terrible wounds marring his face, neck and chest began to knit.

"That's it, love," she crooned. "You're going to be just fine. Drink from Zane, and then we'll be able to take you home, okay?"

He gave a slight nod and tried to fix his gaze on her face, but couldn't quite manage the feat yet.

"No, don't try too hard. Rest, dearest." She closed her wrist and motioned for Zane to give his to her. To his credit, he didn't flinch as she tore the flesh.

Zane gave to his friend, letting him take all he needed. When Johan's lashes drifted downward to curl against his pale cheek, Raina took Zane's arm and sealed the cut.

"He's sleeping," she said softly, lifting Johan's shoulders to cradle him in her arms. "We'd better get him home and cleaned up before the sickness hits. The next few hours will be rough."

Alexi took Zane's arm. In a flash of light, the foursome appeared in Raina's spacious bathroom. Zane ran a warm bath, and the three of them washed the unconscious man with care from head to toe, cleansing his body of the last traces of the horrible ordeal. On the outside, at least.

Once clean and dry, they placed Johan in the center of Raina's big bed. Zane eased his dark head onto the plump pillows while she tugged the crisp sheet over his naked hips.

"That's it," Alexi said quietly. "Dawn is approaching, so I thought I'd turn in, unless you two need me."

"Goodness, I can't believe it's been hours." She smiled at her old friend and kissed his cheek. "Go ahead. We'll call if we have trouble. In fact, let's all get some rest."

"All right, dear. Until the evening." With a wave at Zane, he left.

Zane looked at her in concern. "How bad will his sickness get?"

"Honestly, I don't know. I've never nursed anyone through it, but I've heard there's fever, aches and pains. Not to mention the rising of the *ardin* as it becomes part of his genetics. When he awakens, he'll be randy as a stallion in full rut. If he thrashes around, he'll hurt himself and we'll have difficulty calming him."

"Then we'll need to bind his wrists," Zane muttered. "Dammit, I hate that he has to suffer."

"Me too, sweet. All we can do is try to make this a little easier for him." Striding to her dresser, she opened the top drawer and dug through her trove of toys. Locating what she needed, she held them up. "Will these do?"

"Oh, boy. Can we use them on me?" His green eyes lit with hope.

"Patience is a virtue, as they say."

"And sadly overrated," he grumped.

Yes, indeed. The idea had merit, and they'd have to put these to good use. Returning to the bed with a pair of soft, padded cuffs, she slipped Johan's wrists into them. Each resembled a wide wristband with straps to adjust the fit. She secured them snugly, but not too tight. Attached to each wristband with a length of chain was a regular metal handcuff. This end, she fastened to a headboard slat over Johan's head, making sure his arm wasn't stretched so much he'd be uncomfortable. Zane secured the other arm.

"Wow, he looks like a Pagan sacrifice," Zane observed with no little appreciation. "Or a fallen angel."

"Just wait. When he awakens, he'll feel like both, and then some. Shower?"

"Yeah." He glanced at himself. "His dried blood is all over both of us."

She and Zane took turns in the shower so the other could keep an eye on Johan. She went first, slipping naked under the sheets and curling against Johan's side afterward. Whether to comfort him or herself was anyone's guess.

Zane returned, padding across the room to the bed, naked and glorious. A big, sleek, jade-eyed cat. For a moment, he just stood beside the bed and looked down at her and Johan. The sheen in his gaze now wasn't from fear, but from love so powerful, the emotion bathed the three of them. A warm, gentle wave.

Without words, an understanding passed between them as Raina returned the warmth. She welcomed him, and he slid into the bed on the other side of their lover. A place he'd never be asked to leave.

Take a chance, allow yourself to be happy.

But what about the law? These men were still slaves, and royalty was forbidden to take slaves as mates. She could free them...and lose them both forever. Zane might want to stay, but Johan would tear out of here as though Satan were gnashing at his heels. Zane would follow him, just as he'd done all their lives.

Blazing Hades. Wasn't refusing to give all of them a chance at real happiness—and yes, love—the same as losing them anyway?

I'm strong enough to take the risk! I can do this!

The real question was, could they convince Johan? Such a proud, stubborn man. Headstrong, self-assured. Dominant, sexually explosive. Her match in every way.

Her mate.

She'd hinted to no one. Not even Alexi, though he might suspect. She'd known almost from the first. In their decadent bath last evening, she'd come close to letting the truth slip.

Exhausted, she rested her head on Johan's shoulder and laid a palm over his heart. Zane's hand covered hers, his quiet, easy strength giving her the courage to do something she should've done a thousand years ago.

Raina sent a prayer to the kingdom where great, brave men spend their eternal rest.

And bid Marcus goodbye.

Chapter Ten

A few hours into their daysleep, the sickness hit Johan's system with the force of a freight train.

A hoarse cry jerked Raina from uneasy dreams of shadows and death. A faceless demon stalked her warriors, all the more terrifying for his anonymity. As the cobwebs cleared, she realized with a start the harsh, guttural moans weren't just part of the daymare, but were being wrenched from the man thrashing between her and Zane.

"Nooo…stop!" Johan twisted in the restraints, tossing his dark head from side to side.

Sitting up, Raina swept the mass of her unruly hair over her shoulder and splayed a hand on Johan's bare chest. His skin burned like the sands of Death Valley and his handsome face, shadowed with the stubble of his beard, was contorted in agony.

"Shh, warrior," she soothed. "You'll be all right."

Zane sat up, rubbing his eyes. "Damn, this is it. What can we do to help him?"

She shook her head. "Nothing much at this stage except talk to him, touch and try to comfort him as much as possible."

Johan gave another harsh cry, jerking his bonds in a futile attempt to escape the clutches of his torment. The headboard rattled and the entire bed vibrated with the violence of his struggles, every hard muscle in his arms and chest straining. Thank goodness they'd had the foresight to restrain their lover, or he'd surely harm himself.

"I can't stand to see him like this," Zane murmured in worry. "I wish I could endure it for him." He laid a hand on

Johan's heaving shoulder, tentative at first, as though adjusting to this new level of intimacy. Keeping his touch light, he began to stroke his friend's heated skin.

Raina massaged Johan's chest over his heart and leaned close to his ear. "Easy, love. Stop fighting and grab hold of the bond. Feel us, we're here. Reach out, Johan, let us help you."

She repeated the words several times, watching intently for signs of improvement. Gradually his struggles quieted and he appeared to listen and make an effort to heed her words.

"That's right." She smiled, stroking his fevered brow. "You're doing fine."

"Hurts," Johan whispered, surfacing from the depths of his pain.

Raina's heart wrenched at the soft, bereft plea. "I know, darling. But not for much longer, I promise."

"Raina?" Johan's eyes opened, his pupils dilated, the amber rings of his irises a thin thread. Turning his head slightly toward her voice, he attempted to focus on her face, but failed.

"Right here beside you. Rest now."

"Thank...you." Another spasm of pain chased off the small smile that tried to curve Johan's lips.

Warmth curled through Raina's breast. Did she dare hope for the beginning of a truce between herself and this stubborn slave? Or the start of something more?

Zane caressed his friend's arm, wretched with worry and struggling not to show it. "Hey, I wasn't exactly chopped liver out there," he teased, voice gruff. "Get some sleep, my badass friend. You're going to need it."

Johan's lashes drifted down and he sank into exhaustion once more. Raina feared the demon's poison wasn't finished ripping the warrior with vicious claws. Her blood was capable of healing terrible physical wounds, but held no power over either a demon's toxins or his *ardin.*

The next few hours were more horrible than she'd imagined. Alexi had been well past this adjustment by the time she'd swept him under her protection all those years ago, so she'd never witnessed this. The sickness racked Johan's body again and again. She and Zane soothed him each time, yet the damnable poison persisted until, finally, it began to lose ground. At last Johan quieted and fell into a deep, restful slumber.

"So, you can mind-link," she mused aloud, studying Johan's friend during the lull. "Just before we healed Johan, you read my thoughts of guilt over his attack. Mind-linking is a handy gift for a human to possess in a harsh world filled with dangerous creatures. But very risky as well, should an enemy learn your secret."

Zane returned her regard, expression sober. "Yeah. The kind of ability that can get a guy's head separated from his shoulders—or worse, taken captive and used like a puppet. Forgive me for not telling you, my lady. Johan has always known, but I've grown so accustomed to guarding my gift, it's second nature. And we had no idea what sort of mistress you'd be."

Curious, she cocked her head. "What sort am I?"

"Strong, passionate and fair." His green gaze warmed. A smile played about his sensual lips, revealing an alluring dimple. "I've known from the first that we could trust you with our lives. Forgive me for holding out on you."

"A rather glowing assessment, but I should still lay a few lashes across your backside." She arched a brow, managing to hide how very much his words pleased her.

Zane sent her a boyish grin. "Don't threaten me with a good time if you don't plan to follow through, beautiful. It just ain't fair."

She stifled a laugh. "Impertinent slave, we'll soon see what you're made of. Get some rest, because your friend isn't the only one who'll need his strength."

Raina and Zane took advantage of the reprieve while they had the chance, snuggling in on each side of Johan's big body to sleep. They'd need plenty of strength when his *ardin* rose and seared itself into his DNA for good.

As she began to drift off, Zane's hushed voice caressed her. "He knew he was dying. In what would've been his last moments, Johan asked me to bring his body home...to you. His words. I thought you should know."

Home. To me. "Thank you for telling me," she murmured.

"He's not such a hard man, you know, once you get past that proud exterior."

Zane yawned and fell silent, his breathing evening out in slumber within minutes. Raina lay awake, mulling over what she'd learned. The last request of a dying man was often the most telling, and Johan had made a special effort to emphasize those wishes.

Still, she tamped down the wondrous joy surging in her breast. Perhaps it meant nothing at all, except that he hadn't been able to think of anywhere else for Zane to take his body. Too tired to contemplate the matter anymore, she sank into oblivion.

When Raina awoke next, she didn't know whether hours or minutes had passed. She lay still and listened, her palm resting over Johan's thundering heart. His skin burned with a fire not borne of sickness. He moaned, tugging on the restraints, his agony clearly for a very different reason than before.

Pushing to sit upright, Raina peered into the blackness. The faint slivers of day that had slipped past the edges of the heavy draperies were gone. She snapped her fingers and several fat candles on the dresser and bedside table flared to life, dispelling the night.

"Johan?" She looked down at his trembling body and her breath caught. Zane was right. On the verge of waking, broad chest heaving with mounting desire, bound spread and helpless, Johan did resemble a Pagan sacrifice.

His head was thrown back, raven hair tangled about his face and shoulders. Every muscle in his gleaming frame stood out in relief, licked by the candlelight. His erection curved upward, arching over his taut belly, demanding.

Johan Stone was the most beautiful man she'd ever seen, bar none. A man in desperate need. *Mine.*

She leaned over him, placed a gentle kiss on his gorgeous mouth. "Wake up, Johan. It's time to let me take care of you."

* * * * *

No matter how hard Johan struggled to escape the thousands of knives stabbing his body, the awful heat boiling the very marrow of his bones, the blessed relief of eternal sleep eluded his grasp.

Never any pain like this. Flaying him from all sides, ripping every cell apart. Endless, unrelenting agony mingled with images of horror.

Red eyes, slashing claws. Blood and bone. Screaming.

Why can't I die?

Dimly, he heard Raina and Zane urging him to hang on, giving him comfort, nursing him through hell. His companions' worry and caring — and something much deeper — washed over him in waves, bathing him in light. Driving back the pain to fortify his strength, inch by torturous inch. He tried to express his thanks to them both, but couldn't maintain a conversation, or even summon a smile when Zane called him a badass.

At last the terrible nightmare abated and he tumbled gratefully into the peaceful abyss of healing sleep. Some time later, consciousness began to return, and with it the awareness that his body was on fire.

The fever and pain that had torn at him were gone. What

was this? As Johan came more fully awake, he took stock of his situation. Healthy didn't begin to describe how he felt. More like *electrified*.

A new entity sizzled in his tissues and blood, burrowed into his cell structure and became part of him. Or at least that's what he imagined, so deep and profound was the change. The merging was swift and powerful, and Johan moaned with the awesome sensations sweeping him from head to toe. The flames quickly spread from his gut outward to his limbs, his groin. Licked between his legs like a long, hot tongue. He reached to palm his aching shaft, only to discover that his arms were stretched above his head in a Y position, wrists secured.

A kiss, soft as rose petals, brushed his lips.

"Wake up, Johan. It's time to let me take care of you."

He opened his eyes, blinking to adjust his vision. Raina leaned over him, candlelight dancing on the wild red hair curtaining them both. A lock trailed over one creamy breast, the pink little nipple peeking through the strands. Heat speared his cock, stiffening his member like a divining rod.

"Raina, what's happening to me?" As he yanked on the padded cuffs, a tinkle of chain and scrape of metal on the headboard slats mocked his predicament. Fear coiled in his gut, intensifying the unbearable arousal rather than lessening it. "Why am I bound?" he rasped.

Her fingers smoothed his scorching forehead, the magic of their bond assuaging his mounting panic. Gods, that felt damned good. He turned his face into her touch, seeking more.

This seemed to please Raina, and her lips turned up in a gentle, sympathetic smile. "Don't worry, love. The *ardin* is binding with your genetics, and we can't risk letting you loose during your first full rut. The adjustment will be quite intense, but extremely pleasurable. Zane will help."

"Hey, big guy." Zane sat on the other side of Johan, jade eyes sparkling with happiness at seeing his friend awake. "You're one lucky bastard, you realize that?"

133

"The jury's out." First full rut? Ah, shit. Johan studied his friend with growing unease. "How exactly are you going to help with my problem?"

"No," Raina ordered, placing a finger over Johan's lips. "Don't think anymore, just lie back and concentrate on relaxing your muscles. Let the fear and tension go."

"How can I?" he blurted. Reality crashed in, misery and despair clogging his throat. "Whoever the fuck that demon is, he's evil, and now the sonofabitch is a part of me. Why didn't you both just let me die?"

"Oh, Johan." She cupped his cheek, the gesture tender, a mysterious sheen in her lovely blue eyes. "You're not a quitter, and you're not evil. Demons *choose* to use their *ardin* for vile purposes, but you don't have an ounce of malice in your soul, Johan Stone. If I'd believed that for one moment, I'd have ended your suffering."

Absolute truth resonated in her voice. Still he had to be sure. "You mean that? You'd end my life before allowing darkness to own me, or to prevent me from becoming other than a man? My present status as a slave excluded, of course. I'm not a coward."

"Yes, I would," she affirmed gravely.

"And when the day comes that you must choose between your desire to keep your slave at your side for eternity or allowing me to die with honor? When even your blood won't heal my wounds or halt the mark of age on my body, will you turn me against my wishes?"

A spasm of pain flashed across her face. "Not if you don't want the gift."

"I don't, and I never will," he asserted, even as his heart lightened. When his time came, Raina would place his wishes above her own. She'd let him go.

"Then you have my word, I swear it." She looked unhappy about her promise, but steadfast. Leveling her gaze on Zane, she asked, "Is this your feeling on the subject as well?"

Nonplussed by the topic, Zane raked a hand through his shaggy, brown-gold hair. "Saints, I don't know. Do I have to decide right this minute?"

"No, of course not. Just don't wait too long to come to a decision, or you may not have one to make. Case in point, tonight's near-tragedy. Now that the issue has come to light, I'll do whatever is necessary to save you, including turning you vampire, unless you've expressed wishes to the contrary."

"Fair enough." Zane nodded.

"If we're finished with the morbid stuff, I'm in a bit of a situation here." Johan gritted his teeth, so embarrassed he wanted to vaporize. "Why don't you two just let me go and I'll…tend to my problem myself."

His friend gazed down at him in sympathy. "No can do, pal. The rut is going to get a helluva lot worse before your system adjusts. We let you up and you'll be out the door, humping everything from here to the Canadian border."

Well, wasn't that flattering? "Goddammit, I—"

A wave of heat and lust rolled through his body, choking off his protest. Along with the blinding need came anger. The beast's howling rage at the delay in seeing his urges satisfied, demanding that he savage everyone within reach to take his fill.

They're right. I'm dangerous. A man sworn to protect, now a threat to all within his reach. The knowledge suffused him with shame, but the rising beast eclipsed even that emotion. Obliterated all thought, leaving nothing except flesh and blood, straining toward the ultimate goal.

Raina bent, whispered into his ear. "Easy, my beautiful slave. You cannot swim against a tidal wave. Ride the crest, accept this new darkness, because that is the only way you'll learn to master it."

135

Her mouth captured his, sweet tongue sweeping past the seam of his lips, tangling with his. Ride the crest. That meant opening himself to this foreign entity, letting go, becoming a man he didn't know. As a warrior who, until recently, had been in control of every aspect of his life, he didn't have the slightest clue how.

He needn't have worried. The powerful forces seizing control, rooting deep into the marrow of his bones, his psyche, drove his body. Conqueror or conquest, the distinction hardly mattered, not with Raina's tongue down his throat, the hard pebbles of her nipples grazing his bare chest. Twin points branding his skin, sizzling to every nerve ending. Arching his back, he dug his heels into the mattress and lifted his hips, moaning in frustration.

Leaving his mouth, she trailed licks and kisses down the column of his throat to his chest. Her attention traveled to his pierced nipple, flicking the ring and taut copper nub with that clever little tongue. She drew both between her lips, sucking with enthusiasm, using the ring as an implement of torture. Small shocks of pain radiated from the sensitive peak, merged with the desire driving him to desperation.

A hand smoothed his hair, and it took Johan a moment to realize the gentle touch wasn't Raina's. Zane scooted close and looked down at him, bottle-green gaze swirling with emotions. Concern and empathy were etched on his boyishly handsome face. And unmistakable desire.

Johan's breath caught. Awareness hummed along their bond, new and electric. Zane started to bend to his friend, but stopped, glancing quickly at Raina, awaiting permission to proceed. Releasing the throbbing nipple, she nodded, a small smile playing about her lips.

Zane lowered his head and Johan stiffened out of pure knee-jerk reaction. Warm, firm lips pressed against his, seeking, urging. *Oh gods, my best friend—another man—is kissing me.* Johan's brain short-circuited and he lay frozen in a maelstrom of confusion and pleasure, reason flashed-fried.

"Johan," Raina said softly. "You've loved Zane all your life, and he feels the same. The bond has merely strengthened this connection and made physical expression between you possible. Even necessary. Darling, stop fighting and let go."

Her words flowed along the golden thread between the three of them, bathing her men in love and approval. Zane sipped at his lips, coaxing patiently. Breaking down his resistance.

This strange new loving felt...wonderful. Very different from a woman's touch, and more meaningful by far than the few females he'd been with before Raina. Zane moved over him, tasting. Bare chests brushed together, nipple rings grazing sensitized pectorals, Zane's huge shaft resting on Johan's stomach. His friend was all hard muscle, bunching and flexing, fascinating planes and angles. Yet the man's heart was as soft and beautiful as Raina's lithe, curvy frame. Zane was the perfect complement to their mistress. *And to me.*

The *ardin* spiked higher, stretching and purring like a big, hungry cat. His wicked new companion wanted feeding, demanded Johan's surrender. The darkness spread through every part of him, not evil in the least, but lovely and decadent as a moonlit night full of promise.

Because Johan had no choice, he surrendered.

Only then did he fully understand why Raina and Zane bound his wrists. Raw power and white-hot lust blasted through his body and along the bond with the force of a megaton bomb. Zane's harsh gasp echoed his own and Raina gave a startled cry as tremors shook the three of them, similar to the aftershocks of an earthquake.

Zane recovered first, burying his hands in Johan's hair and renewing the kiss with a ferocity Johan had only witnessed in battle. He reveled in the other man eating his mouth, his lover's unique flavor, like brandy and sex. In the pungent, spicy scent of aroused male. Of Raina's lips blazing a path to his navel and beyond.

His mistress positioned herself between his spread thighs and cradled his aching balls in one hand. Long fingers manipulated the sac, eliciting a growl of impatience from his chest. The damnable cock ring performed its job admirably, squeezing his tortured shaft and balls in tandem with her ministrations, heightening his awareness of total vulnerability. He no longer cared.

With a throaty, feminine laugh, she nibbled and nipped. Sharp fangs grazed the sensitive flesh of his scrotum, and he shivered in delight as she laved the tiny, stinging cuts. Savoring him like an appetizer before the main course.

Ahh, yesss, the beast goaded his captors. *Be glad I'm tied, at your mercy…for now. Do me, anything you want, I can't stop you. Just remember, paybacks are a motherfucker.*

Zane chuckled, breaking the kiss, and Raina smiled, leaving no doubt they'd heard his thoughts. Good. Whatever these two had in mind for him, he was ready.

Raina slid off the bed and padded to the dresser. Johan turned his head to watch as she opened the top drawer, digging in her naughty treasure trove. He drank in the sight of her, wild red hair licking at her hips and lush buttocks like flames. When she spun around holding aloft the object she'd sought, his eyes widened and his rampant cock jerked in anticipation.

"Ready to eat your bold words, slave?" she drawled, returning to the bed to crawl between his legs once more.

Johan stared at the black marble phallus in her delicate, pale hands. The thing was enormous, about eight inches long and almost as thick as a man's wrist. Larger than the one Alexi had presented to him that first evening. Speech deserted him.

Her cobalt gaze flicked to Zane. "Place a pillow under his hips, then hand me the little bottle of oil there on the nightstand."

"Yes, ma'am." Zane grinned, grabbing a pillow.

"And take note, my pretty slave," she replied, arching a burnished brow. "Compared to your impending initiation as a submissive, what we're doing to Johan is so vanilla, one could eat it on top of a waffle cone. Savvy?"

Zane sucked in a breath and lowered his eyes in respect. "Yes, mistress."

Johan raised his hips as Zane pushed the pillow underneath. The position made him even more vulnerable, completely accessible to her in a way he'd never allowed any woman to have him. But Raina wasn't just any female, she was his as much as he was hers. *Mine.*

He groaned, pumping his erection into empty air, desperate to bury himself in her slick heat. His poor cock curved over his clenched abdomen, flushed deep crimson and leaking pre-cum from the broad head.

"Hmm. Johan has too much freedom of movement in his legs," Raina observed, taking the bottle of oil from Zane's outstretched hand. "He's keeping himself too tense."

"Want me to fetch an extra pair of bindings from the drawer, my lady?" His friend seemed pretty damned cheerful at the prospect.

She nodded. "Yes, something soft. We don't want his wrists and ankles damaged by his struggles."

Oh, shit. A bead of sweat trickled down his temple into his hair.

Zane returned in a moment with a pair of black velvet ropes. "Will these do?"

"Perfect. Loop one around each ankle and tie the other end to the bedposts."

Zane complied, spreading Johan's legs wide, effectively immobilizing him. Now he really was at their mercy, with no leverage whatsoever. His entire body thrummed with need, and he fought not to come.

Raina dribbled the clear oil onto the phallus, used her palm to coat it all over. "Cup your hands underneath him and spread his ass for me," she said to Zane.

Big hands worked between his butt and the pillow, strong fingers exposing him. This also put Zane's face in close proximity to his raging erection, warm breath fanning across his groin.

Raina slid two fingers between his cheeks, rimming his puckered entrance, then pushed just inside. Unable to help himself, he gasped, tensing in defense.

"Shh, love. Relax your muscles, open for me." Massaging, she worked past the taut ring, delving deeper into his channel. Stroking, stretching the virgin flesh. "Very good, that's right. Give yourself over to us, darling. Your beast needs this, *you* need this."

Yes. Her voice, husky with desire, hypnotized him. His muscles went liquid, accepting the sweet burn in his ass. Whorls of ecstasy swirled through his sensitive flesh, spiraled around his balls and cock as her fingers slid in and out. Left him craving more, so much more.

She removed her fingers, replacing them with the tip of the phallus. "This will hurt at first, my love. I need for you to trust me, to know I'd never allow any real harm to come to you."

"I trust you, my lady," he whispered, and realized he meant every word.

The cool hardness nudged his entrance, and he resisted the natural urge to grip the chains attached to his wrist cuffs. *Trust your mistress, give yourself to her.* She pushed the broad tip into his anus, gently working the massive oiled device into his passage. Slow and easy, deeper, the burn quickly becoming fire that torched his ass in spite of her care.

Johan cried out, tears rolling from the corners of his eyes and into his hair. He yanked at his bonds in a futile attempt to escape the agony as his mistress seated the phallus to the hilt.

Impaled, split in two. No escape. Panic threatened to suffocate him.

"No, don't," she crooned. "Calm, Johan."

Heaving in ragged breaths, he feared his thundering heart might explode. He'd never been so conflicted, so afraid of the shadow on his soul. The dark, sexual nature of the demon, a phoenix rising from the ashes of the man he'd been. Reborn.

Johan only thought he'd surrendered before. The beast opened his arms, beckoning. Unable to battle against the onslaught any longer, he went willingly into its embrace. His final submission, and he shuddered with delicious joy. The beast's roar of triumph became his own as the agony knifing his ass danced along the razor's edge of intense pleasure.

"Ahh, fuck yeah!" Johan threw back his head and closed his eyes, gasping. "More, damn you!"

The slick hardness pumped his channel, filling him, sending him to madness. Thrashing, he strained against the bonds, instinct driving him in a useless effort to thrust. From the red haze, his mistress whispered, *Help Johan…take his cock, slave.*

Strong fingers encircled his shaft as the rasp of a tongue explored his balls, laving the heavy orbs with relish. Johan shivered in delight as the journey traveled upward, licking his rod from base to tip again and again. Eating him like a lollipop. *Zane.*

Warm, moist heat enveloped his throbbing cock. Sheathed him to the base and held there for a moment, very still. Letting him bask in the mouth worshipping his body, his engorged shaft stuffed down that lovely throat. Johan moaned in misery and ecstasy, recognizing the act of submission on Zane's part. Deferring to Johan as the dominant male, awaiting his command.

"Suck me," he rumbled, the low, gravelly voice of his beast strange to his ears. "Do it now."

Johan opened his eyes, lifted his head to watch. Zane's sun-streaked head bobbed up and down over his lap, paying homage to his cock with lips and teeth. Scraping and sucking in tempo to the phallus fucking his ass. Harder, deeper, taking him higher. Cum boiled in his testicles and he panted, desperate for release.

Raina laid a hand on Zane's shoulder. "That's enough. We don't want him to come yet."

A snarl of frustration erupted from Johan's chest as Zane released his dick, leaving it on fire and desperate. Raina shoved her toy deep enough to tickle his tonsils, lodging the damned thing firmly in place as she crawled to his side. Straddled his lap, guided the head of his cock to her slick folds.

And sank, impaling herself on his eager shaft.

"Oh gods," he groaned. "Fuck me, Raina, please…"

Johan's head fell back into the pillows and he gazed at her from under his lashes, wondering if he'd fallen into a wild dream. If so, he didn't want to awaken. Ever.

Bracing her hands on his stomach, Raina began to pump. Sliding up and down, her hot, wet little pussy clenching his throbbing cock. Long, curly hair lapped at their joined hips, and her ripe breasts begged for his touch. Creamy thighs hugged him as he lost himself in his mistress. His beautiful lady.

Mine.

Just when he thought his mistress might allow him release, she rocked forward on her knees and nodded to Zane.

"Take me from behind, my pretty slave. Complete us."

Zane's jade eyes widened. Beside his companions, he stopped stroking his erection and swallowed hard. "I would be honored, my lady."

He crawled between Johan's spread legs, positioning himself behind their mistress. She gasped, long red fingernails digging into Johan's abdomen as Zane dipped his fingers between her legs, rubbing her wetness. Slowly he used Raina's cream to lube her taut entrance, then pushed into her tight hole.

Johan felt his friend inch deeper into Raina's backside, careful not to hurt her. Zane's shaft slid along his own through the thin membrane separating them. In to the hilt, and out again. In, out. The wicked, wondrous sensation was unlike any he'd ever known. Two cocks filling their lady, hers for the taking.

The golden thread between them all flared as though doused with kerosene and a match. The bond burned brighter between Johan and Raina, but he couldn't sort out why.

The dark beauty of their joining shook him to the core, wound tendrils of something around his heart, an emotion he couldn't name. This had become much more than sex, more than the *ardin* rushing in his veins. A sacred act between bondmates.

They are mine, and I'm theirs.

Raina rode him faster, slamming onto his cock without mercy, finding a rhythm with Zane. Each time she sank onto Johan, Zane pounded into her channel, merging the three of them as one. The slapping of flesh, Zane's balls rubbing his as they fucked him, was too much. Johan came undone, spiraling out of control.

The powerful release rocked his world, twisted him inside out. The beast roared, pulling against the restraints. Helpless, he writhed as the waves crashed over his shaking body. His cock pulsed on and on, jetting more semen into her welcoming heat than he'd ever believed possible.

Raina's vaginal muscles spasmed around his shaft as she exploded, Zane following her into oblivion. Their cries mingled, the three of them clinging to one another through the storm until all had quieted. Spent at last, Johan lay quivering and bathed in sweat, lungs heaving like a bellows. Sated for the moment, he drifted in a fog of satisfaction and self-discovery as his lovers separated and snuggled on either side of him.

He'd do anything for Raina. For Zane.

Anything at all, no matter the cost to himself.

Was this…love?

Yes, he'd always loved Zane. Raina had him pegged on that score. If not for the extraordinary circumstances they'd found themselves in, would he ever have expressed those feelings toward Zane physically? Probably not.

But what about Raina? Truth be told, she'd done nothing but try to protect her men since she'd rescued them from Lash and whisked them from Drakkon's clutches. She'd tried to comfort him, to convince him she wasn't the enemy. Had worried over their safety as they'd gone into the night poorly armed to search for a killer. With Zane's and Alexi's help, she'd healed him from the demon attack, then saved his sanity when the *ardin* merged with his DNA.

Being the Vampire Queen, she must conduct herself in accordance with the law, but she wasn't at all selfish and cold as she'd have others believe. Raina was sexually free, compassionate, beautiful—

Two truths hit Johan between the eyes like twin hammers.

Hadn't he already guessed? The thread glowed brighter between him and Raina, illuminating his heart and soul, every fiber of his being, because she was…his mate. *My mate!* He couldn't explain how he knew, but he did. The other truth?

Johan, former warrior-turned-slave, was falling hard for Raina Zharov.

Gods, how is this possible? My Queen, my mistress, my mate.

And he didn't have a fucking clue how to avoid becoming entangled in her silken web. A bitter laugh escaped his lips. Too late. Damn it to Hades, he should leave. Take his chances and just go, as soon as possible.

At once, the bond screamed in protest and terror, a white-hot lance skewering his brain. The beast added to the cacophony, roaring in displeasure, coiling his muscles into a knot at the very idea of abandoning his mate. *Mine!*

Gritting his teeth, Johan gripped the chains and rode the agony, muttering a foul oath. Didn't Raina know the shackles at his wrists and ankles were no longer necessary?

His own traitorous heart had performed the task just fine.

Trapped like the animal he'd become, with no way out.

Chapter Eleven

ဆ

Sweet Virgin, he knows.

Raina saw the raw emotions play over Johan's weary face. An upset and angry male she could handle. She'd rather deal with his stubborn alpha attitude any day over the defeat clouding his golden eyes.

She'd known the instant he recognized her as his mate. For a few brief seconds after their earth-shattering climax, new emotions zipped along the bond from him. Wonder, even a nudge toward acceptance. But the reprieve hadn't lasted. The bitterness and despair returned full force, seizing her heart in a ruthless fist, stealing her breath.

Trapped...animal.

His anguish reverberated in her head and she quickly shut his thoughts out, not wishing to intrude. Learning to enjoy his enhanced sexuality wasn't the same as accepting the life changes that had stripped away his freedom, in his view.

Her man was lost, confused. He longed to be anywhere but here, a slave mated to his mistress. And though she understood, his rejection hurt far more than it should have.

Not since Marcus had she allowed a man to turn her inside out this way, and the growing power Johan held over her was frightening. Recalling her promise never to turn him, she could've wept. Seeing how very much this meant to him, she hadn't been able to refuse, and her impetuous decision ensured Johan would one day be lost to her forever.

Clever Vampire Queen, what will you do now?

Any fool could see he'd been pushed to his limit and should he snap, giving free rein to his beast, the fallout didn't

146

bear considering. She'd wait him out, hope that he came to accept her as his mate and embrace what nature had decreed. He must learn to trust her, let the walls around his heart crumble. Once he did, if he did, the rewards to them both would be without measure.

"Let me go."

Johan's quiet demand startled Raina from her thoughts. As he rattled the chains at his wrists, she realized he meant freedom from the bindings, not from her. For the moment, at least.

Propping herself on one elbow, she studied his anxious face. "The rut isn't over, darling. Learning to control your new libido will be no easy task."

Johan sighed. "I'm not going to turn into a homicidal maniac. Give me some credit."

"I don't know…"

"Let me up. *Now.*" An angry glare punctuated the demand, along with the erection reviving to lengthen against his thigh.

Raina arched a brow. Any other royal would've strung a slave up and doled out twenty lashes across his broad back with a barb-tipped whip for daring to speak as an equal. And to Johan's thinking, that's precisely what he was, his fallen status a mere technicality.

Privately, she agreed, but was no closer to an acceptable solution for them all than she'd been before. Johan was a beautiful eagle beating his wings against his cage, and he'd continue to fight until she let him fly, or his spirit broke. Either way, he'd be destroyed. Unless she won him over.

"Zane, love, get his feet."

Casting a dubious glance at his friend's arousal, Zane removed the ropes from Johan's ankles while Raina took the cuffs off his wrists and removed the phallus. Johan sat up, rubbing the reddened skin, chafed during his ordeal of the past few hours.

Raina took one of his big hands in hers, carefully brushing his wrist with her fingers. "I'm truly sorry about having to use those. As hard as this might be for you to believe, I do not enjoy seeing you suffer."

Golden eyes probed deep into hers, searching for the truth. "I know," he murmured at last.

Leaning into her, Johan cupped a hand behind her head, pulled her against him. The naked desire etched on his face, the renewed strength of his arousal, set her heart fluttering in her breast. Stirred feelings she hadn't experienced since her youth.

Since Marcus. Except these emotions were mature and complex, not the giddy notions of a silly, vain girl. He was *real*. And hers.

Johan lowered his head, took possession of her mouth, and she didn't once think of resisting. Of even trying to fend off one hundred percent pure male, determined to have his way. Pressing his body into hers as they sank onto the bed together, wrapping his solid weight around her.

So much man, all hard planes and angles of muscle and bone. Perfection. A symphony of movement as he parted her legs with one hand, stroked the silken curls between her thighs as his kiss became fierce. Possessive. His caresses dipped lower, fingers rubbing her slit, already hot and wet for him, spreading her cream. Performing magic with his touch, making her writhe and whimper for more.

"Beautiful Raina," he whispered into her lips. "My mistress, my love. Always in control, so contained. Let go for me. Trust *me*."

"Yes, Johan…"

His kisses blazed a path of wildfire down her throat to her breasts. She buried her hands in the luxurious thickness of his long black hair as his mouth took one nipple. Liquid heat melted her limbs as he laved and suckled, the scrape of his whiskers delicious against the sensitive skin.

Releasing the nipple, he moved lower, lips and tongue exploring her flat tummy, tickling her belly button. She giggled and he smiled up at her, literally taking her breath away. *Oh, my.* Had she ever seen him smile? With the shadow of his beard darkening his cheeks, eyes glittering and feral beneath a fall of black silk, that sexy, roguish smile slipping beneath her defenses...gods, yes. Johan was every inch the conquering barbarian she'd dreamed of, the man who'd take what he wanted and damn the consequences.

And he wasn't taking anything she wasn't more than willing to give. She'd waited many lifetimes for a man strong-willed enough to match her fire, even best her. This man. Somehow, she'd find a way to keep him, make him happy. But for now, she'd do as he asked and trust him. Let go.

Johan crawled between her thighs and cupped his big hands under her ass, lifting her backside off the bed, her sex so near to his lips, his warm breath fanned against the scorching flesh.

"Pretty," he praised, baritone voice rumbling with pleasure. "So pretty and pink, already hot and wet for me. Spread for me to feast on your lovely pussy, completely at my mercy, isn't that right?"

Raina shivered, a thrill shooting through her fingertips and toes. She needed him like this, confident, seizing control. "Yes."

Pulling her to his mouth, he gave the slit a long, slow lick from the crack of her ass to the tiny, throbbing clit. Just the tip of his tongue, enough to tease and torment. His gaze remained locked on hers as he licked again. And again. Unraveling the last shreds of her composure.

"Like that, my lady?" he grinned.

"Johan..."

"Mmm, sweet." His tongue delved into her slick, dripping folds, and out once more. "I'm going to eat you until you scream, baby. Until you come, crying my name, begging me to replace my tongue with my cock. Do you understand?"

"Y-yes." Her entire body strained, taut as a bowstring, yearning.

"Good. Because when you do, I'll continue feasting until you fly apart, mine for the taking. Know what I'll do then?"

"No...yes, I..."

"I'm going to fuck you," he whispered, nuzzling her sex. "So hard and deep you won't know where I end and you begin."

With that promise, Johan fastened his mouth to her sex, drawing the vulnerable nub between his teeth. Grazing and sucking in turn, sending spirals of decadent pleasure to every nerve ending. Her limbs went boneless, her brain floating somewhere outside her body.

Vaguely, she was aware of Zane stretched on his side nearby, watching, desperate arousal crackling along his thread. Ordering their companion to take his leave had never occurred to her, nor would she have done so. Zane's place was by their side, ready to please them in every way, and fleeting thoughts of the wicked play she had planned for them all fired her blood even more.

The gentle waves quickly gathered with the intensity of a roiling storm threatening to break over her head. True to his word, Johan used his mouth and tongue as a weapon of destruction, merciless. Lashing and sucking, he buried his face in her pussy, dined like a man savoring his last meal. Propelling her higher, faster.

Writhing under him, Raina tugged at his shoulders. "Johan, please..."

"Please what?"

"I need you inside me!"

"Not yet," he laughed softly. "First, I'm going to lap your sweet honey, take all you believe you have to give. Then I'm going to take more than you dreamed possible. Come for me, baby."

Lowering his dark head once more, he fucked her with his tongue, delving into her slick channel. Again and again, relentless. Tremors began to shake her body and she gripped the sheets in a futile, instinctive attempt to retain the iron control she'd possessed for eons.

No use. The tremors became quakes and Raina cried out, bucking under Johan's glorious assault.

"Oh, Johan! Yes, yes!"

The explosion rocked her world, shook her to the core. He did not let up for a moment, but drank her essence, a parched man dying of thirst for too long. His name was a mantra upon her lips as he drove her to the peak and over the edge repeatedly. Until there had never been another, only Johan, conquering her body and soul. Shattering centuries of loneliness and making her new. Whole. *His* woman.

At last, Johan crawled up her body, nestling the unyielding length of his huge erection just at the entrance between her wet, pouting lips. Bracing his elbows on either side of her head, he gazed down at her, expression fierce.

"You're mine," he growled, low and dangerous.

Raina shivered. "Yes. Please, Johan—"

"Tell me who you belong to."

She cupped his shadowed cheek. "I belong to you, Johan...my mate."

With a snarl of sheer male triumph, he drove his cock to the hilt, seating himself as deeply as possible. He began to thrust with languid strokes, shafting her, sliding his cock along her clit. Driving her mad, higher than before.

Gathering her against his broad chest, Johan pumped his hips, increasing the tempo. Raina clung to his shoulders and buried her face in his neck, loving the feel of his strength enveloping her, the play of his lean muscles under her fingertips. His beast roared, sweeping them both into his dark embrace, hungry for her flesh and blood. But Johan reined in his violent new counterpart with ease, leashing the beast's power to hurl them both toward the razor's edge of pain and passion.

He fucked Raina hard and fast, pounding her into the mattress, driving into her hot pussy. Filling her so deep they became one heart and mind. New threads wound unbreakable tendrils between them, leaving no division between souls that had once been separate.

Mated.

The word whispered along their bond and Johan surged with renewed fury. "Mine!"

"Oh, Johan, yes!"

Raina bucked wildly underneath him, unable to stop herself from flying apart. He thrust once, twice, then buried himself to the balls. Their cries mingled as they exploded together, his cock pulsing hot jets of semen into her womb. On and on, giving as much as he'd taken, until they lay panting and spent.

Johan didn't move for a long while. She held him tight, stroked his hair, kissed his temple. Loved him with all her being, but dared not speak the damning truth. Not yet. Reality seeped back into her awareness, unwelcome. Nothing had really changed about their situation, and she was more confused than ever regarding what to do with her mate.

And by law, her slave.

"Holy shit," Zane rasped, finding his voice.

Johan raised his head to glare at his friend. "Shut up, brat." Then his lips twitched, betraying rare humor. Chuckling as he relieved Raina of his weight, he shoved Zane's chest, then settled in on the opposite side of her. His friend laughed and flopped onto his back, hooking his hands behind his head, revealing an erection that could've hit a home run out of Busch Stadium.

"Ooh, poor baby," Raina sympathized.

Zane made a face. "You guys are a tough act to follow. St. Peter's balls, I'm in serious pain."

Arching a brow, she gave him a sly smile. "Not yet, but you will be. Here, take your blood reward because you're going to need it."

His face brightened. "Really? When?"

"Patience, darling."

With quick efficiency, Raina sliced her wrist and offered it to Zane. After he'd taken a few fortifying sips, she withdrew her arm and closed the small cut.

"Saints, one taste of you is better than a glass of the finest wine," Zane sighed happily.

Leaning to him, she kissed his cheek. "Sweet talker. Now, get showered but don't dress. Next, find Alexi and tell him I said to take you to the parlor downstairs and prepare you for initiation as our thrall."

"Thrall?" he repeated.

"The proper term for a true submissive, remember?"

"Oh, right." Zane swallowed hard, paling a bit. "Will you two be down soon?"

"Later, after Alexi helps ready you, physically and mentally. The correct harmonious zone, acceptance of your decision to eagerly open your mind and body to others' sexual desires is most important, and we can't begin until you've reached that place. Do you understand?"

"Yes, but I'm ready." He frowned. "I mean, I think so."

"No, you aren't," she countered softly. "Go and let Alexi see to your needs. Johan and I will be along in a while."

With a nod, Zane pushed from the bed and strode for his own room. To his credit, he refrained from asking the zillion questions Raina knew hovered on the edge of his tongue. He was scared, but excited and eager to please. Zane would make an excellent thrall, one who'd be very popular.

"That boy worries me." Johan frowned after his friend left.

"*That boy* faced down a murdering demon last night and saved your life."

"I'm not talking about his courage and you know it." He shook his head, concern clouding his gaze as he looked at her.

"In spite of the horror of his childhood, or perhaps because of it, Zane has always been led by his kind and gentle heart. He has this deep-seated need to please and he likes structure, discipline. I'm not an idiot, I know why our new status appeals to him. I see those needs becoming something more intense, darker, and it scares the shit out of me. He's braver than ten men, but hides a vulnerable center that could be easily exploited in the wrong hands."

"Like Drakkon's."

"Exactly. What does he truly know of being a slave? I won't always be around to protect him and neither will you. Raina, I'm so damned afraid he's going to get hurt," he finished in a hoarse whisper.

Scooting close to Johan's side, she laid a hand on his chest. "You've been watching over Zane all your lives, haven't you?"

"Yes. I've done my best, but lately…my best isn't fucking good enough."

"People get hurt, love. You can't keep them in a glass cage forever."

His lips turned up in a sad, lopsided smile. "Can't you?"

Raina stilled, the quiet accusation laced with irony cleaving her breast. "Touché."

The expression on her face stopped him, and he swore. "I'm sorry, that was uncalled for. When you purchased us at Lash, you saved me and Zane from suffering unimaginable hell at Drakkon's hands. Given the alternative, I can hardly complain. Especially now."

"The she-devil you know, with fringe benefits?" she quipped, unable to mask her disappointment. She didn't want to be Johan's best alternative, his safe haven by default. But what had she expected? She'd created this mess.

Instead of denying her words, Johan reached out and cupped her cheek, stroking the fullness of her lower lip with his thumb. "Who hurt *you*, baby?"

The earnest question and his unexpected tenderness blew her reason to bits. The warmth in his golden eyes, his voice, sounded just as it did when he'd spoken of his worry over Zane.

Johan cares, she realized. *He's my mate, he's reaching out to me, and he cares.* The stunning notion thawed the ice around her woman's heart once and for all. Here was a solid place for them both to begin.

"The Vampire King who killed my fiancé and turned me on the very same night, one thousand years ago," she heard herself answer. And marveled that for once, speaking of the horrendous evening she'd lost Marcus brought only the soothing peace of closure.

"Oh, Raina, I'm so sorry," he said quietly, taking her hand. Comforting her as though the event took place yesterday and not a millennium past. "What happened?"

Staring at his big hand swallowing hers, she shrugged. "The oldest story in creation. I was the crown princess in my home country, a small land bordering old Russia. Marcus was a lowly soldier assigned to guard my family's palace and our love was forbidden. Of course, in our foolish belief that we could beat the system, rules didn't stop us. The Vampire King, however, did."

"He wanted you for himself," Johan guessed.

"Yes, and he was used to taking what he wanted. He paid a royal visit to my family, took one look at me, and our doom was set in motion. Leaving Marcus alone and simply petitioning my parents for my hand in marriage never occurred to a vain, vicious monster like him."

"I think the vampire saw your fire, your love for the soldier, and knew you'd rather die than give in," Johan mused.

"Actually, you're right. Somehow, he learned I'd planned to run away with Marcus. He stopped us before we left the city limits and the bastard made sure my lover would not rise again. He...he ripped Marcus apart. Then he turned me."

"I can't imagine how horrible it must've been for you, seeing the man you loved suffer such a hideous death." Johan squeezed her hand, sympathy etched on his face. "Obviously, the vampire didn't succeed in making you his. Or did he?"

"No. When he arrived back at his palace, his right-hand sentinel learned of what the Vampire King had done to two innocent people. He'd been waiting for the opportunity to rid all vampires of an evil leader, and a terrible battle ensued between them. The sentinel won his place as King, and remains in that position to this day."

"Zoltan! No wonder you're as anxious as us to free our friend." He looked at her from under sooty lashes, unable to squelch his curiosity. "He made you his Queen, or ruling counterpart, but you never became his mate. I've heard women seem to find him pretty irresistible."

Raina heard the unspoken question hidden in the statement, tinged with an endearing touch of jealousy, and smiled. "We've never been lovers. Zoltan became a good friend and close advisor over the next two hundred years as I matured enough to become Queen, but nothing more. He's like a brother to me."

"And Drakkon?"

Ooh, now that tone held more than a smidgen of male ire. "Has been a wart in the ass crack of the world the entire six hundred years of our acquaintance. He's a fact of life, like human disease or the national debt. He's tried to seduce me over the years, but has never succeeded."

The tension in her mate's shoulders eased and he kissed her knuckles, an extremely satisfied expression on his sexy face. "I guess I'll have to find another justification for sending him down the River Styx."

"If my plan to thaw relations between Drakkon and me is going to work, you'll have to get a handle on your emotions," she warned. "We'll have to play his game to get inside his inner sanctum and find out what he knows about this demon killer."

Johan's face darkened. "And how do you propose I charm my way inside his lair? Because you are not going within ten miles of his cave, and that's final. I don't give a fuck what he knows, it's not worth risking your life."

"Neither of us is going inside. I'd never step foot in his cave, and he'd never believe otherwise. You'd work, but you're not the best candidate."

"Why the hell not?"

He was so going to despise this. "We must play to the Demon King's greatest weakness, his lust for slaves."

"To him, that's what I am," he argued, black brows drawing together.

"Yes, but you're not a thrall."

Comprehension dawned swiftly, transforming his handsome face into a mask of thunderous anger. "You suggest sacrificing Zane to this monster? Knowing how much he means to me, how worried I am about him falling prey to the wiles of an evil creature like Drakkon?"

"Zane is a warrior, first and foremost. He's smart and brave. Drakkon won't be a able to resist my offer of the loan of my thrall, then Zane will get a look at what's going on inside. Keep his ears open."

"And when my best friend isn't able to withstand the demon and falls under his spell? If he sees or hears something he's not supposed to and Drakkon finds out?" he gritted. "The bastard and his brethren will tear Zane limb from limb!"

"That won't happen. Drakkon has coveted an alliance with me for centuries. He wants me too much to damage his chances by murdering my slave."

"Are you willing to bet a good man's life on that?"

"Do you have a better idea?" she countered. "Or would you prefer to drop the whole investigation? You've hit the wall, Johan."

For a long while, he remained silent, fear and rage warring in his eyes. Battling the truth of her words and coming up short. Coming to a decision, he nodded.

"If Zane agrees to this scheme, I'll do everything in my power to keep you both safe. But if Drakkon harms one hair on his head, I'll rip his black heart from his chest with my bare hands." His eyes shot golden fire, his hand tightening around hers as he delivered a final promise.

"And if the demon touches *you*, I'll make the sonofabitch scream for death first."

Chapter Twelve

~

The ear-splitting screech of rage barreled through the tunnel with the decibel level equivalent to a supersonic jet. The walls shook, sending a shower of little pebbles tumbling to the dirt at Delilah's booted feet.

The little vamp froze in the middle of the passageway, eyes widening, heart jackhammering against her breastbone. *What in the holy fucking hell was that?*

A demon, what else? After all, she was sneaking around in a lair full of the beasts. Well, not sneaking, exactly. She'd never entered Drakkon's domain without being summoned first, and considering she'd come to break off as his date for Raina's gatherings, the fewer demons encountered on the way in, the better. Among her top five rules was *always leave an escape route.*

Right up there with *never date your best friend's enemy.*

Spreading her legs for Drakkon upon occasion to keep him happy and off her case was one thing. For all his disgusting faults, including a total lack of conscience, the demon was a skilled, mesmerizing lover. Not a hardship by any means. But to come out in public with the Demon King as his female, to see the hurt and betrayal on Raina's face tomorrow night at Lash…

No. She wouldn't do it. Even a mercenary had standards, and Raina was her only real friend in this whole lonely world. Delilah wasn't willing to risk losing that, even if Drakkon decided to throw her to his clan and let them devour her for dinner.

Which left her hovering in the corridor, ears ringing from the awful racket, wishing she'd sent Drakkon a note instead.

159

He'd have summoned her anyway, but she might've managed to avoid him until he cooled off. Now what?

Shouts drifted down the tunnel between deafening roars, followed by one heavy crash after another. *Time to go.*

Delilah hesitated. Whatever was happening down there wasn't any of her business. Unfortunately, she'd never been very adept at resisting an opportunity to learn something an adversary wouldn't want her to know. Damnation.

Hugging the rocky wall, she crept forward, keeping to the shadows as much as possible. At an intersection of three passages, she stood debating which one to take, until another angry roar blasted from the one on her left. Cursing herself for a fool, she hurried in the direction of the cacophony, rather than away.

The cave floor began to slope downward, taking her deeper into the bowels of the earth. Her skin prickled, every nerve ending on high alert for disaster, not just from danger of discovery, but from the very real possibility of being caught as a bystander in the fallout of Drakkon's wrath.

The Demon King despised disorder, chaos. He ruled his kind with cunning and cold calculation. The penalty for opposing him was death, in most cases slow and agonizing. He knew how to drive a point home, and did so while betraying no emotion in those onyx eyes. No soul.

Drakkon would not, under any circumstances, tolerate the madness taking place below. Such a scene called his authority into question, whether he was actually present at the moment or not. The idea of finding a chink in Drakkon's armor, something juicy enough to get Delilah out from under his thumb, was a delicious prospect that proved more powerful than fear.

The mouth the passage loomed a few yards ahead, emptying into a large chamber lit with torches braced on the rock walls. Flames licking at the gloom gave the impression of descending straight into Hades, and she knew that wasn't far off the mark. Delilah moved toward the entrance with the stealth of a small black cat, but she needn't have worried. She could've arrived on a motorcycle and they wouldn't have heard her approach with the hair-raising screeches and ongoing battle drowning out all else.

"Hold him, moron!" a desperate voice boomed.

"I'm trying, damn you!"

Using the lip of the entrance for cover, Delilah peered into the chamber...and her mouth fell open in shock. Inside a prison-type cell carved into the far wall, fifteen or so of Drakkon's sentinels and dungeon guards were engaged in life-or-death combat with a demon the size of a tank. A very pissed-off purple demon with boulders for muscles and a baseball bat for a cock, who towered head and shoulders over his captors. Even in true form, the lot of them were facing a near impossible struggle.

The demon under siege threw back his massive head and let out another shriek, straining against the numerous thick chains wrapped around his hulking body. Drakkon's minions were frantically trying to secure a few remaining loose ends to huge metal bolts in the cell floor. One sentinel slipped in the dirt and fell on his bare ass, losing his grip on the length encircling their captive's forearm. Before they could pull him back, the crazed purple demon lunged, grabbed the fallen sentinel by one ankle and slung him through the air. The sentinel's body slammed into the cell bars and bounced off to hit the dirt. Hard. Bellowing and cursing, the rest redoubled their efforts. Two guards grabbed the loose chain and one by one, the links were secured to the bolts.

The Demon King stood outside the cell and off to one side, observing the melee with talons clenched and leathery black wings folded against his ramrod-straight back, expression grim. Pensive. Delilah had never seen Drakkon so...unnerved, for lack of a better word. What was this rogue demon to the King? Clearly, the giant was one wire short of a closed circuit. Why didn't Drakkon just order the thing executed?

Weary and battered, sentinels and guards trudged from the cell, sporting a variety of injuries for their trouble. Some limped, nursing tattered and broken wings. Others were marred by deep scratches where the rogue had managed a swipe or two of his talons. One stopped to help the shaken sentinel, the one who'd been tossed like a sack of grain, to his feet. Several shot their Lord furious glares beneath lowered gazes, but only when he wasn't looking.

So, Drakkon's men were unhappy with their King. More food for thought. A horrible suspicion began to form, too vague as yet to support without details. Delilah bit her lip, knowing she should leave while her luck held, but she was determined to glean something useful. Drakkon's features hardened as his bedraggled troops lined up before him, ready to face his displeasure. Their wait was brief.

"Would one of you care to enlighten me as to why it took twenty-four hours to catch him this time?" Drakkon said calmly.

No one did. They knew their Lord's deceptive tone of pleasantness well, and not one of them was eager to place their balls on the chopping block volunteering answers they couldn't possibly get correct.

Drakkon gazed at his right-hand sentinel, expression closed. "Charon?"

Charon, cradling his mangled right arm, stared back at his King, equally cool. "For all his great bulk, Grog moves like lightning and is as elusive as the wind, Your Magnificence. He's grown to possess the strength of twenty demons. What would you have us do that has not been attempted?"

Delilah could've sworn a flash of pride lit Drakkon's face before he masked the emotion. That gave her pause. She glanced past the group to the demented creature still fighting the chains and screeching his rage. Drakkon taking pride in such a monster disturbed her on a whole new level.

The Demon King laughed, a cold, brittle sound. "Grog also has the mental capacity of a two-year-old fledgling. Can you not outwit a simpleton?"

Charon stiffened. "Were this a matter of wits, your unit wouldn't appear to have been run through a meat grinder. Grog is out of control, my Lord, as is the enhancement potion you blackmailed out of that sly warlock. Should your progeny's strength double yet again, we'll not be able to subdue him."

Progeny! *Grog is Drakkon's son!*

Delilah stifled a gasp, pressing trembling fingers over her mouth as the terrible suspicion began to solidify into a horrible scenario. The wary demons flicked their attention from their Lord to his right hand, like spectators watching a deadly tennis match in which the loser might find himself headless.

The Demon King narrowed his gaze. "Are you suggesting that I allowed Roland to swindle me?"

The sentinel kept his reply even, his gaze direct. "I'm saying something has gone wrong with the enhancement experiment. Perhaps it is not the fault of Roland's potion, but you cannot deny the results. Grog's mind was not right before the treatment, but he was not violent. Now we have five slain human women as proof of the spectacular failure of this test. Those girls were *innocents*, my Lord, not warriors," Charon spat in disgust. "I cannot think such needless loss of life is worth a fruitless endeavor to create an invincible immortal army."

Delilah's eyes rounded, as did several of the demons'. Charon was indeed treading on paper-thin ice with their Lord. She sagged against the cave wall, head reeling with the terrible information she now wished to be rid of. Drakkon's poor, mentally challenged son had been a guinea pig, a sacrificial lamb for his father's twisted cause. And the Demon King had ruined two good warriors for getting too close to the truth.

"What is your recommendation, then?" Drakkon said softly to his most trusted sentinel.

"That we cut our losses. Your position with the Council, our entire clan, is endangered. I request we turn Grog over to the Council for trial. We will play to the individual Superior's sympathies by revealing you were suspicious of the close match of the murderer's DNA to yours. You tracked the rogue demon, only to discover, much to your grief, that the perpetrator of these horrible crimes was your long-lost son. Grog cannot speak for himself, and the Council will not be able to disprove your story. We will all back your claims, Your Magnificence."

Charon shot the silent demons a pointed glare, and they promptly nodded in agreement. Delilah held her breath along with the others, waiting to learn whether Drakkon would approve this scheme. Charon's idea was a viable solution, given the situation rapidly spiraling out of control. Of course, no one knew their secrets had been overheard, or that Raina, her fallen warriors and the Council would soon be set straight.

You're going down, you sonofabitch.

The Demon King studied his sentinels and guards for several long moments. Weighing, calculating. "Request denied."

A ripple of shock and dismay passed through the gathering. Charon's mouth fell open, revealing the tips of two sharp fangs. The expression on his angular blue face, handsome even in demon form, was comical. No one felt like laughing.

"But Your Magnificence—"

"This conversation bores me," Drakkon announced, waving his claws. "See that Grog is secure. Should he escape again, the ones responsible will find themselves roasted and served for my feast."

Without a second to spare, Delilah spun and fled up the tunnel in the direction she'd come. If Drakkon found out she'd heard enough damning testimony to get him executed, the bastard would feed her to Grog without a wisp of remorse. Despite her shaking, rubbery legs, she fled, running faster than any human was capable. She could've just bolted herself to another location. Home, anywhere but Drakkon's vile lair. But she needed to run, and not only to escape being caught.

To escape...herself.

She'd lain with this evil male, allowed him to use her mind and body for a decade. Knowing what he was but playing his games. Straddling the fence between right and wrong, light and dark. Always looking out for number one.

You lie down with dogs, Delilah girl...

At last she gained the Mississippi River and slowed to a walk. A hysterical laugh bubbled in her chest, then another. Anyone watching would've believed her a crazy lady, walking in the darkness by the water, laughing like a loon. Maybe she was insane, and worse.

Somehow, hilarity became wrenching sobs. Delilah wrapped her arms around her aching stomach and doubled over, mired in a sudden wave of self-disgust so powerful, she wasn't sure she could go on. Didn't know whether she wanted to. Epiphanies sucked, and she guessed this was her stinking wake-up call.

The tears subsided to hiccups and she stood looking out over the black water, letting the desolation wash over her head. The loneliness she so richly deserved. *If* she were a quitter.

Now what? There was really no question. For the first time in centuries, she'd been seized by the annoying need to do the right thing. To make good on her useless existence. Problem was, following through with the urge to play heroine had never brought anything except sorrow to her doorstep.

Letting out a shaky sigh, she wiped the stupid tears with new determination. Satan's cock, the night wasn't getting any younger, and she had a visit to make. One that would bring Raina and her delectable slaves a great deal of satisfaction.

"Drakkon will kill me," she whispered to the darkness. The cool breeze tossed back her answer.

Nobody gave a damn, except maybe Raina.

So be it. In no great hurry to hasten her own doom, Delilah began the long walk to her friend's palace.

* * * * *

Can a man die of sexual sensory overload? Zane wondered. Maybe all of his pleasure receptors would short-circuit and he'd dance as his system fried from the inside out. He'd explode into a ball of flames and burn until nothing but a pile of ash marked where the man had once been.

What a way to go.

Zane closed his eyes, took a deep, calming breath and exhaled slowly, attempting to purge his nervousness. To allow self-doubt to flow from his body, leaving only a core of acceptance. Of peace.

To his amazement, the static in his brain faded to silence and the tension drained from his muscles. Even standing naked with his arms and legs spread and chained to silver bars above his head and between his ankles, vulnerable to whatever anyone wished to do to him, he wasn't afraid nor did he feel victimized in any way. Oddly enough, he'd never known such freedom. All his lonely life, he'd needed to be wanted, desired. Now the void in his soul would be filled forever.

Picturing the various methods Raina and her followers might employ to take their pleasure with him, Zane's aching cock lifted several degrees higher to curve toward his taut belly. The erotic images might've made him come prematurely, if Alexi hadn't bespelled his cock after binding him. A bit of magic, he'd declared with a predatory smile, to ensure Zane received the maximum sexual torture. Oh, the spell wouldn't compel or coerce his arousal, that was genuine. He simply wouldn't be allowed to come until he'd earned the right. Besides, no human male could withstand the initiation from slave to thrall otherwise.

"Saints," he muttered, glancing down at his rod with a sigh. "Can't we get on with this?"

Alexi paused in the act of spreading an array of scary devices on a nearby table and turned toward him with a grin. "Eager, aren't you?" he teased, tucking a wayward strand of white-blond hair behind his ear that had escaped his chic ponytail.

"I am," he admitted, flushing. The vampire stalked forward with the grace of a lean cat, frank appreciation lighting those pale blue eyes.

"You relish your place as Raina's slave," Alexi mused, laying a hand on his cheek. "You need this like a plant needs sunlight and water to flourish."

Zane nodded, tilting his face into the vampire's caress. "Yes."

"Why?" The vampire seemed genuinely baffled.

He blinked, considering how to give a simple answer to such a complex question. Memories flooded him, but without the cold edge of horror they'd wielded to gut him in the past. The squalid apartment piled with rotting garbage where he'd lived in hell for the first decade of his life. The beatings, years of emotional torment. Finally, starving on the streets, abandoned and half-dead...until he met Johan Stone.

His friend saved his hide, and the two became inseparable. They grew to manhood knowing they always had each other. But they belonged to no one. Two men, missing a vital connection, surviving together in a harsh world.

Until Raina.

Zane looked into Alexi's patient gaze. He could lie, but why bother?

"Belonging to Raina means nobody will ever throw me away again," he said quietly.

Alexi's expression warmed in compassion and understanding. He stepped close, leaned in to brush his lips against the supple skin at the curve of Zane's neck. "Ah, lovely man. This is no easy path you've chosen. The life of a thrall is physically grueling, and as a general rule you'll receive no mercy from anyone. You'll be fucked until you can't walk, your body used until you collapse in exhaustion. But thrown away? Never. You are much too valuable."

Zane shivered as the vampire's teeth scraped his neck and a palm skimmed his backside. Cupping one ass cheek, Alexi drew him in, fitting the bulge in his black pants to Zane's throbbing erection.

"I wish I'd gone into Lash that night and bid on you myself," the vampire murmured, kissing Zane's jaw, grinding his hips in tantalizing circles. "Do you have any idea what I'd do to you right now if you were mine, slave?"

Zane gave a shaky laugh, miserable for relief from the mounting desire. And the torment would only get worse. "I have some idea."

The vampire raised his head, a feral glint in his pale eyes. "Oh, I don't think you do, young pup." He brushed a featherlight kiss across Zane's lips, gentle in contrast to his electrifying promise.

"If you were mine, I'd sink my cock into your sweet virgin ass. I would fuck you until you screamed for mercy, but do you know what I'd show you instead?"

Zane swallowed the lump in his throat. "None."

"None," the vampire repeated, taking the captive's face in his hands. "Riding you hard, I'd tear into that delectable throat and drink, hurling you into the mind-blowing release only a vampire can give you. And your cries of ecstasy would call to my beast, fuel my hunger to the point I couldn't control my bloodlust even if I wanted to. Driven past reason, I'd bury my cock in your ass, drink until your heart struggled to beat. I'd pump my seed deep inside my pretty slave, even as you drew your last breath."

Zane stared at the vampire. "Y-you'd kill me?" he whispered.

Alexi dipped his head, sipped at Zane's lips. "Yes, but you needn't be afraid. You'd awaken as a vampire, my slave for eternity. *If* you were mine, which you are not," he added with a sigh of great regret.

The vampire took possession of his mouth, tongue sweeping past the seam of his lips to taste and explore. To rasp behind his front teeth and stroke his own tongue, deeper, making love to Zane with his talented mouth. A skilled seducer who'd no doubt be an unequalled lover. Zane moaned, leaning into the vampire, losing himself in something as vanilla as a kiss, craving more. So much more—

Alexi pulled away, leaving him breathless. Flashing Zane a grin, he returned to the table and began to sort through the toys. Dildos, anal plugs and beads, leather straps, a choke collar. Blazing Hades! Damned wicked vamp knew exactly what he was doing, ramping up the anticipation.

"How does this initiation work?" Zane flicked his gaze to a spot on the wall above the parlor fireplace. There, mounted on a horizontal rack, a variety of whips were on proud display just as a hunter might show off his rifle collection. He'd never been into bondage other than to play light games with the few women he'd dated, but he recognized a cat-o'-nine-tails and one with a barbed tip among them. Saints, why hadn't he noticed those before? His cock twitched.

"The process isn't random, and even our Queen doesn't get the option of going easy on you," the vampire answered, inspecting a plug. "All prospective thralls must endure the same test. First, you'll be adorned with more ring piercings than Johan, as befitting your elevated status. A preliminary honor, if you will, that also serves as the beginning of phase one."

"Which is?" He was almost afraid to ask.

"Pain, dear boy." Alexi strode over, large plug in hand, and circled around to stand behind him. "Methodical sexual torture designed to increase in intensity until your body is pushed past the limits of human endurance. You'll either break or cross the threshold into Rapture."

Zane flinched as the vampire's palm skimmed a buttock. "And if I break?"

"I remove the piercings and life goes on. Not everyone passes the test, Zane. Nobody in this household will think any less of you should you fail, but I don't think that will happen. I know how badly you want this, and more importantly, you have the proper mindset. Now, take a deep breath, then let it out slowly."

More questions were put on hold as he obeyed, concentrated on keeping his muscles relaxed. Deft fingers parted his cheeks, rimmed his tight hole, spreading cool lube, preparing him for the inevitable. Zane lowered his head and leaned forward as far as the bonds would allow, giving the vampire better access.

The vampire began to work two fingers into his anus, inching past the resistant ring of muscle. The lube helped slick his passage for their invasion, but Zane couldn't stop a gasp from escaping. The penetration burned, a gentle blaze firing his blood, his cock and balls. He moaned as his tormentor stroked rhythmically, found the sweet spot he'd heard about but never experienced, and marveled at the pleasures he'd been missing.

"Very good, pup," Alexi praised. "Your body is receptive to pain, and instinctively understands how to use it to create sexual gratification. Watching you achieve Rapture will be beautiful indeed. Easy now."

The vampire removed his fingers and replaced them with the anal plug, pushing the tip inside, then working the broadening base past his sphincter. Zane sucked in a sharp breath as the device slid in place with a pop and held fast. The plug was nowhere near as large as a well-endowed man's cock—Johan's, for example—and if his ass burned enough to make his eyes water this soon, he wondered whether he'd be able to take the real deal. In spite of Alexi's vote of confidence, he wasn't sure.

What if I can't do this? He raised his head and found himself looking into the vampire's gaze.

"No, no. The evening is much too young to let ugly doubt poison your efforts. Relax, dear one," Alexi soothed, reaching for Zane's cock.

The vampire's warm palm encircled his turgid erection, fingers squeezing, caressing the silken length with delicious pressure. Worry fled under his tutor's expert touch, his muscles gone molten.

"You won't be needing this." With his other hand, Alexi reached between his captive's legs, removed the cock ring he'd been wearing since his arrival and tossed it aside.

"Wh-what's phase two?" Zane managed, relishing the ease of his freed balls.

Alexi rubbed his sac in tandem with pumping his cock to the broad crimson head, and down again. "When you achieve Rapture, and that will be obvious to everyone, Raina leads us in celebration of your new status. This is the Unity, in which you obey her every command, your delightful body used in every conceivable manner by whomever she chooses, until your strength is spent. At that time, you have earned your status as a thrall. Raina administers the brand to your groin area, where the mark will remain always. As a final touch, she'll present you with a jeweled collar to wear permanently."

"W-will she allow me to come?" Oh, *please*.

"Perhaps, perhaps not. The decision belongs to your mistress. Further questions?"

Could a man die of blue balls? If so, at least he'd be the prettiest jeweled corpse around. "No."

"Good," Alexi said, continuing to shaft Zane's erection. "No more talking from you for the duration. Clear your mind of needless garbage such as worry and doubt. Focus on nothing except the extremes of sensation, the rise and swell of agony lifting you to greater heights of gratification than you've ever known."

Zane felt his tension drain once more, no match for the vampire's seductive, hypnotic words. Alexi released his cock and returned to the table, picking up a needle and a gold hoop identical to the one gracing his left nipple. The significance of that barely registered when Zane heard the parlor door behind him open then close with a soft snick.

"Great gods, what are you doing to him?" Johan sputtered. He strode into the room and came to stand before his trussed-up friend, Raina at his side.

Both were naked and beautiful, the perfect complement to one another. Fire and moonlight. Zane noted the scent of fresh soap and the damp ends of their hair. A moment of self-pity assailed him, knowing they'd loved without him. And possibly loved once more. Did Johan even realize how he'd planted himself next to Raina like an overprotective alpha male, how she burrowed close to his side in deference to him? Whether they knew it or not, these two were made for one another's arms, their souls meshing before anyone with eyes. *Oh, gods, they're becoming a couple. Where does that leave me?*

More than ever, Zane was determined to pass this test and become a thrall. He would not survive being cast out in the cold a third time.

Johan fisted his hands at his sides, frowning at Zane. "Are you all right?"

Zane nodded, not daring to break his order of silence.

"Is this truly what you want?" his friend persisted, unconvinced.

Again, Zane gave the affirmative with a bob of his head, adding what he hoped was a reassuring smile.

Johan was not reassured. "What the hell is wrong with him?" he boomed at Alexi. "Why doesn't he speak? If you've harmed him, I'll cut out your heart and eat it for my goddamned dinner! I don't give a flying fuck if you're a prince or a bloodsucking—"

"Darling, Zane is fine," Raina soothed, laying a comforting hand on his big biceps. "Alexi will explain what is happening."

Unruffled by Raina's big, angry male, the younger vampire detailed the process of initiation for a thrall just as he had for Zane. Johan's expression became more grim as he listened and by the time Alexi finished, Johan looked ready to tear the bonds from his friend and beat a hasty retreat, taking their chances in the streets. Which, of course, was no longer an option because of their bond with Raina.

"This is Zane's choice," Alexi concluded, cocking his head to study Johan. "You ought to understand his reasons better than anyone."

Uncertain, Johan glanced around the room, taking in the preparations. But when he looked into Zane's earnest face, his apprehension changed to reluctant acceptance.

"All right. I'll abide by Zane's wishes," he murmured. "Proceed."

Zane lifted his brows in surprise, not because of his friend's agreement, but because Raina and her young vampire companion seemed completely unaware that Johan had just given permission as though he were the ruling male of the household, not a mere slave. And they'd subconsciously acquiesced to his pronouncement. Interesting.

Zane reached for his center of calm as Alexi stepped forward bearing the gold ring and needle. The vampire pinched his right nipple to attention, then jabbed the sharp tool through his sensitive flesh. Zane gasped, blinking as stars danced in his vision. How could something so small hurt so damned much?

In a matter of seconds, the ring was threaded through the nipple and secured, making him the proud owner of a matching set. The vampire bent to the smarting nipple and licked the wound, healing it in an instant. But his relief was short-lived.

The vampire fetched two more rings and knelt between Zane's spread thighs. "Breathe deeply, young pup. This will hurt."

He complied, willing his body to relax as Alexi kneaded his testicles, searching for the perfect spot. Finally, the vampire took a piece of skin at the base of Zane's scrotum and before he could react, lanced the tender flesh.

Zane whimpered, waves of sickness roiling in his belly. Thank the saints he hadn't yet eaten tonight, or he would've lost every morsel. He caught the wave, rode it. *Calm, you can do this.* Johan took a step forward, fists clenched, handsome face a thunderous mask, but Raina pulled him back with a shake of her head.

Alexi attached a ring, sealing the wound with a touch of his tongue. Lingering, he licked Zane's balls in lazy circles, teaching his pupil's body to make pleasure from pain. Nausea receded under the vampire's attentions, need tightening Zane's groin. His flushed cock lifted another notch.

Alexi sat back on his knees and held up the last ring. Studying Zane's cock, he circled a finger around the broad head, then down the smooth length. Zane's eyes widened as he realized the vampire's intent.

Johan paled. "Surely you don't mean to—"

"Quiet, slave," Alexi admonished. He glanced to Raina. "Where, my lady?"

She tapped a red nail on her lips, considering. "Hmm. Just behind the head, I think. The piercing will not only look lovely gracing the end of his magnificent cock, it will be functional as well."

Johan made a strangled noise and Zane swallowed hard, swamped with images of what decadent uses the ring might have. But first, he had to endure the needle's penetration of the most sensitive spot on his body without passing out cold.

"You're right as always, dearest." Alexi smiled at her, then turned back to his work.

Zane jerked his chin up and stared at the ornate tapestry on the opposite wall next to the bed. He couldn't watch. Gripping the chains at his wrists, he filled his lungs with air, let it out slowly. Ignoring Johan's vicious curse, he blanked his mind of all except humble thoughts of servitude.

Raina is your mistress, and you are pleasing her.

"Very good," Alexi murmured, feeling behind the head of his shaft for the perfect spot. "Steady."

In one swift movement, the vampire lanced the needle through his target. A harsh cry erupted from Zane's chest and darkness curled the edges of his vision. Unbelievable agony, twisting him inside out. His knees turned to water. Sweat dripped off his jaw, trailed down the cleft in his back. Had he not been bound, he would've fallen.

Despite the excruciating waves battering him, he felt the cool invasion of metal slide into his cock. A symbol of ownership, of his willingness to surrender totally. His erection was hard and hot as a branding iron, arousal throbbing in tempo with the pain. Alexi's warm mouth closed around the head, suckling, tonguing the ring. Zane groaned and tilted his hips forward, begging without words. *Take all of me, please...*

To his distress, Alexi released him and stood, laughing softly. "My lady, what do you think?" He swept a hand to indicate Zane.

"Beautiful," she breathed, cobalt gaze raking him hungrily from head to toe. A feral smile curved her full lips. "Now, old friend, take our slave to Rapture."

Alexi turned to inspect the array of whips with a grin. "Name the instrument, love. The barb-tip?"

"We want to bring him to Rapture, my mischievous prince, not tear him to shreds. We'll save that one to use on him another time."

Zane's pulse skipped a beat. They had to be joking.

"Killjoy," he pouted. "You know I'd heal him after. Which one, then?"

"The two-inch-wide leather strap will do nicely."

The pair might've been discussing which steak to order for dinner. Still, Zane was calm. Aroused to the point of self-combustion, but enshrouded in a weird sort of tranquil fog, the peace that had eluded him all his life finally within his grasp.

Alexi removed the strap from the wall and came to stand behind Zane. Raina and Johan lowered themselves onto plump pillows a few feet away to watch, curling against each other. Zane raised his eyes to the tapestry once more, concentrating on his will to succeed. He'd be a good thrall, the best—

The first stinging blow caught him across his buttocks, making his eyes water. The next snatched the air from his lungs, though he suspected the vampire was holding back, getting him used to the contact before increasing the power behind the blows. Each strike sent electric jolts singing through his balls and cock, and he reveled in the wicked torture.

After applying a few more strokes to heat Zane's ass, the vampire moved upward. Methodically, he struck the tender flesh of their captive's back in a crisscross pattern. Up to the shoulders and down again. More and more powerful with each stoke. Zane cried out as the pain intensified. Relentless with his punishment, the vampire pushed Zane to the final threshold. Using every ounce of brutal strength, Alexi flogged his ass and naked back.

"Ahh, gods!" Zane heard himself shout.

Gripping the chains so hard his nails dug into his palms, he closed his eyes. His head fell back and tears streamed down his face. *I'll break! I can't do this, can't take this!*

And then, something strange happened. A luminous glow enveloped his body, became a brilliant light, bathing him with serenity. The agony fell away, the light whisking him into another realm. No human boundaries such as pain or fear. He was nothing more than flesh, blood and bone. A pulsing cock, ready, eager to serve his mistress or master in any way. Even death.

Zane moaned, lost in euphoria. "Ohh, yes, yesss..."

"Alexi, hold!" Raina called. "Lower the bar and bring him to his knees."

Zane felt himself sinking, his knees coming to rest on soft cushions. His entire body trembled with tiny aftershocks, the awesome experience almost too big to contain. Someone cradled the back of his head, lifted to support him. A masculine hand cupped his jaw, thumb stroking his cheek.

"Zane," Johan croaked. "Talk to us. Are you hurt?"

Blinking his eyes open, he gazed into his friend's anxious face and gave him a tremulous smile. "I'm great."

"Praise the Virgin," Raina sighed, nestling in next to Johan to peer at Zane. "Oh, my! Look at his eyes."

Johan's mouth dropped open. "Gods, they're...glowing. Like green fire."

Raina gazed at Zane and touched his hair, her smile gentle. "Congratulations, my beautiful thrall. Tell me, how will you serve your Queen?"

Searching his heart, he answered. "In any way you desire, my lady. I'm yours to command."

Approval flashed in her blue eyes, and no small amount of hunger. She glanced from Johan to Alexi over Zane's head.

"Gentlemen, prepare for the Unity."

Chapter Thirteen

ဆ

Johan wouldn't have been surprised to look in the mirror and find that his black hair had gone shock white. He didn't know about all this thrall initiation shit, but he knew a man who'd completely surrendered ownership of his soul when he witnessed the transition in Zane.

He didn't recognize the man kneeling before them in supplication, bound in chains yet more at peace than Johan had ever seen him. The change was strange, seductive...and terrifying. As a thrall, Zane would be in more physical danger than ever before, within the palace walls or not. Not even the strongest-willed creature would be able to resist the lure of this thrall's beauty, charm and desire to submit.

"This Unity will be a celebration," Raina said softly, threading slender fingers through Zane's thick, sun-kissed brown hair. "An act of joy, an extension of our love for this man who has made the ultimate sacrifice of body and soul. He has given his very life to my keeping, and I treasure the gift."

Johan's throat tightened with unexpected emotion. She meant every word, and Zane's expression radiated pure happiness. This wasn't about using or brutalizing her slave for her own purposes, but rejoicing in a man who'd finally found a true home and a calling.

"Shall I remove the plug, my lady?" Behind Zane, Alexi bent to nip at his bare shoulder, skim a palm down his broad back.

"Yes, then remove your clothing if you'd like to join us."

"Oh, I'd like very much." The vampire beamed, flashing his fangs. "Who am I to refuse such a delicious invitation?"

"Yeah, right," Johan snorted, surprised by a rush of jealousy. "You've been itching to get your hands on Zane since Raina brought us home. Don't think I haven't noticed."

"Careful, human," Alexi teased, batting his long, dusky eyelashes. "Green isn't your color."

Cocky punk. The young vamp was too damned pretty and ethereal, like that blond elf pipsqueak in *Lord of the Rings*. Just the type of creature that would overwhelm Zane, sweep him off his feet. *If you were human, I'd snap you like a skinny little twig,* he projected mentally, not sure it would work.

Alexi dimpled. *You could try.*

"Boys, boys," Raina admonished, smothering a laugh. "Goodness, I'm suddenly drowning in testosterone. I'll never understand why males must turn everything into a competition. Alexi, get on with it. Johan, behave yourself."

Johan bit back a retort, fascinated in spite of himself as the vampire removed the plug and eased a finger into Zane's passage. Or at least that's what he gathered from this angle, judging by the slow back-and-forth motion of the young vamp's arm. His friend arched his spine, lips parted, head tilted back, sheer bliss etched on his face.

Johan's erection, awakened the second he'd walked into the parlor, hardened fit to jackhammer into concrete. Before his joining with Raina and Zane earlier tonight, he'd never seriously considered fucking another man. But now he envied the vampire his position behind Zane, kneeling between his spread legs. Working the tight hole, putting that awed look on his face, like a man who had been to the other side and witnessed Elysian Fields.

The bond flared along the triad, each feeding off the needs of the others, desire blazing like a match struck in a room full of propane. Johan was aware of Raina's pussy, hot and wet, throbbing with arousal as though her slick folds rested between his own legs. Felt the slide of Alexi's fingers deep inside Zane's ass, massaging in and out. Incredible.

The beast roared, demanded he plunge his cock into the thrall, fuck him into oblivion, master him so he'd know what male belonged there. *Mine.*

Alexi stood, walked to the sofa and began to remove his clothing. Raina touched Johan's arm. Her sweet honey-almond scent teased his nose, an aphrodisiac winding every sinew in his body like a corkscrew.

"You want the thrall."

A statement, not a question. A sarcastic retort came to mind, but all he managed was a terse nod.

His lady arched a serene brow. "Well, what are you waiting for?"

Johan and his lusty beast needed no further encouragement. He moved into the place the young vamp had vacated, staring at the crisscross pattern of red welts left by the strap. Just starting to bruise, the marks would be purple by tomorrow. How had the man borne the pain, used it to fulfill his craving?

"Brave and beautiful," he whispered, tracing a bruise across the heated flesh with the pads of his fingers. "I'll take your pain away."

He admired his friend's back in wonder, as if he'd never seen him before. Damp tendrils of hair curling against his corded neck. Strong and lean, muscles rippling under tanned skin gleaming with sweat. The ornate tattoo of the black dagger adorning the cleft at the small of his back, deadly tip resting at the part of his firm buttocks. Pointing the way for a dagger of another sort.

His fingers swept downward, skimming the tattoo briefly, then lower. His hands trembled as he parted Zane's ass, found the tender skin of his anus, began to rub in a circular motion. The thrall whimpered, backed into his touch as far as the chains would allow.

"Yeah, you want me right here, don't you?" he growled, thrusting the finger inside the lubed hole. "You want this to be my cock."

"Y-yes," Zane stammered.

"Tell me. *Beg me.*"

"I've wanted this for so long," he said in a broken voice. "I need you inside me, Johan. Fuck me, please! Saints, please..."

Johan removed his finger, pressed the head of his straining cock to the entrance and gripped the thrall's hips. Ever-so slowly, he pushed inside. Groaned at the sight of his captive's ass parting to admit him. The tight glove squeezing his aching length as he sank deeper.

"Ahh, gods, yes." Seating his shaft to the hilt, he shut his eyes. Lost himself in the flames licking his body, the wicked pleasure of taking the man writhing underneath him. "Other males will burn to have you like this, to fuck a lovely thrall, and I'll accept that because we're bound by the law and it pleases our mistress. But you'll always be *mine*. Never forget whose cock belongs up your pretty ass, do you hear?" he rumbled, low and dangerous.

Zane shuddered under him. "I-I won't, I swear. I'm yours, always."

Yes. He withdrew, then sank. Again. Out, and in once more, a long, glorious slide to the balls. Grinding his heavy testicles against the thrall's, skin to skin. Pumping. So good, so right.

And so very different from fucking a woman. Hard planes and angles meeting his thrusts rather than soft curves, but no less delicious. Gods, he burned. Higher, hotter.

He opened his eyes to see Raina standing over Zane, straddling her thrall's head, bracing herself on his shoulders. Zane lifted his face to her sex, buried his nose in her burnished curls, flicked the folds with his tongue. At her breathless encouragement, he lapped her pussy, a man dying of thirst.

Plunged his tongue between her dripping nether lips and into her vagina, tongue-fucking her and rasping the tiny clit. Eating her cream.

Johan felt the dual action of Zane's attentions to her pussy whisper against his own cock. The little sucking noises of moist flesh and Raina's whimpers of pleasure drove his beast wild. His hips pistoned faster, harder into Zane's channel, causing the thrall to groan in helpless ecstasy.

Raina stepped back, motioning Alexi forward. "Darling, fill our thrall's mouth with your big cock."

"My pleasure, dearest." He grinned, releasing his impressive erection from the stroking he'd been giving it.

The young vampire took her place. His toned body was lean and graceful, like a runner's. He'd unbound his flaxen hair, letting the silken tresses fall about his shoulders. His pale eyes darkened as he eased his cock into Zane's eager mouth, pushed deep. Began to fuck their thrall in tempo to Johan's thrusts.

The sight nearly finished Johan, but what he saw as he peered around Zane took all of his restraint to keep from coming. Raina knelt on all fours between Alexi's legs, and impaled her juicy pussy on Zane's iron-hard cock. The three of them now owned the thrall, stuffed him full in every possible manner. At their mercy, theirs to do whatever they wished.

"Ohh, yeah..." Johan's body went taut. He fought for control, tried with all his might to leash his beast.

And lost.

With a feral snarl, he lunged deeper, hammering his cock into the thrall with all his strength. Nothing but this, the slapping of flesh as they fucked their captive senseless. Nothing except the beast driving relentlessly, mastering his prey. So close...

Molten fire boiled in his sac, drawn tight and flush, ready to explode. His body quickened, the mystical trigger sending him over the edge. Slamming home with a shout, he held on fast as sweet release rocketed from his balls. His cock pumped on and on, deep into the thrall's channel. Filling him until the spunk streamed from his ass to coat their balls like warm, wet silk.

Above him and Zane, Alexi stiffened with a hoarse oath and let his head fall back. Lips parted, breathing hard, he cupped the back of Zane's head and pinned the thrall's face into his groin. Locked deep in Zane's throat, he poured his seed, shuddering. The thrall choked once, then drank obediently.

At that moment, Raina cried out. Johan sensed the walls of her slick passage clenching, spasming around Zane's beleaguered cock.

"You may come, thrall," she panted, releasing his shaft from the spell.

Zane's eruption powered into her pussy, stunning all four of them with the intensity of his release. He opened his emotions to his companions, bathing them in love. Even Alexi, not actually part of their bond, was swept away by his passionate response. His absolute joy in serving as their thrall.

Gradually, Johan's beast subsided, sated for the time being. For a few moments, silence reigned as the aftershocks faded and temperatures cooled, broken only by heaving breaths. The musky scent of sex and sweat threatened to arouse him again, but he squashed the temptation with an effort. Zane must be exhausted and sore.

With great care, he eased his shaft from Zane's backside. "Did I hurt you, old friend?"

"No." A pause. "Well, maybe a little. But I liked it."

Hearing the smile in his friend's voice loosened the knot of guilt in his chest. "Yeah? If I'd known you were a pain slut I'd have beaten you a long time ago and saved you all this trouble," he teased gruffly.

The other two disengaged themselves from Zane to kneel in front of him. Johan crawled from behind his friend to do the same, anxious to be reassured that he was really all right. Zane gazed at the three of them, green eyes normally sparkling with humor, glassy and tired. Johan knew that expression well. His friend was done, near collapse. *What if he can't handle this life he's chosen?*

Johan cast a worried glance at Raina. "He needs rest."

"I agree. But first his gift, then his thrall's mark," she replied. "Gentlemen, you may free him from the chains."

Johan helped Alexi do as their lady bade while she stood and retrieved a rectangular black velvet box from a table by the sofa. When had that arrived? Perhaps Hope had slipped in and put it there. The idea of the housekeeper getting an eyeful of their session had heat creeping into his face.

Once freed and sitting on the pillows, Zane tried to remain upright, but couldn't. He toppled over with a groan of pain and Johan caught him, pulling him into his arms, back resting against his chest. Not long ago, the idea of holding his best friend in such an intimate embrace, the two of them naked, would've seemed absurd. Now, seeing to Zane's comfort was the very least he could do.

Raina returned to sit comfortably next to them, box in hand. "Would you like for me to open this for you?" Zane nodded, so she flipped the lid and presented him with the contents.

Zane gasped, eyes widening in shock. "Oh, my lady. That's...mine?"

"Tradition dictates a new thrall to be presented with a gift from his mistress or master. Something that will make a bold statement to everyone of the thrall's great worth. This is my gift to you."

Smiling, she lifted a jeweled choker from the box. Square-cut emeralds and diamonds glittered, millions of facets catching and reflecting the light. "To match your eyes, love."

Johan's brows shot up. "Holy shit." That baby set her back tens of thousands, no question. Not that she didn't have money to burn.

"I-I don't know what to say," Zane whispered, overcome. "Nobody's ever given me anything so fine."

Pleased by his reaction, she waved a hand. "Don't say a thing, just enjoy wearing the piece. You may take it off to sleep and should leave it at home when I give you unaccompanied leave from the palace. We don't want you getting mugged or kidnapped, for pity's sake."

"Other than when you suggest, I won't ever take it off. Thank you, my lady." He gave her a heart-stopping smile. "Help me put it on?"

Laying the box aside, she reached around his neck and fastened the clasp. The choker fit snug against his throat, resplendent. "Not too tight?"

"No, it's perfect."

"Wonderful!" Leaning forward, she sobered, studying him for a long moment. "The thrall's mark is the last part of your initiation. I will lay my palm next to your groin and call upon my magic to burn my brand into your skin. Another master or mistress might not tell you that even at this point, you can change your mind."

Zane shook his head. "I won't."

"Be very sure, love. While this is your choice, the thrall's mark is permanent and the decision is irrevocable. Once I place the brand upon your skin, you'll be a thrall for the rest of your existence, whether you are turned vampire or not. I plan on being around for centuries to come, but what if I'm not, Zane? I may not always be here to protect you, and there are masters such as Drakkon, indeed hundreds like him, who'd die to get their vile claws into you. Are you willing to take the risk?"

Zane paled, but held steady. "Yes, my lady. I'd risk anything at all to remain here as your thrall forever, with Johan and Alexi."

"What if you find your mate?"

That one threw him. "Mate? I don't..."

"For the sake of argument, let's say you find your mate and the two of you wish to acknowledge your union. What do you think happens then?" she pushed.

Johan's respect for Raina rose several notches. She was truly determined to make him see all angles of the consequences. Her honesty and concern touched him, tugged at his heart.

"I don't know," Zane said, looking from her to Alexi in confusion.

"That's the point," she said gently. "Another master could refuse to allow the union, or worse. You or your potential mate could be punished for insubordination. Either one or both of you might face execution, but in reality that tragedy would likely befall your mate because an excellent thrall is hard to replace."

"You'd never hurt me that way." His voice was quiet, but confident.

"True, *if* I'm still here. We never know what road we'll travel or what evil will befall us. I'd be remiss in my duties if I led you to think you're going to live in Utopia. As open as I am to expanding my coven, a thrall finding a mate is a tricky thing."

"How so?"

"I would approve the union, with your mate's understanding that your status as my thrall is not open for discussion. You will entertain my guests or members of our coven as before, your body shared. She—or he—would have to accept and willingly embrace other lovers in your bed. In *hers*."

Whoa. The import of what she was saying smacked Johan on the forehead. "Hang on a sec. Does that pertain to me, should I choose a mate?" *To me and Raina. Gods!*

"Yes, darling. Vampires are highly sexual creatures, our coven members enjoying relations with one another as well as our slaves. A coven is close, a family of sorts, like me, Alexi, and whomever we might invite to join us. We trust each other implicitly and view sex as an act of love and devotion, never a betrayal. An extension of our emotions."

Zane's brow furrowed. "Let me get this. As the household thrall, I submit to whomever wants me. In addition, any coven member can fuck my mate. And neither of us is supposed to get jealous?"

"That's the short version, yes," Raina laughed. "And that rule applies to all of us."

Blazing Hades. Johan's cock stirred anew at the picture she'd painted. Talk about the proverbial having your cake and eating it, too! But could he handle Alexi or Zane spending time alone with Raina, covering her, bringing her to orgasm? And what if this fictitious mate of Zane's were female? Would it turn Raina on to know that he, Johan, sank his cock into her welcoming heat, taking his pleasure? The beast purred, loving the arrangement.

None of that mattered. His decision remained steadfast. He'd do anything to make Raina happy.

Zane's expression cleared. "My mate will understand our way of life, or the union is not meant to be. I know all the consequences of my actions, and I'm ready to be marked, my lady." He looked content, and incredibly tired.

"So be it. Gentlemen, hold him."

Johan locked his arms around Zane's middle. His friend leaned back, his head resting on Johan's shoulder. Alexi laid his hands on the thrall's chest to keep him down.

Raina placed a palm against Zane's groin, next to his flaccid penis. "I'm sorry, love. Steady."

The acrid smell of burning flesh reached Johan's nose. Zane cried out, muscles bunching and straining in his embrace, struggling to escape this last round of agony. The area under Raina's hand glowed red, burning her brand into her thrall for all time. Johan held him still with Alexi's help, heart breaking to hear his hoarse screams, weakening as he lost consciousness. At last, Zane went limp, lapsing into merciful oblivion.

Raina removed her hand, revealing a simple design of a shield bearing her initials, *RZ.* "Even if I'm long gone, his origin as a thrall can always be traced to his original owner," she explained.

"Nifty premise, but you're not going anywhere," Johan informed her. For some reason, his declaration made her dimple prettily. The sight of her kneeling there buck naked, creamy breasts peeking through her mass of red hair, made him feel weak.

Her gaze fell to Zane's prostrate form, and her expression melted. "Oh, poor baby. Let's get him up to his room."

"I'll bet he sleeps until tomorrow evening," Alexi put in, looking upon their burden with unmistakable tenderness. "Here, I'll take him."

Johan opened his mouth to protest, but Raina's slight shake of her head cut him short. He relinquished Zane to the young vampire's care with a frown and no small amount of worry.

"He'll be fine," she said softly as Alexi disappeared through the parlor door with his best friend. Scooting closer, she trailed a blood-red nail down Johan's chest to scrape one nipple and toy with the gold ring there. "It's been a long, nerve-racking couple of days for us all. What do you say we retire to my chambers and snuggle?"

Without hesitating, he hooked an arm around her waist, yanking her close. Her breasts crushed against his chest, emblazoning laser twin points of heat into his skin. "How about we snuggle...after I have my way with you?"

"My, you beast!" she quipped, fanning herself.

"Hazard of the job, sugar. Shall we?"

Johan stood, scooped Raina into his arms and bounded for the stairs, her merry squeals ringing in his ears.

The sudden, weird feeling of impending disaster yawning in front of him like a black hole meant nothing. He wouldn't let the ridiculous woo-woo shit mar this moment. Nothing would stand in the way of Raina's or Zane's happiness. Everything would turn out fine for all of them. Or at least for the ones he loved.

Even if he had to die to make it so.

* * * * *

"You're insatiable," Raina sighed, pillowing her head on Johan's big shoulder. She'd never taken a shower quite as stimulating as that one. Who knew so many positions were possible while lathered with soap? "I've created a monster." His rumble of laughter echoed under her ear, the warm, pleasant sound making her tingly all over. Less like a queen and somehow more womanly.

His arm came around her, anchoring her snug against him. "All your fault."

"Hmm, you're sounding awfully cheerful about your dire fate. And it's not all my doing that a good stiff breeze stands your penis at attention. I'm not the demon who attacked you and left you with a supercharged libido."

Chuckling, he kissed the top of her head. "I guess I'll have to thank him for that…before I lop off his head."

The reminder of how close to death Johan had come after his encounter with the rogue demon sent an ominous chill of dread down her spine. "I can't allow you to go after him again. It's too dangerous."

He stiffened, good humor deserting his tone. "Allow?"

"You swore loyalty to me," she reminded him. "And I can ill afford to have you chasing a maniacal killer."

"Afraid you'll lose your million-dollar investment, Highness?"

The cool accusation dispelled the easy warmth blossoming between them. Dammit to Hades, she'd used the wrong tactic and offended Johan on several levels in the bargain. Levering onto his chest, she took his face in her hands. The hurt in his amber gaze steeled her resolve to make him understand.

"I don't care about the money, Johan, I care about *you*. I don't doubt your abilities as a warrior, but I couldn't bear it if you were killed. Don't you see? This has nothing to do with your being my slave."

"I don't see squat. Suppose you spell it out for me," he said, doubt still lingering.

"I went about this all wrong. This is a female's concern for her mate," she whispered.

His expression softened the tiniest bit.

She took a deep breath. "Somewhere along the way, I realized...I've fallen in love with you."

With a tortured groan, he pulled her in for a sweet kiss. Pushing a strand of hair from her face, he looked up at her, eyes solemn. "And I love you, my lady. Tell me, is love enough for us?"

"Wh-what do you mean?" Oh, but she did know.

"Will you claim me as your mate before the Council, release me from service as your slave? Do you trust me enough to watch me walk away, knowing I'll slay my demon and return to your side safely, and of my own free will?"

Oh, sweet Virgin. Her worst nightmare reborn. True, this wasn't the exact scenario in which she'd lost Marcus, but the result might be the same. A good man, a man she loved with all her soul, cut down by the evil she'd sworn to protect him from. She'd let Marcus take the reins of their predicament and he'd been butchered for his efforts.

"What about you?" she countered. "Do you trust me enough to allow me to drain you, turn you vampire? If I give you my word I'll speak to the Council about our union and release you to fight your monster, will you turn? Give me that much, knowing you go into battle with all the preternatural strength and magical abilities becoming vampire will give you, and I'll let you go."

Another mistake. His face hardened more with every word, until a stranger stared back at her. "Blackmail doesn't suit you, Raina. I already told you how I feel about turning, and I don't need your fucking magic to dispatch my enemies. I suppose I have my answer."

"I suppose I do as well. You don't trust me either," she shot back, horrified by the wobble in her voice, the damnable tears suddenly filling her vision.

Rolling, Johan pinned her underneath his big body, his arousal heavy between her thighs, expression fierce. "Feel this," he snarled, grinding his shaft against the wet folds of her pussy. "I'm a man, damn you, not a slave. You can imprison me in chains, starve me, beat me within an inch of my life, and it would not change the truth. I'm your mate, the man who loves you, but never your slave. *Never.*"

She gave a startled squeak as he crushed his mouth to hers, sheathed his cock to the base in one long, forceful stroke. After a couple of halfhearted shoves at his chest, she gave up the pretense of fighting him. She could blast him across the room and through the wall and they both knew it...just as they both knew she wouldn't.

Parting her thighs, she melted in his arms. This wasn't the dark, carnal pleasure they'd experienced with Zane and Alexi. Nor was this the playful lovemaking they'd enjoyed in the shower.

This was a warrior giving his woman a good, sound fucking. Plunging into her again and again, conquering her body and soul. A male proving he'd not be cuckolded, soothing his wounded pride.

Opening herself to the bittersweet assault, she met his powerful thrusts. Clinging to his shoulders, she relished the flex of muscle beneath her hands, the incredible feeling of one hundred percent raw male wrapped around her. Driving into her like a piston, spiraling her higher, out of control.

"Ohh, Johan, yes, yes!"

Crushing her to his chest, he went rigid, burying himself as deep as possible. They exploded together, shattering into a zillion pieces. She held him tight as he spurted hot jets of semen into her womb, pulsing until he collapsed on top her with a final shudder.

Silence fell, reality intruding. A hot, rough coupling changed nothing. They were at an impasse, the chasm between them wider than before, impossible to breach. Johan was right.

Without trust, their love was doomed.

A knock on her chamber door interrupted the uncomfortable moment. "Yes?" she called.

"Raina," Alexi's muffled voice answered. "Delilah is downstairs in the foyer."

"St. Peter's hairy balls," she muttered as Johan withdrew. Sitting up, she yelled back, "I don't have time for her shenanigans. It's almost dawn, so tell her I'll see her tonight when—"

Alexi strode into the bedroom uninvited, rumpled and clad in his robe, not contrite in the least. Concern marred his brow. "I tried. She's really upset, dearest. She wants to speak to all of us, right this second. I've never seen her so undone."

Raina blinked at her longtime companion, dread pressing on her lungs. "All right, but don't wake Zane. He's got to have his rest or he'll never make it through tonight."

The young vamp made a face. "Oh, gods. Your date with Drakkon the Disgusting. Don't make me gag."

She blew out a weary breath, not up to sparring with Alexi. "Go put on some clothes and tell her we'll be down in a few minutes."

They cleaned up with quick efficiency, neither speaking as they dressed. Raina donned a pair of black pants and a white cotton blouse. Johan ducked into his room and returned with a pair of crisp blue jeans and a dark T-shirt rather than his required robe and boxers. He'd removed his cock ring, but left the one in his nipple, she surmised, to prove he could. Pulling the jeans on and zipping the fly, he arched a brow, daring her to reprimand him for such bold defiance. Next, he yanked on the shirt.

Holding her tongue, she turned to go. Unfortunately, Johan was in a nasty mood and not quite done beating his breast.

Grabbing her arm, he spun her to face him. "What, no uppity comment? No punishment for your naughty slave? That's all I'll ever be to you, Highness. A possession, not a man."

That's not true! her heart cried. *I'm so afraid of losing you. I love you!*

How to make him see? But she'd hesitated too long. He let go of her arm and jerked back, sucked in a sharp breath as if she'd shot him in the heart with his blaster. The raw pain in his golden eyes made her want to weep.

She reached for him. "Johan, I—"

"Let's find out what has Lady Delilah in such a state, shall we?" He laughed coldly. Dropping his voice, he gave her a grim smile. "Maybe she needs a hot-blooded slave to give her a big dose of comfort up her luscious little backside. Does the image make your panties wet, baby? Does it make your cunt burn to picture me eating her sweet pussy, taking her again? Because the idea makes my beast hotter than the center of the sun, may the gods forgive me."

The pole forming behind his zipper gave credence to his hoarse words. He appeared wild, beautiful and miserable. Heartbroken. After a pause, he stalked past her and left.

Raina staggered, clutching the bedpost for support. Oh, saints, she'd hurt him so very badly. She'd shoved a proud lion in a cage and tried to turn him into a house cat. She couldn't blame him for lashing out, going straight for the jugular.

Johan wasn't the type of man to have sex with another just to get back at her, no matter what he implied. But in his hurt and disillusionment, he might seek to soothe his wounds. Use his slave status as an excuse to give his beast free rein. If he took another to his bed while filled with pain, he'd be eaten with guilt afterward. A human reaction steeped in human mores, and Raina hadn't been human for one thousand years. He'd only punish himself more.

"Oh, darling. What have I done to you?"

Johan was caught between roles, battling his conscience. His longing to lose himself in the freedom of the open sexuality of her coven was etched in every taut line of his aroused body. He wanted to explore his desires, but not as a slave. Johan Stone was a dominant alpha male, and wouldn't settle for less than ruling the coven as such.

So, that was the crux. Step aside as coven ruler and take Johan as her mate, her equal before the Council, or lose him. Was there any other decision to be made?

Relief and happiness spread through her. As soon as Johan dealt with this rogue demon, when his anger had a chance to calm, she'd speak with him.

Johan's parting words reverberated in her brain. Yes, indeed, her sex was hot and wet at the image he'd conjured. Now she just had to help him come to terms with his own sexual desires.

One day soon, Johan Stone would rule their coven as the dominant male, with an iron fist.

And a rock-hard, very happy cock.

Chapter Fourteen

The grim little assembly waited in silence as Raina descended the staircase and stepped into the grand living room. If the irrepressible Delilah had ever appeared more subdued, she didn't recall the occasion. Alexi sat next to her on the sofa ready to offer comfort or support if needed, but she didn't acknowledge his concern. Other than a fleeting glance of longing at Johan perched on the arm of the sofa, her friend remained mute, hands clasped in her lap. A dark silk waterfall curtained her shoulders and part of her tearstained face.

Tears? From the ice princess?

Bracing herself for whatever dire news had brought Delilah so low, Raina closed the distance between them. "Oh, sweetie. What brings you to my door looking so glum? Surely it can't be that bad."

"Raina!" Delilah shot to her feet and launched herself into her friend's arms, clinging like a cocklebur. "H-he's going to k-kill me but I c-can't live with this anymore. Not after what I s-saw. What I h-heard in the cave—"

"Slow down," she ordered firmly, setting Delilah back and tilting her chin up. She had a good idea what this was about, and the hair on the back of her neck prickled. "Tell me what's happened."

Delilah's mouth trembled. "I've deceived you, my lady."

Ah, here we go. At last. "In what way?"

A long silence. The little vamp heaved a hitching breath, looked Raina squarely in the eye, her remorse bare for all to see. "Lord Drakkon," she whispered, the name encompassing the sum of her shame. An explanation unto itself.

But the vixen wasn't about to get off so easily.

"How long?" Raina asked, keeping her expression neutral.

"I met him a decade ago, when I first immigrated here from Arabia. Months before I met you," she emphasized. "I didn't know the history between Drakkon, Alexi and you for a couple of years. The subject never came up, and I didn't realize at the time he was grooming me, digging his claws deep, using me as his eyes and ears to spy on you both. He seemed so handsome, charming, and had an edge of danger I've never been able to resist. Later, it was easier to give in to his occasional demands than rock the boat, especially since the sorry bastard could fry me with a flick of his finger. But I didn't know…"

"And by the time you did, you were caught in his web," Raina finished, taking her friend's hands in hers. "Delilah, part of being your Queen means I must be more proficient than my subjects at spy games or I won't survive. I've known about you and Drakkon almost from the first. Why do you think I've never officially invited you to join my coven and live at the palace with me and Alexi? And why have you confessed to me now?"

Her face crumpled. "I'm so sorry. I'm a spoiled, selfish idiot and I deserve whatever punishment you decide on. I honestly don't know if I ever would've told you, except Drakkon came up with a scheme to present me as his date for the two invites you sent to him. He wants to use me to get in your good graces, lower your defenses."

"*He's* the idiot to believe I'd ever fall for that," Raina scoffed, pulling her to sit on the sofa between her and Alexi. On Raina's left, Johan remained quiet on his perch, his earlier erection abated, expression inscrutable. "But the Demon King's stupid plot isn't what brought you here at this hour so badly shaken. Tell us what this has to do with the cave."

"Well, I went to Drakkon's lair tonight intending to break off as his date. His plan crossed the line for me. I thought you'd be shocked to see me on his arm, advocating a liaison between the two of you, and I couldn't bring myself to hurt you," she sniffed, miserable.

Raina could smell a lie with ease, and her friend was telling the truth. She patted Delilah's back, encouraging her to continue. "You *intended* to break your dates. You didn't see him?"

"Yes, but he didn't see me. When I arrived and started into the tunnels, I heard the most awful screeching and terrible sounds of a huge battle in progress deep in the bowels of the earth. I investigated and discovered Drakkon's sentinels trying to subdue the biggest freaking demon I've ever seen and getting the shit beat out of them. Of course, Drakkon wasn't lifting a talon to help."

Johan bolted to his feet, all semblance of calm vanishing. "This big demon, what did he look like?"

Delilah's speculative gaze met his. "Massive. He stands head and shoulders above the others in true form, at least nine feet tall to their seven. Dirty black hair, broad bulldog-like face, yellow teeth, purple skin. And he's, um, circus-freak endowed. His tool alone is probably a lethal weapon."

"That's him!" Johan punched a fist in the air. "He's our killer and the sonofabitch who attacked me, and Drakkon's in on everything somehow, just like Zane and I believed all along. Their asses are *mine*."

Delilah gaped at him. "You fought that thing and survived?"

"Two nights ago," he confirmed, pacing the floor in excitement. "I should've been a dead man, except Zane summoned Raina and Alexi, and they got to me in time. The demon got the jump on me, but I won't let it happen again. Damn, I need to find out why Drakkon is jeopardizing his Council seat and risking execution to protect the rogue, and I need solid evidence."

"I don't have your proof, but I can answer the first," Delilah said softly. "The rogue's name is Grog, and he's nothing more than a mentally challenged misfit who fell victim to his sire's evil scheme."

"His sire," Johan repeated, the revelation sinking in. "Drakkon is Grog's father. Zane and I considered the killer's DNA might belong to a brother or son, but the Demon King claimed he had no family and we couldn't prove otherwise."

"I don't know the details of Grog's parentage or how long dear old dad has been hiding him, but I overheard that much. What he's done to his own son in search for absolute transspecies domination is truly sinister."

Johan crossed his arms over his chest. "Start with them battling Grog and tell us everything you heard and saw."

The three of them listened in mounting disgust and outrage as her friend repeated every word of the encounter. By the time she finished, Johan was seething.

"There's a special place in Hades for Drakkon and I'm going to love sending the motherfucker there," he hissed. "To use anyone as a lab rat, much less your own flesh and blood, a mentally challenged fledgling who doesn't even understand what's happened to him...that's just so fucking sick I want to vomit."

"Great leaping gods," Alexi breathed, breaking his silence. "They both have to be stopped. What's our plan?"

"Nope, there's no *we* involved." Johan swiped a hand down his face. "Since demons, like vampires, are more active at night, Zane and I will go into the lair after sunup tomorrow. We'll get video of Grog being held captive and hopefully take hair samples for a DNA match, then get the hell out. I'd go today, but my partner needs time to recover from his initiation and we have to be at full strength, tread carefully."

"What initiation?" Delilah frowned, sidetracked.

Raina patted her knee. "Zane became a thrall tonight, dear. He's a bit indisposed at the moment." As she'd expected, her friend's dark eyes rounded and sparked with keen interest. No doubt Delilah, a strong dominant female, would investigate this development at the very first opportunity. Poor Zane would need extra supplement from his blood reward to keep up.

"Fuck that," Alexi argued, bringing the topic back to Johan's plan. "What happens if one of you is badly injured like you were the other night? Raina and I can't walk in daylight, but the demons can. You'd be screwed without a kiss, my badass friend."

Johan swore a vicious curse. "You're right. Dammit, that means finding a time when their guard is down. After hearing Delilah's account, I won't hold my breath."

"What about tonight?" Raina suggested. "We're having drinks at Lash with Drakkon, and he always takes his top sentinels everywhere he goes. The cave will be understaffed for a while."

Alexi grimaced. "Ugh. You're going through with this meeting?"

"Why not? Delilah never canceled and he has no idea we're on to him. The only problem is, I can make an excuse for one of my slaves to be absent, but not both. Knowing his inflated ego, Drakkon is expecting to be entertained and we'll need to keep him distracted while either Zane or Johan visits the lair and gathers the evidence."

"I have a feeling I know which one of us you think should stay behind and play boy toy to *His Magnificence*," Johan spat, voice dripping with sarcasm.

"Zane is a true thrall, love," Raina reminded him. "Drakkon will be so completely taken with him, he won't object to your absence. I'll say you were defiant and I had to leave you at home in chains, which I don't think anyone will have trouble believing, then you go do your thing."

Johan shot her a dark scowl, jaw clenching in anger. "I don't fucking like it, and I don't want the dirty bastard touching Zane. Does anyone have a better idea?"

No one did. There simply wasn't time to come up with anything else and pull the mission off fast. Not to mention Zoltan's trial looming in a matter of days. If the Vampire King was found guilty, he'd be executed immediately.

"Once you get the evidence, who can you trust to place it in the right hands? The Council's in Drakkon's hip pocket and they might decide to shut you up for good," Alexi pointed out.

"One of the Superiors, Logan Alexander, is a good friend of mine. He's an eagle shifter, and a damned fine man. He's the only one who voted against the others when Drakkon persuaded the rest to railroad me and Zane."

Raina nodded. "I've heard of Alexander. Why didn't you both go to him for help after you were put out on the streets?"

"Fair question. Logan offered us sanctuary, but he's earned a deadly enemy in Drakkon by going against him on our behalf. Zane and I thought it best to stay away from him, let the Demon King's anger toward him cool off since he has to work with the asshole. Logan has big personal issues right now as well. His older brother Kieran is dying and the clan is really torn up. Imposing on them was not an option."

How sad. A wave of sympathy for the Alexanders tugged Raina's heart, as well as admiration for the two new men in her life. They'd sold themselves into slavery rather than burden a struggling family, and Johan had never let on.

"Anyway, Logan will see the evidence gets to the Exodus liaison with the St. Louis police and officially bring it before the Council. Once it's a done deal, both factions will decide how to proceed with Drakkon and Grog's trial and punishment. The other Superiors will be secretly relieved to get rid of Drakkon, even if they didn't have the balls to take him on themselves."

"Except for your friend, the fools should all be removed from office," Delilah fumed, apparently forgetting her own delay in opposing the Demon King.

Johan smiled down at the little vamp in amusement. "One battle at a time, sugar. We all make mistakes, right?"

The wry comment missed its target. Delilah was too busy staring at Johan's sensual lips, seemingly stunned witless at the first scrap of positive attention he'd shown her. Being forced to fuck her as a slave wasn't the same as noticing and appreciating her without coercion. The air between them suddenly crackled with tension. Delilah's hungry gaze raked his chest, six-pack stomach, thighs...and the rod pushing behind his zipper.

Johan's beast wanted the little vamp straddling his lap. The heady musk of his *ardin* wafted from his skin, undetectable to the human nose but clear as a beacon to the vampires assembled. Their bond telegraphed to Raina his surge of barely controlled lust, and a mountain of guilt and confusion over his desire to taste such dark, forbidden fruit.

Johan hooked his thumbs in his jeans, drew himself up and broke eye contact, dispelling the supercharged moment. "I guess we'd all better get some sleep if we're going to be one hundred percent for tonight."

"Count me in, too," Alexi said, pushing to his feet. "No way will I allow our females to meet that fucker with only Zane for protection. No offense meant to your friend."

"None taken. Not to sound chauvinist, but every effort must be made to ensure the women's safety. If the meeting goes south, you and Zane get them the hell out of there. I'll meet everyone back here when I've got the evidence. If I run into trouble, I'll send a call through my bond with Raina and Zane." Johan looked to Raina, wary. "Shall we turn in, my lady?"

Everyone would've had to be struck deaf and dumb not to notice Johan had acted as an equal since the start of this gathering. And it hadn't occurred to any of them to question his authority or put him in his place as a slave. Indeed, her mate had taken charge of the group and the impending situation like the warrior he was born to be.

Raina couldn't be prouder of this man she adored to distraction.

She stood, taking his arm. "Yes, love, let's get some rest. Alexi, would you show Delilah to the guestroom on the other side of Zane's? She'll stay here for now."

"My pleasure." Alexi grinned at Delilah's astonishment.

"What about my punishment?" her friend asked, visibly nervous.

Raina studied the contrite, worried expression on her small face. "I'll sleep on it and let you know. Goodnight, sweetie."

Johan took Raina's arm and she was content to let him lead her from the room and upstairs like the lord of the palace. Perhaps that wasn't so far from the truth. His large presence at her side made her unbelievably happy.

"Sleeping on it was the worst punishment you could've devised," he mused. "She'll toss and turn all day."

"Zoltan taught me the value of patience. He always says consequences are more meaningful when leveled by a fair mind, and never in anger."

"Ah. If the method is good enough for unruly children, it's good enough for your subjects."

"Exactly."

From under her lashes, she tilted her head and sneaked a covert peek at her mate. His handsome face was pensive but relaxed, showing no trace of their earlier...disagreement. On the outside, anyway. Inside he still churned, a stormy sea of conflict.

In her chamber, Johan turned and ran a work-roughened palm down her arm. The hand of a skilled fighter who'd vanquished many an enemy.

"I don't know where I stand anymore, and that's a damned hard thing for a man to take," he whispered, golden eyes haunted. "Do I sleep here with you or am I banished alone to my cold bed? Do I await your command like a dumb animal? What do you want from me?"

"Oh, my darling." Killing him outright would be kinder than the slow death he'd suffer as her slave. Had there ever been any other option? Hands shaking, she reached out and cupped his beard-shadowed face, so dear to her.

"Nothing you aren't willing to give. I want you at my side and in my bed, but only if you want to be there. I didn't mean to fall in love with you but how could I not? I can't free you from the blood bond so you can leave here, and for that I'm deeply sorry. You'll always need your blood reward from me to survive. But I will grant your freedom before the Council so you may come and go about your business as you wish. You're my heart, Johan, and the choice to be with me is yours."

"Oh, gods, Raina…" His voice broke and he pulled her into a bone-crunching embrace. "I'm sorry about the nasty things I said to you earlier. I was a real bastard. Forgive me, please."

"There's nothing to forgive." She nuzzled his neck, clinging to him, wallowing in the wonderful feeling of Johan's big body wrapping around hers. A lean, hard wall of protective strength under his soft cotton T-shirt. Holding her close, his love washing over her like a warm tide. There was no greater power on earth than devotion freely given. And to receive those gifts from such a fiercely independent man, a warrior of great worth…her heart was near to bursting with joy.

He pulled back and gazed down at her, stroking her hair. "I want to be with you as your mate. This coven stuff is all new to me, though." He gave a wry laugh. "With my horny new beast always raring to go, the sex alone will probably give me a heart attack."

"You're *such* a human." She grinned. "Once you get used to the open ways of our coven, sharing our love for one another, you'll enjoy taking your place as the dominant male. Just don't forget who your mate is, buster."

"Never," he vowed, kissing her on the nose. Growing serious again, his smile faded. "But I meant what I said before about not turning vampire. I can't see myself doing that, baby, even for you."

The one barrier still remaining between them. A huge one. "You've never said why you feel this way."

He shook his head, searching for an explanation. "Maybe I'm overwhelmed by the idea of living forever, of taking an irreversible step. Of quite possibly being around to witness the end of the world. Fatalist bullshit. Yeah, I know most people wouldn't feel the same, but I can't change the fact that the mere thought makes me break out into a cold sweat. Can you understand?"

"Yes," she said, determined not to cry in front of him. He'd just feel bad and tears would change nothing.

He tilted up her chin and ran a thumb over full lower lip, expression hopeful. "Alexi said because of our blood bond, I'll live close to two lifetimes. Most people don't get so many years together, right?"

Slipping on a mask of calm, she fought to keep her voice even. "You don't have to sell me, love. I made a promise to you, and I won't break it."

Even when losing you shatters my soul into tiny pieces and there is no reason for me to exist another day.

Lowering his head, he pressed his mouth to hers in a slow, gentle kiss. She fisted her hands in his black hair, letting the strands slip through her fingers like the finest silk. She remained pliant in his arms, encouraging him to call the shots, lead her where he desired.

"To bed, my lady?" he murmured, his sex pressed to her belly through his jeans.

"At your command, my love."

They undressed quickly and he carried her to the bed, laid her upon the soft down like a precious treasure. She sank into him, pushing aside the lurking shadows, vowing to live only in this moment.

To love and honor this man for as long as the gods granted them.

* * * * *

Raina hadn't killed in fifty years, since the night she tore apart the sentinels chasing Alexi, the demons intending to take the brutalized fallen prince back to Drakkon. Or so the story went.

The fact didn't comfort Delilah. Keeping her association with the Demon King a secret from her Queen was tantamount to treason, made worse by their friendship. Oh, she didn't really believe Raina would sentence her to death, but the Queen could make her life miserable for the next century or two.

Flopping onto her back in the comfortable guest bed, she stared at the vaulted ceiling and tried to pinpoint what really had her so unsettled. The actual punishment? No. More like dread of how her stupidity would affect their friendship. If Raina never extended the invite for her to officially join the coven, chose to banish her, she had nobody to blame but herself.

In spite of the mess she'd created, a strange lightness eased the terrible weight in her breast. No anvil crushing her lungs. She'd carried a load of hidden remorse over Drakkon for so long, the absence felt odd. Like gravity no longer had any pull on her body and she'd fly off the earth.

"Great. After he kills you, at least you'll be a guilt-free corpse," she muttered.

In spite of the daylight outside, sleep wasn't in the future. And lying here brooding sucked. Not her forte. Sitting up, she swung her legs over the side of the bed with a frustrated sigh. If she didn't expend some pent-up energy, she'd go nuts. Going for a walk in the gardens was out of the question unless she wanted to become vampire stir-fry, so she'd have to content herself with prowling the palace. Not an optimal solution, but better than nothing.

Pulling on a short silk robe Raina had loaned her, she belted it loosely at her waist and padded from the room. In the darkened hallway she paused, tucking a stray lock of hair behind an ear. Where to? She'd fed on one of her own servants before the eye-opening visit to Drakkon's lair, so she wasn't hungry. And she didn't care to watch television. The programs were beyond asinine, and their creators should have their beating hearts carved from their pale, scrawny chests and devoured.

Unless one of them conceived a show called *Surviving Vampire Bitch Island*. Now *that* might be interesting.

Faint, telltale sounds of feminine giggling and a male groan of pleasure drifted from the end of the corridor. Raina's bedroom. The regal Vampire Queen, *giggling*? Well, her friend had certainly worked a miracle on the dangerous, brooding Johan, hadn't she? Or perhaps it was the other way around.

Self-pity stabbed under her breastbone sure and true as a stiletto, unfamiliar and unwelcome. Johan Stone was a damned fine man, proud and tough. Virile. Any woman and a great many men would kill to have him…his heart as well as his cock.

And Johan's heart would have to be involved for him to fuck any coven member other than Raina from now on. He'd die before being forced again, and he'd telegraphed his dominance to Delilah downstairs, loud and clear. Oh, he'd burned to ride her, long and hard. But he would not become a slave to his sexual urges. No one owned him.

Raina deserved this happiness. Finding her mate and solidifying her coven was a long-overdue dream about to become reality.

A reality that won't include you, Delilah girl. Because you're a selfish bitch and—

A low moan drifted into the corridor from somewhere nearby, interrupting her pity party. She cocked her head, listening. There, again, too soft for human ears. The miserable groan of a man in pain, or perhaps having a bad dream. Homing in, she realized the sound was coming from the thrall's room next door to hers. What was his name? Zane.

Intrigued, she walked to his door and hesitated, hand on the knob. In truth, during her visit the other day she'd been so dazzled by Johan she'd hardly noticed the other slave. Clearly, Johan's friend held quite a polar opposite view of their circumstances. What drove a trained warrior to desire life as a thrall? For this was his choice and no one else's.

Unable to restrain her curiosity, she went inside. Thanks to her sharp night vision, she didn't need to turn on a light to see the tall man lying prone in the big bed. He was stretched out on his stomach, long legs tangled in the sheets pushed low on his naked hips sometime during an obviously restless slumber.

A quiet whimper escaped his lips and he flinched, reacting to some unnamed terror. Drawn to his bedside, she approached silently, her gaze immediately settling on his back.

"Mother of Creation," she gasped, clapping a hand over her mouth.

Zane's smooth back was a mass of deep purple bruises made by a wide belt or strap. The marks crossed back and forth in an even pattern from his shoulders downward to disappear under the covers, so dark they nearly obscured the striking tattoo of the Exodus dagger in the small of his back. The sheet had fallen away to reveal the curve of one firm buttock, decorated by yet another purple stripe snaking around to his hip.

Delilah knew what a thrall's initiation entailed but she'd never witnessed a ceremony, much less the direct results. She had a house slave and a couple of servants to see to her daily needs, nothing fancy. Thralls were so rare, only a handful of the city's high-class members owned one. She'd never touched a thrall and suddenly she itched to let her fingers explore this marvel of male beauty.

Hoping not to wake him, she perched carefully on the edge of the bed at his side and turned her attention to the rest. A jeweled choker of green and white fire glittered at his graceful neck. And his face...oh, the gods had favored this man! Long strands of golden brown hair fell over his arched brow and fine nose. Thick, dusky lashes any female would kill to possess rested against lean cheeks. Grooves bracketed his sensual mouth, marking him as a man of laughter and love. The kind, gentle face of a poet, not at all similar to the dangerous magnetism of his friend. How on earth had she not noticed Zane before?

In four hundred years, he was the loveliest male she'd ever seen, bar none.

"Watch...out...*nooo.*" Zane's brow furrowed, his mouth opening in a soundless scream.

Concerned, Delilah reached out to push the wayward strands from his face, stroked his hair. "Shh, it's all right. Delilah's here, sweetheart." Which normally was cause enough to send any man fleeing in fear, not wallowing in comfort. But for some reason, she longed to erase whatever shadows had overtaken his dreams.

"Nooo...don't leave me," he whispered brokenly, clutching his pillow tight. Tears clung to his lashes, and a lone drop leaked out to trail down his cheek.

Oh, mercy. She'd rather face a horde of crazy demons than one man's grief, even if he was only dreaming. What was it about the sight of a man's tears that turned even the most hardened female's insides to mush?

"Zane, wake up." She shook his arm gently, the only visible area besides his face not bruised. He shuddered. "Zane?"

His lashes fluttered open and he blinked in confusion, cobwebs from the nightmare still clouding his gorgeous jade eyes.

"There, you see? It was only a nasty dream," she soothed, brushing away the moisture on his face. Why did she have this strange, inexplicable urge to place herself like a snarling tigress between this thrall and any creature that might dare to hurt him?

"What..." Turning his head, he gazed up at her as his wits returned, recognition dawning. "Lady Delilah! Forgive me, I—" His apology ended on a strangled gasp as he pushed up.

"Slowly," she scolded, helping him sit up. Reaching past him, she plumped two pillows against the headboard and eased him back. "Can you sit up like that with your back so bruised?"

"Yes, my lady," he hissed, gritting his teeth in pain. "Thank you."

"You're welcome, now stop squirming." To her surprise, she enjoyed fussing over him, pulling the sheets up and tucking them around his hips. But not before pausing a beat to admire his package, his long, thick cock magnificent even in repose. Just like the rest of a mouthwatering body to inspire the most decadent of fantasies.

What would it be like to see the thrall's head thrown back in ecstasy as she rode him, the jeweled collar winking at his throat? To command him totally, knowing he'd willingly submit whether she chose to take him to the heights of passion or the abyss of physical punishment? Her nipples pebbled and her sex heated at the idea of taking him, sinking her fangs into his throat, savoring him like crème brûlée, smooth and sweet on the tongue.

Ohh, if Raina didn't banish her to Siberia, she'd do just that. But not today. Johan was right when he declared his friend needed time to recover. More like days...which Zane didn't have.

"How are you ever going to get through tonight's ordeal with Drakkon?" she remarked, suppressing a shiver.

"What?" he frowned. His puzzlement cleared and he snorted. "Oh, right. Drinks at Lash with *His Fugliness*. Raina told you, huh?"

"Ah...not exactly. What is fugliness?"

He rolled his eyes. "When *ugly* doesn't cover the sentiment, there's *fugly*—fucking ugly."

A laugh escaped, taking her by surprise. When was the last time she'd laughed out loud? "You are an impertinent one. Raina's going to have her hands full with you."

"Not just her hands, my lady." He waggled his brows. "If I'm a good boy."

His impish grin was so infectious, she found herself smiling back.

Plucking at the sheet over his lap, Zane slanted her a curious look. "So, what brings you here? You heard about Raina's new thrall and rushed right over to have your wicked way with me?"

"Hmm, tempting." She ran her tongue over one fang, contemplating. "But no, that's not why I'm here, more's the pity. Actually, I made a rather startling discovery last night that, unfortunately, forced me to make a confession to Raina in the telling of it. If she doesn't stake me in the sun when this is over, I'll count myself fortunate."

"Wow." Eyes twinkling, he whistled through his teeth. "Sounds like quite a story. Shall we break out a six-pack?"

Bemused, she shook her head, completely disarmed by his easy charm. What a novelty to feel as though she could tell this man anything and he wouldn't judge her. Must be the warmth in his lovely green eyes, his innate kindness. Or those dratted dimples slashing either side of his kissable mouth.

Guard lowered, she told this human male, a mere thrall, the truth about the past miserable decade under the Demon King's thumb. Every last ugly detail. She spared herself no embarrassment, made no excuses.

"I used to be so full of arrogant pride. But I've learned there's always someone stronger," she finished, unable to squelch the note of wistful sadness.

Zane laid one big hand over hers. "Not stronger, Lady Delilah. Just more ruthless." He gave her hand a gentle squeeze, face full of understanding. "Would that we could all afford to cast stones, but the only perfect beings are gods, and we are not fit to touch them."

Oh…oh, my. For the first time in several decades, her caustic wit and sarcasm fled. What could she say in response to such eloquence and compassion? The heat from his palm sizzled up her arm to french-fry her brain. "I…thank you."

"Forget it. You're the one who made the decision to break away from him once he finally schemed to use you to get to Raina," he emphasized. "That's commendable, but you know as well as I do, if you'd gone through with it nobody would've found your corpse. The bastard would never have been under suspicion of your disappearance because nobody except his own sentinels knew you were seeing him."

Her stomach lurched. "Blazing Hades, I never thought of that!"

"Things turned out for the best." He sobered, going into warrior mode. "Okay, you arrived at the cave to give him the boot. What stopped you?"

Heaving a weary breath, she went over the covert visit once more, describing the discovery of Grog and Drakkon's vile plot. Zane's reaction mirrored everyone else's, and the determined glint in his eyes when she outlined tonight's plan worried her. A lot.

"You're in no shape to suffer his cruel attentions, Zane," she fretted. The prospect seemed even more horrifying than it had earlier. "Sweet Virgin, if he takes you to one of the club's private rooms—"

"Then I'll be able to buy Johan more time to get the evidence we need to put them both away," he said quietly.

Zane wouldn't be swayed. Her gentle thrall possessed a backbone of solid steel and a wealth of foolish courage that would probably get him killed.

And Zane is not your thrall. Raina will never let go of a treasure like him.

Still, Delilah had the strong urge to protect this man however possible. "One piece of advice, since you're obviously set on going ahead with tonight. If—no, *when*—Drakkon gets you alone, no matter what he does to you, regardless of the terrible agony he inflicts…do not scream."

Zane paled, but his resolve remained intact. "Why?"

"Screams and blood drive him to a frenzy of lust. If he breaks you, he'll be driven past all reason and will not stop until you are dead."

"Game over," he muttered, raking a hand through his shaggy hair.

"Yes. The only way to keep him intrigued is to take the harsh punishment he metes out with bravery. You'll have to delve deep into your psyche and employ all of your skills as a thrall to survive. Be the true submissive you are, push aside fear to achieve sexual rapture, and you'll wrap him around your little finger. And I must caution you, that invites a whole new set of dangers where the Demon King is concerned."

Zane grimaced. "In other words, if I light Drakkon's fire, so to speak, he won't stop until he satisfies his obsession to own me permanently."

"Worse." Leaning forward, she laid a hand on his chest. She had to make him fully comprehend the mastermind he'd be dealing with. "Drakkon in his handsome, more human, form can quite charming, lethally so. He'll do more than own you physically, Zane. Unless you keep your mental shields solid every moment, he'll take over your mind, compel your devotion. The desire to serve him will become a fever in your blood until you can think of nothing else, until you no longer remember who you were. May the gods help you then. Just ask Alexi."

"How did you avoid that sorry fate all those years?"

"I'm not human. Those sorts of mind tricks won't work on me, so he resorted to old-fashioned threats and blackmail," she said ruefully.

"Well, you're going to be free of that bastard soon enough." His eyes hardened to match the emeralds at his throat. "Raina, Johan and everyone in the coven are my family for the rest of my days. I don't give a shit what happens to me as long as they're safe. That includes you, Lady Delilah," he added softly.

She swallowed hard, unexpected tears stinging her eyes. Pushing from the bed, she hastily dashed them away, falling into her only method of self-defense. "Don't waste your efforts on me, young thrall. I've been taking care of myself for centuries."

He crossed his arms over his smooth chest, arching a brow. "And doing a piss-poor job of it, too."

"Impertinent," she purred, showing some fang. "Good way to get your tongue cut out."

"Sorry, sweetheart. All of my appendages are valuable tools of my trade."

Oh, that adorable grin! Hellfire and damnation. "Get some rest," she snapped. "You'll need it."

Turning on her heel, Delilah sashayed out, nose in the air. She absolutely would not give Zane the satisfaction of seeing how deeply he'd touched her heart.

Damn the lovely man to Hades for reminding her she had one.

Chapter Fifteen

ဆ

Johan was aware of Raina's gaze following him as they dressed. He wished he could erase the stark worry on her beautiful face, make love to her until she forgot everything except his cock driving home, worshipping his mate.

Not gonna happen. She'd picked up on the weight pressing on his chest, this sense of impending disaster that had grown steadily worse since they'd arisen. He'd never been gifted with any extrasensory abilities, especially precognition, but this yawning black hole stretching toward his boots seemed very real, very threatening.

Forget that and focus, dammit, or you're going to get your ass killed.

Johan yanked on a dark T-shirt and black leather jacket, then tucked a blaster into the waistband of his matching leather pants. Next he tugged his necklace from behind his T-shirt, making sure the gold medallion lay properly. The device Alexi brought him a short while ago wasn't just any necklace, but a micro-camcorder. Hidden in the center of the medallion, the recorder stored all incoming data on a sliver of computer chip, useful for leaving his hands free in case of a battle he would, with any luck, avoid.

This was a simple covert information-gathering exercise, nothing more. In and out, just as he'd done successfully on dozens of occasions. This would be no different.

"I have something for you." Raina sauntered past him, mile-long legs encased in tight leathers, high-heeled boots making little indentions in the plush carpet. Her butt swayed back and forth, enticing him to pounce. Again.

And Daddy has something for you, babe.

215

"I heard that!" she called from inside the walk-in closet.

He chuckled in spite of himself, mood lightened somewhat. Yeah, a guy could have a lot of fun with this bond and mating stuff. Just one of the little perks he'd come to appreciate, along with the fortification Raina's blood provided him. She'd given him and Zane an extra amount tonight, and he had to admit the rush was awesome. He'd become addicted to her after all, and he no longer cared.

"What are you doing? Tunneling a hole in the wall?" From the racket she was making, he wouldn't be surprised.

"Something I should've done the night you were attacked." Raina emerged from the closet hiding something behind her back. "A warrior should never be without these."

Stopping in front of him, she brought forth the items in question. Johan gaped in astonishment. In her grasp were his hand blades, dagger and sword. The night he'd surrendered them at Lash, he was as devastated as if he'd been castrated. And now, to have them back...

"Where...how..." Gratitude clogged his throat, and he blinked against the stinging in his eyes.

"I had Alexi go back and fetch them the next evening." A ghost of a smile touched her lips and she looked at him with all of her love shining on her face. "I guess I knew from the first you'd never be tamed."

By the gods, she had his weapons all along. Deep down, Raina knew she'd give them back one day. Overwhelmed with joy, he grabbed her shoulders, pulling her close. "You have no idea how much this means to me," he whispered. "Thank you, sweetheart."

"Oh, it's no big—"

He promptly silenced her protest with a soul-blistering kiss. She melted into him, breasts crushing against his chest. She felt so damned good in his arms. Soft and warm, so right. He never wanted to let her go because their embrace seemed too much like goodbye, the forever kind. More stupid woo-woo shit…but not exactly groundless.

Breaking the kiss, he pulled back and tipped up her chin with one finger. Stared long and hard into her face, memorizing every beloved feature. High cheekbones and an aristocratic nose. Creamy porcelain skin. All of that lush, wild flaming hair perfect to fist in his hands as he took her. Fine, arched brows accenting fathomless blue eyes shadowed with the ache of old loss.

"I know what this is costing you, setting me free to do what I need to do," he said softly. "But I'm not Marcus, baby. I'll come home to you, I swear."

"Promise me." Her voice hitched, composure close to crumbling.

"I promise."

Raina dropped the weapons. They hit the carpet with a clatter as she launched herself against his chest, held him fast. Not anyone's queen, just a vulnerable female scared to death for her mate. His arms went around her and he nuzzled his face into her hair, breathing in the scent of sweet honey-almond. If only he could take her inside himself, carry her with him wherever he went. But in a way, he supposed that was already true.

This time she pulled away first, giving him a watery smile. "You'd better get going. The sooner you're finished, the sooner I can make our excuses to end this farce of a date."

"Believe me, that's all the incentive I need to hurry."

Bending, he retrieved the dagger from the floor and slipped it from the sheath. The dark blade, almost as long as his forearm and wide as his wrist, gleamed wickedly. The weight of the weapon settled into his palm, familiar and comforting, as though he'd never been without it. Satisfied, he sheathed the blade once more and strapped it to his right thigh, nice and snug.

Next, he fetched the sword and tested it in the same manner. The silver blade was straight rather than arced, broad and heavy, so sharp the edge could slice a falling sheaf of paper cleanly in two. Swung with force, it would sever the intended target with the ease of a hot knife through warm butter.

Dagger for the heart, sword for the head.

With a sigh, he replaced the sword, slinging the carrier over his leather jacket and across his back, handle within grasp over his left shoulder. The heaviness of the weapon kept it secure during a fight, giving the rest of his body necessary freedom of movement.

Last, he slipped the black glove fitted with four razor-sharp blades onto his left hand, leaving his right open for the other weapons. The blades curved over his fingertips, extending like six-inch talons. Not quite as dramatic as the dagger or sword, but effective enough to puncture a vital organ or rip out his opponent's throat.

"My, my," Raina breathed, her appreciative gaze raking him from head to toe. "I think I've developed a fetish for dangerous warriors."

"Warriors, plural?" A smile tugged his lips.

"Well, Zane isn't a warrior anymore, so I stand corrected." Stepping close, she took the collar of his jacket in both hands. "I have a thing for one warrior in particular. The man I love."

"And I love you, sweetheart." Framing her cheeks in his big hands, he kissed her gently, lingering for just one more moment. "Damn, I have to go. I need to get into position and be ready to move in when you tell me Drakkon and his cohorts are settled in at Lash and distracted. Are you sure I'll be able to communicate with you?"

"Yes. Even though you can't mind-link and read thoughts on your own, I can hear you and push my words into your head."

"All right." Resting the hand on the hilt of his dagger, he frowned, thinking of Zane facing one of their worst enemies with only his sexual allure as a weapon. They'd said goodbye earlier, and Johan was disturbed to find his friend far from one hundred percent in spite of receiving his blood reward. Whatever happened tonight, the man he loved nearly as much as Raina would get the raw end of the deal. "Raina, if Drakkon starts to go too far—"

"I'll tear the bastard's heart from his chest," she assured him.

"Good enough for me." One last hug and kiss, then he released her and strode for the door. If he didn't go now, he'd never be able to leave.

Just as his hand touched the knob, she called out in a tremulous voice. "A warrior never breaks his promise."

Hesitating, Johan nodded. "That's right, my lady. He never does."

Blending into the night, he sent a prayer to the gods that he hadn't lied to his mate.

* * * * *

"I look like a gay disco pimp from the nineteen-seventies," Zane sighed, glancing down at himself. "Did we have to go with green silk?"

From her seat next to him in the limo, Raina patted the knee of his tailored black pants. "The shirt brings out those striking green eyes, not to mention the jewels at your throat. You look extremely edible."

"Somehow, I don't find that much of a comfort." Her unhappy thrall waved a hand to indicate his chest. "You can see my nipple rings outlined through the material. I feel totally ridiculous."

Across from them, Alexi made a face. "Stop complaining, pup, or I'll have to kill you. There are worse fates than your sex appeal attracting every horny creature within a hundred miles." He sent Raina a droll stare. "Can I please drain him?"

Despite her worry over Johan and the trying evening ahead of them all, Raina laughed softly at their antics. "Not tonight. We'll need every ounce of that sex appeal to keep our nasty demon distracted."

Alexi's humor fled. "I don't like this one bit. Being in a public place won't stop Drakkon from hurting Zane." He pinned their thrall with an anxious gaze. "Delilah warned you to keep your mind shields up, right? And to never, under any circumstances, accept his—"

"Yeah, I know," Zane grumbled, waving off his advice. "Cut it out, you're making me nervous."

"Damnation, I was only trying to—"

"Here we are," Raina said, cutting off the sparring match in progress from the second the limo left the palace. Any fool could see that her longtime companion had fallen head over heels for Zane, and the young thrall was fast becoming enamored of Alexi as well. If Drakkon picked up on the attraction between them, he'd make it his life's mission to destroy the fragile new connection simply to amuse himself.

George came around to open their door, standing aloof and handsome in his dark suit, wavy brown hair curling against his collar. Raina took the hand he offered as she stepped from the vehicle, studying her driver as he, in turn, studied Alexi emerging after her. The poor man had to wonder whether the new thrall would take his place as Alexi's primary food source, but he needn't have worried. Zane belonged to Raina and no human could handle providing regular sustenance for more than one vampire.

Patting George's arm, Raina allowed her mind to brush his, soothing without his knowledge. Immediately he relaxed, calm replacing anxiety. Satisfied, she turned her attention to Zane, who'd gripped the open doorframe to haul himself out of the limo. His lips were compressed into a thin line, face taut with the pain of his screaming muscles, but the stubborn fool ignored Alexi's attempt to help him. The idiot was going to push himself too far.

"I doubt I'll be the one doing the pushing," Zane retorted, grimacing.

"Oh! Do stay out of my head. That's rude and inappropriate." She punctuated the set-down with a glare, hoping to curtail the bad habit that could easily get him killed.

"Sorry." He dimpled at her, dispelling the sincerity of his apology.

She gave an unladylike snort. "What am I going to do with you? Nevermind, don't answer that! Just keep your gift firmly in check while in Drakkon's presence. We don't want to pique his interest in you any more than necessary."

She already questioned the wisdom of bringing Zane here tonight, placing him in the demon's clutches. But Johan was even now awaiting her word to proceed with his mission, and counting on his friend to distract the Demon King. And distractions didn't come tastier than her thrall.

"Did someone mention my name?"

The devil take it, the bastard was early! She'd hoped to have her party safely ensconced inside Lash away from prying eyes before the demon arrived with Delilah and his minions. Now she'd be forced to bestow a cordial public greeting upon him, which was probably what he'd intended. Two royals putting aside their long-standing feud to hold a mysterious conversation over drinks. Before dawn, the city would be abuzz with speculation of their meeting.

As one, her group turned to face Drakkon approaching with his legion of ghouls. Even she had to admit he looked sexy as hell. Designer jeans hugged his muscular thighs and cupped his huge sex like a glove. A long-sleeved light blue shirt emphasized his powerful shoulders and contrasted with the raven hair flowing unbound nearly to his elbows. But his brutally handsome face was spoiled by the cruel set of his sensual mouth and the evil glint in his dark eyes. Drakkon had come prepared to play dirty, and she wished for Zane's sake he'd assumed the ugly, disgusting form he'd been sporting during their last encounter at Lash.

Halting before Raina, Drakkon took one of her hands and brought it to his cold lips. "My dear, you look..." His gaze slid from her face to the full breasts pushing against the midriff-baring red tank top, down to the ruby in her belly button, to her long legs encased in tight black leathers, landing on the toes of her booted feet. He smiled, flicking a pointed glance at her nipples before raising his eyes to hers once more. "...like a biker's wet dream," he finished. "Good to know that vampires aren't completely impervious to the cold."

Tugging her hand from his, she resisted the urge to wipe off his kiss and claw the grin from his face. Instead, she gave him an innocent smile. "Drakkon, you're looking less bloated this evening. Amazing what a bit of diet and exercise will do."

Behind him, a couple of the sentinels snickered. A barely perceptible gesture of his hand silenced them. He shook his head, refusing to rise to the bait. "Come now, that was beneath you, Raina. Everyone expects that sort of cheap shot from me, but you? And I'm here at your invite with total absence of malice, no less."

Raina fought the flush staining her cheeks. They were starting to draw speculation from passersby, and several who'd skirted their group to enter the club glanced back at his comment. *Absence of malice, my ass.* "You're right, forgive me," she said, amazed her tongue didn't shrivel and fall off. "My goal is to end the animosity between us, not perpetuate it."

"Fascinating. Don't you agree, my little desert flower?" Eyes glittering in anticipation of Raina's reaction, he held out a hand to someone hovering at his back. Delilah, who'd been eclipsed by his big body, stepped around her lover.

Former lover, unbeknownst to you, asshole.

Playing her part, Raina affected what she hoped to be an

expression of genuine shock. "Delilah! What are you doing here, with — with *him*?"

Earlier, they'd decided that allowing Drakkon to believe he had the upper hand was the best way to get him to lower his guard. From his smirk, she guessed the deception worked. The demon radiated conceit.

Tucking Delilah's hand in the crook of his arm, Drakkon glowed with triumph. "Raina dear, my poor little flower has been fairly eaten alive with guilt these past few years. Given your friendship with her versus how you feel about me, she has been distraught at deceiving you. However, your invitation filled us both with hope that this olive branch from you would be a new start for us all...and a perfect time for Delilah and myself to declare our love."

Oh, puke. How many times had the pompous jerk rehearsed that speech in the mirror? Lost in himself, the demon failed to see his great love roll her eyes in disgust. Ignoring Alexi's discreet cough, Raina splayed a hand on her chest. "Oh, my. I — I don't know what to say. This is so much to absorb. Delilah sweetie, tell me you don't love this demon!"

"Okay, I won't," she said sweetly, tossing a lock of dark hair over one tiny shoulder. Drakkon, the fool, totally missed the double entendre.

Raina managed to look dismayed. "Well, perhaps we should go inside and sit down. This is much too personal to discuss out here on the — "

"Satan's cock, what is this?" Drakkon breathed, staring past Raina. Disengaging himself from his "lover", he walked slowly forward, leaving her forgotten. "Zane? Zane Ramsey has become...a *thrall*?"

Gotcha. "Oh, yes. It seems my pet has embraced his submissive nature and found his true calling. Isn't he scrumptious?"

On cue, Zane stepped forward and dropped gracefully to one knee before the Demon King. Taking Drakkon's left hand, he raised it to his lips and kissed each jeweled ring on the demon's finger. Then he lifted his head and looked Drakkon in the eye. "At your service, my lord."

Zane was beautiful and ethereal, an angel from heaven with the teardrops of the gods winking at his throat.

"Exquisite," Drakkon whispered, face darkening with raw hunger.

The die was cast. The Demon King had ceased to realize anyone else existed. He'd stop at nothing to have the thrall now. With a predatory smile, he pulled Zane to his feet.

"Let's go inside, shall we? The sooner we dispense with business, the more quickly we can attend to pleasure."

* * * * *

All right, it's a go. We're settled in a private booth inside Lash, and Drakkon is completely infatuated with Zane. He didn't even think to ask where you are.

Unused to communicating telepathically, Johan concentrated hard and pushed his response to Raina. *Okay, going in. Keep that slimeball in line, baby.*

Worry about yourself and be careful!

Always.

Johan crept from his hiding place near the mouth of the cave, unease skittering down his spine. Not a sign of movement since Drakkon and his sentinels vacated the premises. No demons guarded the entrance, but then again, no one except his clan and Delilah was supposed to know its location.

Inside, he chose the left of the three passages as Delilah had instructed, following the tunnel deep into the earth. Keeping one hand near the hilt of his dagger, he sent silent thanks to Alexi for providing the medallion around his neck.

Reaching the end, he paused. Listened. A burst of laughter and ribald comments by several voices were accompanied by one's strident, angry protest at being the butt of their jokes. The merriment was muffled, distant, as though the participants weren't in the main chamber ahead, but perhaps congregated in another room. Peering cautiously around the lip of rock, Johan saw he was correct. The chamber was empty, save for the hulking figure huddled in the corner of a cell on the far end.

With all the stealth he possessed, he moved into the chamber, ready to be discovered at any moment. Making his way closer to the cell, he spied a corridor branching off to the right of it. The noise drifted from that direction and upon closer inspection, he saw a door about twenty yards down the tunnel, open a crack. Investigating further, he had to bite back a laugh.

Poker. Drakkon's guards of lesser rank were taking advantage of King Sleaze's absence to engage in a raucous game of poker. They were hunched over an ancient wooden table littered with beer bottles, shielding their cards from prying eyes, some whooping and slapping the table, a couple frowning. And the naughty demons were making so damned much racket as they partied, the Dark King of the Underworld Himself could stride naked into their midst and they might not notice. His job should be a cinch, especially since the main chamber couldn't be seen at all from this angle.

Retracing his steps, Johan returned to the cell, hoping the tiny recording device was getting all of this. If this worked, they'd have irrefutable incriminating evidence to take to Logan and the rest of the Council tomorrow. At the least, Drakkon would rot in Region Five, the Midwest's maximum security prison for supernatural beings, for eternity. As for Grog's fate, that subject might be a bit more touchy. If the demon weren't mentally handicapped, he'd be executed for the murders. The bleeding hearts were going to shout and beat their breasts over this one, but by then Grog wouldn't be Johan's problem.

Studying the locking mechanism on the cell door, Johan wished for a handy gift like telekinesis. Then he could spring the lock with his mind or better yet, float one of Grog's hairs to him. Almost everyone he knew had some sort of cool ability, but he'd been born just plain human.

No help for it. The lock wasn't the cheap sort he could pick with the tip of his dagger, and waking up the demon to politely ask for a hair sample was not a good idea. He needed...no, they couldn't be that stupid. Turning, he scanned the rock face behind him and shook his head in amazement. There, hanging on a small hook drilled into the wall, was the key. A single key for the only cell in this chamber, which reinforced Johan's belief that Drakkon kept a more traditional dungeon somewhere else and had ordered this cell constructed far away from the others for secrecy.

Lifting the ring, he glanced toward the corridor where the poker game was still in full swing. Stepping to the cell door, he inserted the key in the lock and turned it, slow and easy. He gritted his teeth at the scrape of the mechanism and a pop as the bolt released sounded like a frigging gunshot to his ears. Tensing, he expected a cry of alarm. Nothing. The guards hadn't heard.

Wiping a bead of sweat from his brow, Johan pushed open the cell door, leaving the key in the lock for afterward. Peering inside, he noted the dreary space, enclosed on three sides and on top by rock. The only way out was through the door...or by ripping out the iron bars themselves as Grog must've done before. Johan had been the unlucky victim during that little foray into the city. He could testify to the rogue's brute strength.

Time to get what he'd come for and get the hell out. The hinges gave with a soft squeak, not loud enough to alert the guards or the giant in front of him. He crept inside and got his first good look at Grog since arriving.

The creature sat huddled in the far left-hand corner, head down, raven wings folded around his massive body as though for warmth. Or comfort. Several heavy chains ran from under the wings, likely secured to his limbs, and were bolted to the floor with very little slack. Ebony hair fell forward, obscuring his face as he slept, deep and even. In all, the creature appeared miserable and lonely, every inch a victim. A hellish existence, worse than death. It was by far the saddest, most pathetic sight Johan had ever laid eyes on.

The video would tell the tale for the Council. Squashing the unbidden wave of sympathy for his would-be killer, Johan steeled himself to collect the evidence. Fishing a small plastic bag from the pocket of his jacket, he moved forward on cat feet. Holy crap, even sitting Grog resembled a large boulder. He'd considered scouting the floor for a stray hair, but he didn't want anyone to challenge the evidence as not belonging to the suspect. Which meant he'd have to pluck it. Damnation.

Heaving a deep breath, he reached out, fingered a flyaway strand. The hair was coarse and thick, like a horse's tail. Information he would've been happy not knowing. Counting to three, he gave the strand a quick yank. To his surprise, it came free with little resistance. Evidence in hand, he froze as the demon shifted on his haunches. After a moment, the creature seemed to settle again.

Pulse hammering, Johan forced himself to remain calm and place the hair in the bag when what he wanted to do was run, not stopping until he reached the SUV he'd parked off the road two miles from here. *Steady…done!* He pocketed his prize and began to back away from the sleeping demon.

Or rather, the demon who was no longer asleep. *Ah, shit.*

Through the tangle of Grog's black hair, Johan found himself looking straight into a bloodshot yellow eye.

Chapter Sixteen

ა

Trailing the group through the murky interior of Lash, Zane scoped out the place. Dark, sort of Goth, trendy. A vague memory of a girl with pink hair tugged at him, and he wondered what had become of her. He recalled little else of his previous visit, other than being so sick he was ready to collapse.

Now he did his best not to stare at the generous public displays of flesh. And failed. Many females wore see-through net tops or went bare-breasted. Some males wore nothing except crotchless leathers or jeans. Here and there, the slaves who hadn't yet been invited or ordered to sit at their masters' tables stood with their gazes lowered, some dressed, others naked save for their collars. Never in his life had he seen so many piercings and gold chains. There was enough bling in the room to decorate for a New Year's Eve bash.

Sweet mercy. Would Raina expect him to perform in public? Or at her upcoming party, perhaps? The idea caused his face to heat even as his cock stiffened in enthusiasm. A pain slut and an exhibitionist. Peachy. Thinking of his two-fisted father, he hoped the sonofabitch was spinning in his grave. A psychiatrist would have a field day with poking around in Zane's head.

The group took a C-shaped booth in a private corner of the club, shielded from the other patrons by fichus trees and assorted plants but affording a great view of the now-empty stage. Drakkon's sentinels positioned themselves behind the booth along the wall, ready to come to their lord's defense if necessary. One of them wore a dark T-shirt with red letters that declared, *As a matter of fact, I do give a flying fuck.* Demon humor? The sentinel caught Zane looking and sent him a feral grin. Zane resisted the urge to salute the asshole with his middle finger.

Drakkon slid into the booth, followed by Delilah, Alexi and Raina. Zane stood at the end of the booth beside his mistress, legs spread, hands clasped in front of him and head bowed as he'd seen the other slaves doing. After a buxom waitress descended to take the foursome's drink orders, the Demon King wasted no time getting to the point.

"All right, Raina dear. Suppose you enlighten me as to why, for the first time in six hundred years, I'm suddenly fit to breathe the same air as you? I'm dying of curiosity."

Raina's reply was crisp, businesslike. "Needless to say, we've never seen eye to eye on our treatment of slaves. What is legal isn't always what is right. Staying within the law doesn't mean an individual is a good person. I don't like you and you don't like me —"

"I like *you* just fine," he countered reasonably. "So you've come to debate politics? To yammer at me about how I deserve to rot in Hades because I'm a carnivore?"

"You consume human flesh, Drakkon. That's wrong on so many levels, I can't even begin."

"Why?" He sounded genuinely baffled. "If a group of middle-class humans pickets a meat-packing plant with signs declaring 'save the cows', they're dismissed as weirdoes. I, on the other hand, perform a service to humans and shifters by cleansing the earth of their lesser brethren. Through the slave system, I dispose of career criminals and other foul wretches no one wants littering the streets. They are my cows, if you will. The choice slaves I use for sex, same as any upper-class member. And I do all of this legally. Why is that wrong, yet your consumption of human blood and ownership of that lovely thrall isn't?"

Zane glanced down at his mistress from under his lashes. The demon hit a nerve. Her lips were drawn into a grim line, her face taut with anger. The scary thing was, every word he'd said was true. A prime example of what made Drakkon such a dangerous enemy, of how he kept the Council in his corner. Smooth talker with a forked tongue. Typical politician.

"Touché. Be that as it may, I'm not here to debate with you. I've come to propose a trade, one of mutual benefit to us both."

Peeking to gage Drakkon's reaction, Zane was startled to find the demon's gaze locked on him. His hungry eyes raked the length of Zane's body. A ghostly caress skimmed his chest, curled between his legs, stroked his erect cock. Mesmerized, he couldn't break the demon's solid hold no matter how he tried.

You like that, boy?

Yes, damn you!

The demon's lips curved in a triumphant smile. Zane's heart lurched. Stricken, he realized what he'd just done. Ten seconds under Drakkon's compulsion, and the bastard had stripped his defenses, discovered his most precious secret. The demon's satisfied expression said he'd pay dearly for the mistake.

"I can think of one acceptable trade already," Drakkon replied. "The question is, what could our illustrious Vampire Queen possibly stand to gain from me?"

Raina appeared unaware of the exchange between her thrall and the demon. "You have great influence with the Council."

"Aha! It is politics, then."

"I suppose. I want you to use your clout to convince the Council to reinstate me as a Superior."

Zane silently congratulated her for the brilliant lie. She'd rather be boiled in oil than ask that self-important prick for a favor, but his inflated ego would preen under the stroke, demanding he believe her.

That got Drakkon's attention. Laughing out loud, he slammed a fist onto the table, causing all of his sentinels to jump. "Why in great blazing Hades would I do that? So you can torment me into eternity on a daily basis rather than occasionally?"

"You owe me," she shot back. "I rescued Alexi from your cruelty and was repaid by being stripped of my position." Beside Delilah, Alexi remained stoic. Drakkon, however, gaped at her as though she'd lost her mind.

"You stole one of my slaves! Considering you could've been executed, I'd say you got off easy."

"Alexi wasn't one of the criminals or wretches you referred to! He was a *prince*, kidnapped and sold into slavery by his ruthless brother!" She slapped her hand on the table harder than the demon had. "Illegal or not, I was right to take him from you. If I hadn't, he'd be dead."

Drakkon waved a hand in impatience. "Why are we rehashing this fifty goddamned years later? Your precious companion lives and I have left him alone. He was no more than a slave to me, albeit an unusually beautiful one." Pausing, he narrowed his eyes in suspicion. "You're blowing smoke up my ass."

The demon was full of shit. The only reason he hadn't tried to wrest Alexi away from her was because she'd turned the former prince vampire. Drakkon could no longer compel his former slave.

"Not at all. I want my Council seat back."

"After more than five decades," he mused, not convinced.

The waitress brought their drinks, but no one touched them.

After the girl left, Raina continued. "Several Superiors have come and gone, including my former supporters. Memories of our disagreement have dimmed and I am bored with being a figurehead Queen for a mostly peaceful region of vampires. It's time."

"Hmm." Thrumming his fingers on the table, he considered. "What do I get in return?"

Knowing she'd hooked him, she leaned forward, elbows on the table's polished surface. "Face it, Drakkon. You're the royal who doesn't get invited to the ball. The Council and the other city officials play your power games at work because they have no choice. But that courtesy does not extend to social hour where the real action is to be found."

"And I care, why?"

"Oh, come on," she cajoled with a hint of a smile. "Tell me you don't crave a place among the city's A-list. That you aren't dying to attend the best parties, move in the inner circle. That it doesn't make your cock hard to imagine the sex and the intrigue, thighs parted for you and secrets revealed in your ear."

He licked his lips, hand tightening around the whiskey glass. "You can give me these things?"

"I can. Starting with my party Saturday night." Sitting back, she took a casual sip of her red wine, letting him stew for a few moments. "Since you're here, I assume you received your invitation. Everyone who is anyone will be there. They will see that we have put aside our long-standing feud to become allies. This gesture from me, and the A-list is yours."

She had him. The Demon King wanted this so badly, Zane almost felt bad for the blow he'd be dealt when he realized the offer was a sham. Almost, but not quite. Drakkon was a cruel master, a killer. An accomplice to murder.

And by dawn, he'd find himself rotting in Region Five, along with his spawn.

"Since you made this proposal and will reap the most direct benefit from it, I would add one item more to the exchange," the demon lobbied. "You will sign over your thrall to me."

It was Raina's turn to laugh. "Not a chance."

"For a limited period, then. Three months."

"No."

"I assume you didn't dangle the boy in front of me tonight only to withhold his favors and make me angry. Name your terms, Raina, because I'll have him or this meeting is over," he stated, low and deadly calm.

They had anticipated his reaction to Zane and she was ready with her answer. "You may have Zane all to yourself on three separate occasions, from dusk until dawn. Use him for your pleasure, but to maim or kill him is out of the question. In addition, you are welcome to enjoy his charms at any of my social functions at the palace, provided he is available and you are on your best behavior."

Drakkon's face shone with wicked glee. "Agreed, but I'll sample this treasure now to ensure I'm getting a good deal. This night won't, of course, count as part of my quota."

"Of course." Raina nodded. "We have a bargain."

The Demon King stood without bothering to shake on it. He closed the meeting quickly, eyes burning into Zane like hot coals, not even sparing a departing farewell for Delilah, his supposed date. "I'll speak to the Council *after* the party Saturday night. Ladies, Alexi. I leave you to enjoy the rest of your evening. Wait here for your thrall if you wish, otherwise one of my sentinels will see him home."

Oh, saints. Knowing he'd never have to follow through after tonight didn't subdue the queasiness in the pit of Zane's stomach. The world tilted slightly off its axis, like the single stupid time he'd smoked a joint. Something wasn't right and the creepy sensation wasn't just the prospect of enduring the demon's attentions.

Johan, hurry! What the hell is taking so long?

No response.

"Thrall," Drakkon snapped. "Follow me."

Expecting him to obey, the demon turned and strode for the hallway at the back of the club, just a few feet from the sentinels. Zane glanced at Raina, who squeezed his hand and spoke in his head so the goons wouldn't overhear.

Keep your shields up tight.

It's too late, he knows I can mind-link. I'm sorry, my lady.

Oh, Zane. Her brow furrowed with real alarm. *Be careful. If Johan doesn't call us soon, I'll invent an excuse to interrupt.*

Zane didn't have the heart to tell her this evening wasn't going to turn out like any of them expected, or even explain how he knew. Instead, he raised her hand to his lips and brushed a kiss against the smooth skin of her palm.

With a sigh, he released her hand and hurried after the Demon King before he lost his nerve. So much for testing the waters as a thrall one toe at a time. His first night solo, and he'd drawn a shark.

At the end of the corridor the demon ushered Zane into the last private room on the right. "Make certain I'm not disturbed," he barked, presumably at a couple of his guards. He slid the bolt on the door, then walked to where Zane stood in the middle of the floor, eyes downcast.

The demon circled him, weighing the options, toying with his prey. The hawk swooping down on the rabbit, claws extended. Zane held still, blanked his mind. Willed himself to show no fear though he trembled inside. He was nothing but one unarmed former warrior against an ancient creature housing unimaginable powers. A seductive enemy holding all the cards, capable of rendering his captive insensate with ecstasy even as he dined on his flesh. In spite of his deal with Raina, the demon would do as he pleased. The knowledge sparked like wild electricity between predator and prey, curling around Zane's balls, licking his rigid shaft.

Zane fisted his hands, his breathing coming harder. The demon hadn't touched him, and he was already no match for his compulsion.

Drakkon's voice emerged as a rumble of satisfaction. "Zane Ramsey, Exodus warrior-turned-thrall. Extraordinary. How is it that I've never noticed your potential as a submissive?" he mused. "In retrospect, I suppose I should've realized given the way you were always following around that nosy partner of yours like a lovesick puppy. You were never much of a fighter, come to think of it."

Since the less than flattering observation didn't seem to require an answer, he remained silent. Until the demon's next question took him by surprise.

"Where is Stone, anyway?"

Before Zane opened his mouth, a sharp pain tore into his head. Drakkon was attempting to rip through his shields to see the truth for himself. "At the palace, bound as punishment for insubordination to our mistress," he gritted, gulping back nausea.

He wasn't used to defending his shields against anyone, much less a creature of great power. As the demon's efforts finally broke through, Zane flooded his mind with an image of Johan bound to Raina's bed, a dildo shoved into his anus. The image was from after Grog's attack during Johan's adjustment to the *ardin*, but with any luck, Drakkon wouldn't know the difference.

"I see," the demon chuckled. "Well, too bad he's missing out on the fun. I'd love to exact my own brand of retribution for the needless trouble he caused me during his ill-advised investigation into the murders. He spent months trying to fuck me over, so perhaps at Raina's party I'll return the favor literally."

Zane's knees went rubbery with relief. But only temporarily.

"Take off your clothes, boy, and don't keep me waiting."

He complied, undoing the buttons on his shirt with amazingly steady hands. Shrugging off the garment, he let it slide to the carpet in a puddle of silk. Bending, he toed off his shoes and tugged off his socks. Last, he unzipped his pants, pushed them down and kicked them aside. His erection sprang forth, flushed crimson, the gold ring gracing the fat cap a tempting delight for any master.

"Lovely piercings," the demon said, smoothing his palms over Zane's chest. His thumbs teased Zane's nipples to taut points, flicked the small hoops there. "I won't allow you to hide from me, boy. Raise your head and look into my eyes."

Pulse pounding his throat, he did as he was told. Drakkon's face was a study of cruel beauty, harsh angles and coal black eyes. Against his will, Zane drowned in their onyx depths, sucked into brackish water with no hope of rescue. The demon's hands skimmed his ribs, his flat abs. They roamed between his spread legs to cup his scrotum and give the ring there a vicious twist.

Zane was helpless to stop the soft moan that escaped his parted lips. Pain radiated from the center of him outward, ripples on a pond. One hand continued to use the ring to torture him while the other stroked his shaft. Dark, erotic. Agony and carnal heat melding together to give him what he craved. The demon read the truth, and Zane was lost.

"Ah, yes. I'm beginning to believe you're the real thing, beautiful thrall," Drakkon murmured. "You're already aching to be punished. You recognize me as your master and can't wait for me to hurt you, to fill you. Isn't that right?"

"Y-yes." *What's happing to me? Oh, sweet Virgin, help me.*

"No one can help you now." The tip of one finger swirled a bead of pre-cum all over the head of Zane's cock, tantalizing. "What do you wish for me to do to you?"

His entire body throbbed with anticipation. "Anything...everything," he whispered, shamed.

Drakkon smiled, revealing a glimpse of dangerous fangs. "And I shall, eventually. I'll have many more evenings to grant your wish. Now step over to the rack." He gestured to a device that was no more than two wide poles with a sling across the middle to support his torso. The whole contraption rotated on a base and could be levered forward as far as the master desired.

Heart jackhammering in his chest, Zane stepped between the poles, raised his arms and spread his legs. The demon fastened his ankles and wrists to the poles with strong padded clamps, the position leaving him open, vulnerable. Next the sling was adjusted across his middle, and another strap hooked at the top to support his head. The rack tilted forward and locked so that Zane's body rested at a forty-five-degree angle, feet toward the floor.

Zane's wrists bore the brunt of some of his weight, but the canvas under his stomach and forehead took off most of the pressure. An archaic but effective contraption. He was completely at the demon's mercy, cock and balls hanging free, accessible. His body no longer his own...and he reveled in forbidden longing.

A hand touched his back. "Expert flogging marks, skillfully done. From your ceremony?"

"Yes, my lord." He couldn't see the demon, but sensed him moving to stand between his spread legs. His ass cheeks were parted and the pad of a finger massaged his entrance in lazy rhythm. "Ohh..."

"Respect from my thrall, so eager for his master. I like that. Do you like this?" he purred, pushing the finger in deeper. In a few inches. Out.

"Yes, *please.*" Zane tried to arch his hips, but was held fast.

"Mmm, very good. But you'll have to earn more."

The finger withdrew and Zane made a small noise of protest, evoking a pleased laugh from his captor. Something rattled underneath the rack and he felt a tug on the head of his shaft. Another on his sac. His nipples.

"Wh-what are you doing?" he stammered.

"Anything and everything I wish," the demon mocked. "I'm making use of those pretty rings. I presume you didn't really believe you'd been adorned on four of the most sensitive areas of your body only for looks."

"N-no, my lord." Of course he hadn't, but—

"There. Each of the four rings is attached to a length of chain by a simple hook. The other ends of the chains are wound around an electric spool built into the floor. When I push a button, the spool will wind the chains around it, taking out the slack." Crawling from underneath the rack, he stood in front of Zane and caressed his face with...tenderness.

"I'm going to tighten them until you beg me to stop, but I won't because I understand how much you need this. I'll give you the razor's edge no other master can," he crooned. "And you'll learn to worship me for it."

The demon's promise was hypnotic, dangerous. Zane couldn't shake the fog of eroticism enveloping him, didn't want to. A pop sounded, the hum of a mechanism beginning to turn slowly. Pressure. Pulling...so good. His nipples, scrotum, erect, white-hot cock. He'd become nothing but those four points.

Gentle pressure became discomfort. The wheel turned, stretching him.

Pain, clean like the slice of a knife. Building, feeding his desire.

The demon was wrong, and right. He did not beg. He needed this. Could not speak. Tears pricked his eyes and he gave a ragged moan, craving more.

The spool ceased. Zane focused through the haze to see Drakkon gaping at him incredulously. Raw hunger glittered in his black gaze, and no little possessiveness. Even pride.

"I've never seen a human endure being stretched so fully without screaming, thrall or not," he praised. "You are incredible. A rare gem worthy of reward."

Striding away, the demon picked a whip from a collection hanging on the wall facing Zane. The instrument sported a long, thin tail designed to draw blood. He was past thinking or caring as Drakkon returned to stand at his back. The demon remained still for a long moment. Making him anticipate. Need.

The first blow cut him from the right shoulder to left hip. Clenching his teeth against crying out, he jerked in the restraints. The slightest movement caused additional torture to the four hypersensitive points, scoring his entire being with searing pain. The second and third sent a warm rush trickling down his heated flesh. The fourth pushed the cry past his lips.

"Mercy," he croaked.

"No, because you do not want me to stop. Tell me what you really desire. *Say it!*"

"H-h-hurt me...please..."

The strikes redoubled, falling with ruthless precision. Each one sent shocks to his dick. The fog thickened until he reached and found the prize. Rapture.

"Yes, yesss," he sobbed.

As if sensing he'd broken the thrall at last, Drakkon tossed aside the whip. He dragged two fingers through the blood on Zane's skin and came to stand in front of him once more. Slashing open his own wrist, he watched as the dark liquid beaded on the surface. He rubbed the crimson fingers into his wrist, mingling their blood, then held his wrist to Zane's lips.

"Taste."

On instinct, Zane tried to avert his head. Restrained as he was, Drakkon dabbed his lips with little effort and out of sheer reflex, Zane's tongue flicked out to clean off the droplets.

"Ohh!" His heart and lungs seized, his brain spinning. He'd never mainlined heroin, had avoided that deadly Venus flytrap, but this is exactly what he imagined the high to be like. An addictive rush bleeding to every fiber, carrying him toward his destiny, black and final.

When the demon's wrist touched his lips again Zane didn't resist. He latched on hungrily, drinking with greedy swallows, loving the heady nectar pouring down his throat. Taking the essence of his master inside him.

"Now you are mine," the demon approved, stroking Zane's hair with his free hand. "We will keep our secret for a while, but I am your master in truth. Only I will be able quench the dark fire burning within you. After tonight, I will stay away until your urgency to submit to my touch drives you mad, until your sanity hovers on the brink. And when I call, you'll come to me eagerly. Beautiful thrall...mine forever."

"Yours, my lord, to do with as you wish," he whispered, nuzzling his face into the beloved hand. The awesome instrument of sadistic cruelty, carnality stripped to its most primal elements.

What am I saying? What have I done?

Drakkon smiled, caressing his cheek. "That's right, sweet boy. The others will try to fill your head with lies about me, but you will not listen. If you betray me, you'll accomplish nothing but your own destruction because your body and soul cannot survive without me. Have I given you anything except what you so desperately need?"

"No, my lord."

"Have I done anything to your delicious body that you did not desire?"

He closed his eyes. "No."

The hand left his face and he felt the absence of the sensual touch like a physical blow. Blinking, he sought his captor...and sucked in an appreciative breath. Drakkon stood naked in his most human form, clothing vanished. Ebony hair tumbled past his shoulders, framed his massive, gorgeous chest. He was all muscled perfection and olive skin. The enormous penis jutting between his thighs and the weighty orbs beneath testified he wasn't anywhere near human. In true demon form, supersized all over, could Zane house all of that magnificent length?

A feral, determined expression hardened Drakkon's face. He stepped around the rack, positioning himself behind his prey. He parted Zane's ass, nudging his tight hole. Pushed in just the head, teasing. "My thrall."

"Please," he begged, reason gone. "If you don't take me, I'll die."

"Never forget it."

Gripping Zane's hips, the demon impaled him, deep and true as a mighty sword. A hoarse cry tore from his soul, borne of both anguish and ecstasy. Split in two, set ablaze. Totally controlled by his ruthless, wicked master.

His captor began to thrust slowly, making certain his thrall knew every inch of the cock that owned him. Every ridge and sleek contour, each ropy vein. Skin to skin, heavy balls rubbing his own. Fucking him at leisure, sealing his fate.

"Exquisite," Drakkon breathed. "The way your hole clenches my cock, your body parted for me as I slide in and out, slick and wet."

The decadent picture he painted had every cell in Zane's body throbbing and hot. The dark magic of his master's blood boiled in his veins. "More," he pleaded. "Fuck me harder...I want..."

What little remained of his sanity prevented him from speaking the awful truth. But he couldn't hide from it. His captor took the words from his tongue.

"You need the demon." He gave a low, triumphant laugh. "You crave the danger he represents, his absolute power and domination over you. And so you shall have me as I am."

Fingers lengthened, became talons digging into Zane's sides. The flesh surrounding him expanded, sliding up his back as the creature's height towered above him. Great wings stirred the air, casting an ominous shadow on the opposite wall. Terrifying. But those sensations paled in comparison to the battering ram stuffed inside him. Growing to immense proportions, filling his cavity to impossible depth and breadth.

Like a starving man, he glutted on his master, the brutal punishment flaying every nerve ending. Writhing, he groaned, out of his mind, tears streaming down his face.

The chuckle vibrating in the demon's chest was a rumble of distant thunder, a promise of the coming storm. His master began to pump, slow at first. Then faster, harder, pistoning into his thrall with savage force.

"Oh, gods, yes!" Zane cried. "Yes, yes, *yes...*"

The entire rack shook with the merciless assault as the demon's huge cock slammed him again and again. Breaking him apart to remold his soul, ruining him for all but his dark lord. Riding him past the threshold of pain and raw animal lust.

Hot, so blazing hot. His nipples, his ass, on fire. A large, rough palm curled around his shaft, jerking in rhythm to the thrusts pounding his channel. The yanking motion caused the chains to torture his cock and sac almost beyond endurance. He sobbed openly, not caring. Never wanting this to end.

Cum boiled, tightening his balls. Gathered at the base of his spine. His body quickened, began to spasm uncontrollably. No! But he couldn't stop the explosion that shattered his vision into a million shards of light. The volcanic release rocked his world. Primal screams rang in his ears and he realized they were his.

The demon slammed into him once, twice, the third time burying himself to the hilt, roaring in pleasure as he sent thick jets of warm semen into his thrall. They pulsed together, shuddering, as the waves crashed through Zane.

"Delicious," the demon rumbled, sating himself. "My beautiful thrall." Another languorous slide, out and in, seating himself to the balls. Two final spurts, and his cum overflowed to spill down the seam of Zane's ass, coating them both.

Limp with exhaustion, Zane hung in the restraints. Awareness returned, along with dull horror. Shame was a greasy coil in his gut. He should've been stronger. He'd betrayed Raina and Johan by bowing to Drakkon's wicked compulsion...and he'd do it again.

Because he was addicted to the demon now. The creature had breached his shields, easy as slicing through paper. Had sealed their bond with his blood, delightful as ambrosia on his tongue. Even now the antibodies rushed in his veins, destroying his golden bond with the two he loved. Coating its glow with a black stain from which there was no escape. They would despise him. They would take him from the bliss of his lord's dark mastery if they knew. No!

A talon grazed his cheek lovingly. "You are mine to command, and you will not defy me."

"Never, my lord." His heart twisted, but he could not save himself.

"And this will remain our secret, or I will kill you sooner rather than later."

A jolt shot to his groin. "As you wish."

"To whom does your body and soul truly belong? Say it!"

"I belong to you, my lord. Every part of me awaits your will."

"Excellent, for I am not yet finished with you tonight," his master declared. With a feral growl, the demon began to fuck him into oblivion once more.

Tears of sorrow dripping off his chin, Zane surrendered to dark beauty of his lord and master.

Chapter Seventeen

ഔ

Johan had no clue how long he stood immobile, sweat beading on his face as he waited for Grog to either go back to sleep or come fully awake. Fifteen minutes? A half-hour? He dared not call out to Raina yet and risk interrupting her meeting with Drakkon, lest the Demon King somehow perceive their deception.

The bleary eye remained fixed, lid drooping lower, one nerve-scraping millimeter at a time. The creature was either too slow or too encumbered by the sandman to process his presence. Or both. Didn't matter as long as he went back to dreamland.

The lid closed. Sending silent thanks to the gods, Johan began to inch backward from the creature. Just a few more feet —

"What do we have here?" a voice slurred from behind him.

"Grog's dinner?" another suggested.

Johan bit back a curse and half turned so he could still keep an eye on Grog. The defectors from the card game were giggling and ribbing each other like that was the funniest joke they'd heard all evening. He'd had no idea demons were capable of getting soused, but he hoped the fact worked to his advantage.

No such luck. As he groped for the dagger strapped to his thigh, one of the drunken duo bent to palm an egg-sized rock.

"Hey, Grog!" the idiot yelled. "Wake up, you stupid sonofabitch, it's mealtime."

He launched the missile, striking Grog square in the temple. The huge demon jerked upright with a squeal of outrage, casting about for the offender. His angry gaze fell on Johan and his gaze narrowed. Leaning forward, he sniffed at the intruder. And bared a mouthful of dirty fangs.

"Warrior," he purred happily. "Mine."

Johan stared at the demon, stunned. *He recognizes me.* The dagger was cold comfort in his hand as he glanced toward the cell door. The inebriated fools shouldn't prove too much of a barrier if he could get past them before the others were alerted. The need for stealth gone, he started for the exit, ready to fight his way out if necessary.

"No, mine!" Grog lurched upward, fighting the restraints.

Dammit! Johan spun. "Shh. I'll be back, okay? Quiet—"

"No, no!" The massive demon strained with all his great strength. One chain popped free and sailed past Johan's head, missing him by a hairsbreadth. *"Mine, mine, mine!"*

"Oh shit," one of the drunken demons muttered. They ran.

So did Johan. Another loud pop, the whir of metal slicing the air. Pain exploded in the back of his skull and he went sprawling. Rolling, sick and dizzy, he scrambled backward in the dirt. Muscles bunching, Grog snapped the chains one by one, links flying. Approaching shouts had Johan pushing up, intent on escape.

A black wing swept him off his feet, hurling him into the rock wall. He bounced off and hit the dirt with a grunt, determined not to lose. Not this time. Too many were depending on him to win this round, including his mate. *I made a promise. I will not fail.*

Johan pushed to his knees, studying his adversary in shock. Grog had broken free. The demon swooped on him faster than he could react, yanking him into a crushing embrace. Squeezing the breath from his body. Bringing his right arm up, he thrust the dagger between the creature's ribs.

245

Grog's earsplitting roar shook the cave. Whirling, the creature held Johan aloft, then slammed him bodily to the ground. Searing pain shot through his right wrist and arm as the dagger tumbled from his grasp. Breathing hurt, causing a sharp pinch in his side and a steely band to constrict his chest. Broken rib, punctured lung? Bad, but if his fighting arm was damaged...

Grog loomed over him. A horde of surprised demons stumbled from the adjacent corridor, gaping at the spectacle.

"Where's the tranquilizer gun Drakkon gave us?" one yelled.

"Wait, I want to see Grog eat the human first!"

Johan pushed up again, cradling his right arm, careful of the hand blades. He didn't think the limb was broken anywhere, but sprained was bad enough to give him trouble wielding his sword. If he could manage a quick strike with his left hand, he might be able to drive the weapon into Grog's heart, then use his sword to take the head before the rest of the demons swarmed in and killed him.

Grog, unfortunately, had other ideas. He snatched Johan off the ground by the sword scabbard on his back and dragged him toward the cell door. His would-be captors bunched together as if to herd him back, but scattered like frightened ants when he bellowed a pissed-off roar, slashing at them with razor-like claws and gnashing fangs.

"Stop him!"

"You stop him, dickwad. I'm fed up with this bullshit. Where are Drakkon and his precious sentinels whenever his crazy spawn gets loose and wipes the floor with us?" Several cheered, prepared to head for parts unknown.

As Grog sped through the main chamber, captive in tow, Johan heard the one he presumed to be the leader trying to rally the others to follow. They were going to warn Drakkon of the escape, who'd swiftly join them with his top fighters. The Demon King couldn't allow the public to become aware of

Grog or his secrets would be laid bare. He'd make sure Johan died, along with his own son if necessary.

Since the tunnel was too narrow for the demon to spread his wings, he bounded ahead at preternatural speed, taking only seconds to cover the distance. Johan was along for the ride, bumping and scraping the jagged rock as the creature ran dragging him like a child slinging a rag doll. A foul oath burst from his lips, and not just from the pain battering him. This clusterfuck was his fault and somehow he had to stop Grog from murdering anyone else.

Gaining the mouth of the cave, Grog leapt into the air and took flight. Sick with dread, Johan watched the earth fall away as the creature whirled higher, higher. The city of St. Louis ahead was a blanket of a trillion lights far below. Johan hated heights, never even flew on an airplane if he could drive instead. Of all situations he'd anticipated tonight, dangling a couple of miles above good old terra firma wasn't one of them.

By nothing more than a single leather strap.

Raina, are you there? Because if you are, baby...I'm in deep shit.

* * * * *

Something was terribly wrong.

Raina waited in the booth with her companions, back rigid, shoulders tense. Six attempts to contact Zane over the past half-hour, to get reassurance he was all right, met with a wall of silence. Why wasn't he answering?

"A novice like Zane can't handle Drakkon," Alexi said grimly, giving voice to the fear eating the three of them. "We never should've sent him in there."

"I can interrupt, try to seduce Drakkon into leaving with me," Delilah offered, as worried as her friends.

Alexi shook his head. "No offense, sweet, but do you really believe he'll halt his play session with a rare new toy to be with you?" Delilah slumped.

Damn, he had a point. Raina slid from the booth, eyeing the pair of sentinels left behind to watch them. "I'll go and simply inform him time is up and—"

A brilliant flash of light cut off her words, startling everyone. The sparks cleared, revealing a smallish demon with dishwater blond hair. A very frantic demon. Spotting the two sentinels, he rushed forward.

"Grog has escaped," he shouted. "Some human was nosing around in his cage and he went berserk! He grabbed the man and is headed downtown, toward the river!"

Raina, are you there? Because if you are, baby…I'm in deep shit.

Raina grabbed the edge of the table. *Are you hurt?*

A pause. *I'm all right. Just hurry. It looks like he's taking me to the Arch, and I'm short on feathers, sugar.*

She pressed shaking fingers over her lips. How could he joke at a time like this? If the creature dropped him—

We'll be there as fast as we can. Hang on and…I love you.

Back atcha, beautiful.

Raina looked around. The sentinels were gone and her companions hovered anxiously beside her. "Johan's in trouble. Grog has him and is headed for the Arch. I'll get Zane. Alexi, take Delilah and grab the extra weapons from the limo. We'll meet you out front."

"You got it." Alexi clapped a hand on her arm giving a reassuring squeeze, and the pair took off.

Raina hurried down the corridor glancing in the private rooms left open, listening as she passed the ones that were not. Searching this way cost minutes Johan didn't have, but the bond with Zane was strangely dim. Not as in impending death but a far more serious threat she couldn't name.

She discovered the last door ajar, pushed inside and sucked in a stunned breath. "Oh, honey," she breathed. "What has that bastard done to you?"

The room reeked of sex and blood. Zane was alone, strapped to a rack, cruelly chained and stretched beyond any torture a human should be able to endure. His poor back was a mess, crimson stripes overlaying the bruises. Raina ran to the mechanism in the floor and stomped on the button she prayed was reverse. The chains went slack and she wasted no time unhooking them from his piercings.

His face was turned away from her. She combed her fingers through his sun-streaked hair. "Zane? Sweetie, it's me. I'm going to get you off this thing, okay?"

Slowly, he turned his head and blinked at her. "Raina? Oh, gods, I'm so sorry…"

Her heart thudded in alarm. His face was pale and his eyes, normally sparkling emeralds, were dull. Muddy. Filled with despair. Something horrid had taken place in this room. Zane needed her and it tore at her insides that he'd have to wait.

"Listen to me," she said, bending to unlock the restraints on his ankles. "Grog has escaped and he's got Johan. That's why Drakkon and his men left so suddenly. We've got to get there, fast."

"They'll kill Johan!" Zane gasped. "Hurry, get me down."

She made quick work of releasing his wrists. He slid off the rack and wobbled a bit. Steadying him, she shook her head. "You can't fight if you can't walk."

His expression hardened. "The damage is superficial. Help me dress and give me a boost with your blood and I'll be fine."

She didn't argue. Johan was out of time. Zane leaned against the rack while she retrieved his clothes from the floor and helped him on with them. He flinched as the shirt stuck to his raw skin but his determination didn't waver. Accepting the wrist she offered, he took a couple of quick sips and nodded.

"I'm ready."

His color did look better, his irises not as cloudy. He'd have to do for now. Grabbing his hand, Raina flashed them both outside to where Alexi and Delilah waited at the rear of the limo. Armed. Alexi shoved Zane's weapons into his hands, the ones the former warrior hadn't seen since the night he'd become a slave. Zane took them, his expression mixed with astonishment and gratitude. After he'd strapped the dagger to his thigh and sword across his bloodied back, he yanked the glove bristling with blades onto his left hand. Finished, in less than thirty seconds. No one spoke. Everyone knew what must be done, no matter the cost.

And if Raina's mate was injured, hell itself wasn't deep enough to hide Drakkon from her wrath.

* * * * *

The landing jarred Johan's teeth and just about everything else.

The ground rose to greet him with dizzying speed as Grog approached the base of the Arch, not bothering to slow down. Or to raise his burden to avoid pulverizing him on the concrete walkway surrounding the monument.

Shit! Johan shielded his face with his arms an instant before the impact jerked him from the demon's grasp, sent him skidding. He flew in one direction, his sword skittering across the walkway in the other. The weapon came to rest well out of reach and he cursed. Without it, this would be a short fight.

Lunging to his feet, he steeled himself against the pain grinding every wrenched muscle and stumbled for the sword. Grog landed between him and the weapon, ugly face contorted with anger.

"Bad warrior!" he thundered. "Bad, bad!"

Johan planted his boots slightly apart, narrowing his focus, forcing himself to forget the crappy odds. Wound, cripple, then go in for the kill. Where to strike on a demon this fucking big? Blood, black and oily, oozed from the creature's side where he'd managed to stab it with his lost dagger. The wound hadn't slowed the demon much. He needed to hit a more vulnerable area, and he had to do it quick. He wasn't going to win a contest of strength with this brute.

Grog attacked first, what he lacked in finesse compensated by a lightning-fast strike. Johan ducked as talons whizzed over his head, right where his neck would've been. Using the opening, he stepped into the demon's body and brought his left arm up, angling the hand blades to land a blow underneath the massive sternum and into its heart. But Grog danced sideways at the last second and the blades sank into his right pectoral.

Shrieking, the creature swatted Johan like a fly to dislodge him, sending him reeling backward. While Grog held his chest, bellowing his rage to the stars, Johan dove between his legs. Twisting around to face the demon's rear, he swiped the blades across the back of its left thigh, hamstringing him.

Johan scrambled away from the screaming, hopping demon, intent on retrieving his sword. If he could reach—

Two more demons appeared on the other side of Grog. Johan recognized them from the cave and knew Drakkon wouldn't be far behind. Renewing his efforts, he made desperate grab for his weapon.

"Kill him, you idiot!" one of the demons yelled at Grog.

The beat of wings sounded Grog's swift approach. Just as Johan's hand closed around the hilt, the creature grabbed him by the leg, flung him up, then slammed him into the ground like a human club. His left arm shattered and the leg in the demon's grasp snapped like a dry twig. Johan had no breath in his lungs, couldn't scream. The agony was too great, his tenuous hold on his wits too vital. If he lost the sword again, he was a dead man.

Using his wings to keep himself aloft and balanced on his good leg, Grog reached down and dragged Johan upright by the front of his T-shirt. Malevolent yellow eyes glared into his and hot, putrid breath wafted in his face. A dark haze descended, clouding Johan's brain. He found himself unable to move, the sword hanging useless in his hand. His injuries were worse than he'd realized, his system going into shock.

From his peripheral vision, Johan saw several more demons flash onto the scene to surround the tableau. And there...Drakkon.

"Very good, Grog," the Demon King praised. "Now finish the has-been warrior so I can take you home and reward your bravery with an extra ration of meat."

Johan caught Drakkon's sly smile and understood who'd provide the meal. Sickened, he struggled to raise his sword. Too late.

Claws tore into his stomach, the blow effective as a shotgun blast. A thousand knives ripping, tearing. A strangled cry erupted from his chest, immediately eclipsed by a heartrending wail that shook the heavens. Scored the depths of his soul.

"*Noooo!*"

Raina. Turning his head, he tried to find her. His mate, his love. Though his vision was blurred, he made out the banner of her coppery hair in the lamplight as she led the charge against the demons, Zane, Delilah and Alexi close on her heels. Swords met flesh, heads rolled. The battle was on and three demons fled, apparently having heard their doom in her eerie howl.

Grog jerked his talons from Johan's middle and stood watching the melee in confusion. Johan saw Zane circling a fat demon. He swung his sword downward to cut the back of its leg. As it fell forward, he lopped off the head. In an instant, Drakkon appeared behind him, saying something Johan couldn't hear from this distance. Zane whirled, then froze as he confronted the Demon King. Why didn't he strike?

A sentinel crept up on Zane's back, but neither saw him. Johan tried to call out a warning, but his shout emerged as a whisper as the sentinel grabbed Zane around his chest and plunged sharp talons into his side. Then the weirdest thing happened. Drakkon rounded on his own minion, roaring in anger. The demon dropped Zane and vanished. After looking down on Zane for a moment, Drakkon left as well.

Johan didn't have a clue what he'd just witnessed and didn't have time to think on the strange scene. His mate, Alexi and Delilah were still battling the remaining sentinels, unable to help him or Zane, who lay unmoving on the walkway. Somehow he'd have to take out Grog himself. He was on his own.

As if he'd read Johan's thoughts, Grog launched into the sky with his prey. The figures below shrunk until Johan couldn't tell which one was Raina. He wished he'd been able to see her beautiful face one last time. Tell her how much he loved her. He dared not push the words into her mind and cause her concentration to slip, but she knew all the same.

The beat of the demon's wings echoed the waning thrum of his heart. The tangle of Johan's long black hair blew into his face as he looked up to see where the demon was taking him.

To the top of the Arch. The sword nearly slipped from his numb hand.

Grog alit at the apex of the monument...a structure that cleared the Statue of Liberty by more than four hundred feet. And the creature wasn't going to let go of his prize, not until Johan was dead.

Cold horror bled into his limbs as he realized what he must do. He had to find the strength to lift his sword. And once he did, the creature's release from misery would be mercifully swift, while Johan plummeted hundreds of feet to his death.

So be it. A warrior's job was to protect the innocent, no matter the cost to himself. He'd never allow a killer loose to destroy more lives if he had the power to stop him. Either way, he'd die.

Grog pulled him close and without warning, sank his fangs into the curve of Johan's neck and shoulder. Jaws of steel crushed muscle and bone, ripping him apart, strangling his hoarse scream. Warmth spurted down the front of his shirt, gathered in his throat, choking him. By sheer force of will, he swung his arm, landing a vicious blow, cutting into the demon's back.

Screeching, the creature thrust him away.

And let go.

The moment stilled to a snapshot, the remainder of Johan's life no larger than the head of a pin. His boots slipped on the narrow, shiny surface atop the Arch as the demon threw back his head, squealing. One strike. No margin for error.

With strength borne of desperation, Johan powered the weapon in an uppercut. His aim was true.

The creature's head disappeared, the corpse toppling after. For one brief moment, Johan was poised on top of the world. Alone with the cool night, a blanket of twinkling stars and the gods.

Raina...catch me...

The sword tumbled from his grasp. The impetus of his swing carried him over the side in slow motion. His mind shut down at the horrific sight of his boots leaving metal as he fell.

And fell.

* * * * *

Raina cleaved the head from the last of the hell's spawn, sword dripping with blood. Puddles of the dark stuff fouled the entire area, along with the stinking corpses. She wished there were more to kill, like the one who'd fled with their lily-livered King on their heels. Cowards!

Glancing around, she spied Delilah and Alexi about forty yards away kneeling beside Zane. Her wounded thrall drank from Delilah's wrist. Fear spiked, but Alexi gave her a thumbs-up to indicate he'd be fine.

The hair on the back of her neck prickled. Johan and the huge demon were gone. Frantic, she scanned the whole park beyond the base of the Arch in either direction along the river. No sign of them.

Pure instinct made her look up...and terror exploded in her breast at the sight that greeted her enhanced night vision.

Grog had flown to the top of the monument carrying Johan, who struggled in his grip. Johan's weapon flashed once. Twice. The demon's headless body hurtled from the structure.

Raina...catch me...

Then her mate tumbled from the sky, plunging helplessly toward earth.

"Johan!" Raina flew to intercept him rather than zone-surfing. If she miscalculated and appeared in the wrong place, she'd not get another chance to stop his fall.

Turning on the speed, Raina approached from underneath and caught him easily about halfway down. Any joy she might've felt at success was short-lived.

Cradling his limp body in her arms, she fought the sob of grief and denial burning in her chest. The creature had mangled Johan's shoulder and neck, coming close to ripping out his throat. His shirt and leathers were saturated in blood, a ragged hole torn in his stomach.

Johan gazed at her with such love, tried to touch her face, but couldn't raise his hand. Instead, his lips turned up in a small smile.

"Knew you'd...catch me." He coughed violently, crimson streaking from the corner of his mouth.

"Shh, don't talk, my love." Her throat was so thick with unshed tears, she could barely speak.

Raina lowered her precious burden to the ground ever-so gently, but didn't let him go. She held him in her arms because he didn't deserve to die on the cold concrete.

Alexi ran over to them, fell to his knees. "Sweet mother of the gods," he choked.

Raina ignored him and stroked Johan's silky raven hair, his face. "Your injuries are much more severe than before, more than taking draughts of our blood will heal fast enough. I-I can't save you this time without turning you vampire."

He nodded, pale and weak. "I know."

Despite her best efforts, tears escaped to stream down her cheeks. Her heart shattered, but somehow she had to find the courage to heed his wishes.

"I want you to know—" She broke off on a sob. Heaving a breath, she began again. "You were never my slave, Johan Stone. Not even for one second. You're my equal, my mate…the man I love enough to set free."

"Love you…" Johan's body shook, chilled from blood loss. His beautiful golden eyes dimmed, the light fading.

"Love you more. Sleep, baby. I've got you," she whispered.

"No. A warrior never breaks…his promise." Pausing, he gasped, "Want to…stay." His thick black lashes drifted closed.

Stay. "Johan? Johan!" Panicked, she looked up at Alexi. "He wants me to turn him? Is that what he means?"

Her companion shook his head with regret. "It's too late, sweetheart. He's—"

"Don't say it," she snapped. She still had time to save him, would not accept failure. Not now, when he wanted to keep his promise to come home to her.

Shifting his body, she let his head fall back and pressed her lips to the side of his neck that wasn't ruined. Quickly, she sank her fangs deep and took the rest of his blood in rapid swallows.

But he had so little to give, she drained him in seconds. Withdrawing her fangs, she gazed into his white face, laid a hand on his chest. His great heart was still, his body already cooling.

Raina pulled him close, buried her face in his hair and finally gave in to the sobs. She wept for the terrible agony he'd suffered tonight, for the wonderful light snuffed forever. Grieved for her mate, the man she'd loved and lost.

Deep down, Raina knew Alexi was telling the truth. Johan had been too far gone for even an ancient vampire like herself to turn. He wasn't going to wake up tomorrow night, or the next.

Johan was dead.

Chapter Eighteen

දා

A warrior never breaks his promise.

Want to...stay.

Raina haunted the palace, a pale ghost inconsolable in her grief. For the past seven nights, Johan's last words provided the only beacon of hope, the sole thread to cling to her sanity as she waited in vain for her mate to open those beautiful eyes. To smile and say everything was all right, take her in his arms.

The first night, the awful wounds to his neck, shoulder and stomach had healed by dawn. Hope flared bright and she waited.

By the second night, she scanned his body to find his broken bones and internal injuries mended. But no heartbeat that night or the third. She told herself to be patient. Just because she'd never heard of someone rising after the third evening didn't mean it wasn't possible.

By the fourth sunset, she understood. The magic of her bite had been strong enough to heal his broken body cosmetically, allowing her love to rest with dignity. His corpse remained whole, his handsome face peaceful as though in sleep. But the bite hadn't come in time to turn him.

Still, Raina refused to let go. Sitting by his side in their bed, she held one of his big hands, studying the various tiny scars. Evidence of victory, a warrior's hands. Harsh in battle, his touch blazing when he loved her. Only he had the power to make her tremble.

Raina brought his hand to her face, rubbed it against her cheek, needing some part of him close. Just a bit longer. "I miss you," she whispered. "Everyone does, especially Zane. I'm worried about him, Johan. The spark is gone from his eyes. He won't eat and he prowls the grounds like a caged tiger. He's grief-stricken about what happened to you, but it's more than that. Drakkon did something terrible to him and he won't talk to us. Come back to us, baby. Don't you see how much we all need you?"

He didn't stir. She kept talking anyway. "Alexander called and you're officially not a slave anymore. Zoltan has been cleared of the murders and released. Turns out the demon meeting with him on the damning video was Charon, Drakkon's top sentinel. Charon was against Drakkon's plot to use the enhancement potion from the beginning, said it would lead to disaster, and he was right. He went to Zoltan early on and revealed only that he knew who was killing the women and his King was involved, but nothing else. With all of the Council under Drakkon's thumb except your friend Alexander, the sentinel and Zoltan had no one at the city level they could trust. Zoltan didn't dare give up his sole witness and risk getting them both silenced, so he bided his time and waited for you and Zane to come through. And you did, didn't you?"

She kissed his hand, combed her fingers through the fall of black silk. "The sentinel is in protective custody somewhere and a bulletin has gone out to all Exodus warriors for Drakkon's immediate capture, dead or alive. You don't want to miss out on taking that monster down, do you? Come on, love. We can have a race to see who gets to skewer the pig first."

Raina sighed, sadness threatening to suffocate her. She'd cried enough tears these past nights to overflow the banks of the Mississippi, and nothing had changed. Nothing would. "Alexi says this isn't fair to you, keeping you lying here this way. He says we should honor your m-memory by allowing you to rest, but I felt like I'd be abandoning my mate to sleep alone for eternity in a barren place without love. Now I know that's not true." A single tear welled, rolled down her face as she pressed his hand over her heart.

"You won't be there, but here for always. So you see, my love, I'm not really letting you go after all." Leaning over, she pressed a kiss to his cheek. "I love you, Johan. After I send Drakkon to hell, I'll join you wherever you are. An eternity without you in my arms would be a living death, and I know you'd never demand such a high price from me."

Sliding from the bed, she rose on rubbery legs and went to inform the others.

The vigil was over.

* * * * *

I love you, Johan...I'll join you wherever you are...

Johan struggled from the depths of a murky pit. He'd been listening to Raina's voice for some time, but not much made sense. Until the last bit sent his sluggish pulse racing. He remembered the battle with Grog, falling. Raina catching him.

Dying in her sweet embrace.

Raina must've turned him and believed she hadn't succeeded. By the gods, he felt so awful no one had to tell him it almost hadn't worked. If he didn't manage to rise, they were going to bury him alive.

And his mate planned to destroy herself.

"No!" he croaked, renewing his efforts. One finger moved, then another. Next, he wiggled his toes. After a while, he managed to pry his eyes open. His gritty vision slowly cleared and relief flooded him. The soft canopy of Raina's bed—their bed—hovered overhead. Yes, he could feel the sheets surrounding his body now, warm and cozy. He wasn't in the ground, cold and forgotten.

Strength gradually returned and with new life came voracious hunger. Running his tongue over his teeth, he was startled to discover fangs. He tested one, then the other, marveling at their length and razor-sharp tips. The desire to sink them into willing flesh, gulp the delicious hot blood filling his mouth, overwhelmed him. If his blood reward as a human had been pleasing, he could only imagine the ecstasy of feeding as a vampire.

St. Peter's balls, I'm going to live forever. The idea still disturbed him on a basic level, but with Raina by his side, forever would be a pretty damned fantastic existence. He had a coven now. A real family.

He was anxious to see not only Raina, but Alexi and Zane as well. Had Raina forgone Delilah's punishment and invited her to join them? He hoped so. *Mine to claim, all of them.* His lusty beast awakened, proving that the *ardin* had survived the change.

Excited, he pushed up to a sitting position, taking stock of his naked body. Whole, healthy. A miracle visited him by a blue-eyed beauty with fiery red hair. Positive he could get dressed and go downstairs under his own steam, he slid from bed and stood. Shaky, but he'd do. Now for some clothes.

As he glanced toward the closet, a square of dark material hanging on the door caught his attention. Gaping, he stared in disbelief. No one had to tell him what the item was for. Raina had planned to bury him in a freaking *suit*? He grimaced, thinking of how close he'd come to being trapped alive tricked out like a stockbroker.

Finding a clean pair of jeans, he pulled them on, deciding against a shirt or shoes. As he zipped his fly, he noted the nipple ring was gone and frowned. He'd kinda gotten attached to it and the little sizzle that shot to his cock when Raina twisted it. Well, she'd just have to put the thing back.

Unwilling to delay a second longer, he made his way downstairs in search of Raina. Completely cleared, his vision was sharper than it had ever been as a human, his hearing and sense of smell acute. He heard someone, probably Hope, washing dishes in the kitchen from several rooms away. Voices drifted to him and those were coming from the parlor.

As Johan approached, he stayed out of sight for a moment, listening. A naughty, unkind thing to do to his mate and friends, but curiosity won over, especially since he was the topic.

"You're doing the right thing, love," Alexi said, his tone firm but kind. "No one rises after seven nights under the best of circumstances."

Seven! His second chance was a true miracle.

"Lose the suit." This advice from Zane. "He'd hate being dressed like a dick until the end of time. Jeans, a T-shirt and his weapons. That's what he'd want."

Johan smiled. Yeah, his friend knew him well.

"I c-can't discuss any more details right now. I just wanted you all to know I'd made my decision." A pause, and a sniffle. "It h-hurts so much I can't breathe. When is the pain going to stop?"

Johan's amusement vanished. Raina's voice, so sad and desolate, tore into his gut. Abandoning his post, he stepped into the parlor. Zane and Delilah sat on either side of his mate on the sofa, his friend holding her hand, the little vamp rubbing her back. Raina's face was buried in her hands, shoulders shaking. Alexi stood in front of the fireplace, forearm braced on the mantle, head down. Until this profound moment, Johan never imagined how his "death" would devastate those left behind.

Johan cleared his throat. "How about it stops right now?"

He might as well have set off a bomb in the middle of the room. Four stunned faces locked on him, not quite believing. Raina's hand clapped over her mouth, eyes red-rimmed from crying.

"Holy shit!" Zane whooped, leaping to his feet. He crossed the room in four strides and pulled his friend into an enthusiastic bear hug.

Johan returned the embrace, grateful as hell, love swelling in his chest. "Good to see your ass, too...thrall. Collar still makes you look good enough to eat. Keeping busy?"

Laughing, his friend gave him a playful shove. "Oh, shut up."

Alexi and Delilah took turns hugging him, all smiles and good wishes. With a glance toward the sofa, Alexi gestured toward the door. "Why don't we give these two some privacy. See you guys later." He grinned at Johan. "Much later."

The trio left, closing the door behind them. Raina was on her feet now, staring at Johan as if he might suddenly vanish, never to return.

"You're really here," she whispered, breath hitching.

He crossed to her, took her beloved face in his hands. "Forever, sweetheart. Nothing could have kept me from you."

With a cry, she flung herself against Johan's chest and held on tight. His arms encircled her waist and he crushed her softness to him, inhaling her sweet scent. Hunger rose, wild and uncontrollable. His pulse quickened, iron-hard erection straining to be freed from the confines of his jeans.

"I think this reunion calls for a celebration," he rasped.

Pulling back slightly, Raina gave him a watery smile. "I'd say that's a vast improvement over what I was doing a few moments ago." The smile faded to haunted shadows, the grief she'd suffered for the past few nights not yet erased. "Oh, Johan. I missed you so much and when I thought I'd lost you, I wanted to follow —"

"No, you're stronger than that." He waggled his brows, attempting to lighten the mood. "Besides, you won't ever have to worry about losing me again. I'm superhuman in all the right places, sugar." His stab at humor fell flat.

"What about the next time you go out to fight the monsters? You can't tell me you're not going to petition the Council to reinstate your position at Exodus," she said softly.

"Being a warrior is part of who I am, but you're an even bigger part." Johan buried a hand in her burnished curls, captured her lips in a gentle kiss. "You're the brightest spot in my soul, the reason I fought my way back. Nothing matters more to me than seeing you happy. All you have to do is ask, and I'll never pick up my sword again."

She touched his face. "And that's the one thing I'd never do. I fell in love with the warrior, and he didn't break his promise. I trust he never will."

Unconditional love. A rare and valuable gift among the many he'd been given. With shaking hands, he unbuttoned her pretty red blouse and pushed the material off her shoulders, baring her creamy breasts. He cupped them, loving their ripe fullness, a perfect fit in his palms. Bending, he captured a pert nipple between his teeth, grazing it to a taut peak, flicking with his tongue. Raina arched into him, burrowing her fingers into his hair, practically making him purr like a big cat. He adored when she did that.

Releasing the nipple, he reached for her waistband and unfastened her jeans. He pushed them down and helped her step from them, mouth going dry at the sight of the triangle between her thighs, fiery as the hair on her head. Gods, it had been too long. His own jeans went next, cock bobbing eagerly. The scent of her arousal, the pungent aroma of her sex, hit his system like speed, calling to the beast. But he wasn't going to fuck her. Not tonight. No, tonight was for making slow, sweet love to his mate.

Johan lowered Raina onto the pillows in front of the sofa, eased her back. Parting her legs, he skimmed a palm over her flat tummy, through the springy curls. His fingers found her moist folds, already wet for him. Her slit glistened, pretty and pink, the rosy little cherry of her cunt the treat atop the sundae. He spread her cream, enjoying the sweet sounds of pleasure she made as he teased the button with each stroke.

"Johan, baby, please!"

He needed no further encouragement. Rising over her, he braced his arms on either side of her head, nudging the tip of his cock between her nether lips. With a groan of pure bliss, he pushed home. Right where he belonged.

Raina wrapped herself around him, legs locked about his waist. Johan withdrew, sank into her heat. Slow and easy, again and again. Pouring all of his love for her into each smooth glide of his shaft deep into his mate. His lady, for always.

They moved together in perfect rhythm, soaring higher. Hunger coiled, spiraling with each stroke of their bodies. The primal drive to claim her as only a dominant male vampire can. In tune with his urgency, Raina pushed aside her hair, baring her neck for him.

"Go ahead, my darling. Complete us and become my mate in truth."

"I'm afraid I'll hurt you."

Raina's lips turned up. "You won't."

Cradling her to his chest, Johan lowered his head. Teased the delicate skin with his tongue, craving a taste of her essence. Gentle as possible, he pressed his mouth to the curve of her neck and pierced the flesh, burying his fangs. Nectar flooded his mouth, poured down his throat. Hot and sweet, detonating his senses. He'd never known joining with his mate would be like this. Sublime, making him new and whole.

Raina moaned, clinging to him, meeting his thrusts with abandon. He drove into her, sweeping them toward the pinnacle. Faster, higher. Raina cried out, clasping him tight. Unable to hold back, Johan convulsed, his release exploding. He pumped into her, giving all that was his, mind, body, soul.

They floated to earth, limbs entangled, covered in sweat. Johan withdrew his fangs and brushed her lips in a butterfly kiss. Love filled his soul, so immense he thought his heart might burst. No words were adequate, but he did his best.

"Thank you for loving me," he whispered.

Smiling, she gazed into his eyes. "Thank you for coming back to me."

"I always will, sweetheart."

Always.

A warrior, after all, never breaks his promise.

* * * * *

Zane perched on a bench in the garden near the swimming pool, lost in a maelstrom of conflicting emotions. Saints above, he'd been overjoyed to see Johan walk through the parlor door. A terrible tragedy turned to happiness, the world put correctly on its axis once more for everyone.

Well, almost everyone.

Chilled, he rubbed his arms. How much longer could he hide Drakkon's stain in his blood, black as tar? How much longer could he resist the call of the dark lord, the lure of the melodic voice in his head?

Come to your master, sweet boy. Only I can give you what your body craves.

The Demon King was out there. Zane felt the touch of his gaze surely as a hand caressing between his legs. The tie was unbreakable, his will to resist gradually being destroyed. Whether he sat here in the open or barricaded himself in the palace didn't matter.

Soon, they'd know. And they'd all hate him for his weakness, his betrayal. Johan would be forced to kill him in order to rid his soul of the evil taking root. No one could help him now.

No one.

"Hey, is this a private party, or can anyone join in?"

Zane started. "Lady Delilah! I didn't hear you walk up," he laughed, the sound shaky to his own ears.

"Penny for your thoughts?" She grinned, plopping down on the bench beside him.

"Don't waste your money." He eyed their new coven member's tiny, see-through white top and dark skirt. Dark hair flowed over her slim shoulders, down her back. His cock stirred, proving he wasn't completely ruined. Scrambling, he searched for a safe topic.

"All's well that ends well," he quipped, striving for his normal, cheerful tone. "Think Raina will reschedule the party now that Johan is okay?"

"Probably so," she nodded. "We'll just have to keep a sharp eye out for Drakkon now, in case he doesn't get that a wanted criminal is now uninvited."

Drakkon. Goddammit, the bastard was everywhere.

Delilah didn't notice his distress. "Wanna go for a swim?"

"It's winter, are you kidding? The water's freezing!"

"Drat, I forgot you're just a puny human." She pouted prettily, then her exotic face lit with an impish grin as he held out her hand. "Come with me, thrall. I've got a much better idea than swimming."

He took her small hand in his. "Oh yeah? Is that an order?"

She tossed her head, flashing her best look of bitchy superiority. "It is."

This time, his laugh was genuine. "Your wish, my lady, is my command. Shall we?"

They rose together and Zane let her lead him into the house, where he managed to forget, if only for a while, his life was over.

The bond he'd forged with Raina and Johan was fading.

And the brightly burning golden thread that had flared the night Delilah saved his life at the Arch would forever remain his secret, bittersweet.

A secret lost forever at the hands of a demon.

Drakkon leered at his prey from the shadows, planning. Oh yes, the boy was going slowly insane with need for his master's touch. He'd have Zane soon, as well as his vengeance on Raina and her mate. They'd thought to use and trap him. But the Demon King played that game better than anyone.

Chuckling, he spun and vanished into the night.

Time to prepare for a party he'd not miss for the world.

Why an electronic book?

We live in the Information Age—an exciting time in the history of human civilization, in which technology rules supreme and continues to progress in leaps and bounds every minute of every day. For a multitude of reasons, more and more avid literary fans are opting to purchase e-books instead of paper books. The question from those not yet initiated into the world of electronic reading is simply: *Why?*

1. *Price.* An electronic title at Ellora's Cave Publishing and Cerridwen Press runs anywhere from 40% to 75% less than the cover price of the exact same title in paperback format. Why? Basic mathematics and cost. It is less expensive to publish an e-book (no paper and printing, no warehousing and shipping) than it is to publish a paperback, so the savings are passed along to the consumer.

2. *Space.* Running out of room in your house for your books? That is one worry you will never have with electronic books. For a low one-time cost, you can purchase a handheld device specifically designed for e-reading. Many e-readers have large, convenient screens for viewing. Better yet, hundreds of titles can be stored within your new library—on a single microchip. There are a variety of e-readers from different manufacturers. You can also read e-books on your PC or laptop computer. (Please note that Ellora's Cave does not endorse any specific brands.

You can check our websites at www.ellorascave.com or www.cerridwenpress.com for information we make available to new consumers.)

3. **Mobility.** Because your new e-library consists of only a microchip within a small, easily transportable e-reader, your entire cache of books can be taken with you wherever you go.

4. **Personal Viewing Preferences.** Are the words you are currently reading too small? Too large? Too... ANNOYING? Paperback books cannot be modified according to personal preferences, but e-books can.

5. **Instant Gratification.** Is it the middle of the night and all the bookstores near you are closed? Are you tired of waiting days, sometimes weeks, for bookstores to ship the novels you bought? Ellora's Cave Publishing sells instantaneous downloads twenty-four hours a day, seven days a week, every day of the year. Our webstore is never closed. Our e-book delivery system is 100% automated, meaning your order is filled as soon as you pay for it.

Those are a few of the top reasons why electronic books are replacing paperbacks for many avid readers.

As always, Ellora's Cave and Cerridwen Press welcome your questions and comments. We invite you to email us at Comments@ellorascave.com or write to us directly at Ellora's Cave Publishing Inc., 1056 Home Avenue, Akron, OH 44310-3502.

Make each day more *EXCITING* With our

Ellora's
Cavemen
Calendar

www.EllorasCave.com

erridwen, the Celtic Goddess of wisdom, was the muse who brought inspiration to storytellers and those in the creative arts. Cerridwen Press encompasses the best and most innovative stories in all genres of today's fiction. Visit our site and discover the newest titles by talented authors who still get inspired - much like the ancient storytellers did, once upon a time.

CERRIDWEN PRESS

www.cerridwenpress.com

Discover for yourself why readers can't get enough
of the multiple award-winning publisher
Ellora's Cave.

Whether you prefer e-books or paperbacks,

be sure to visit EC on the web at
www.ellorascave.com

for an erotic reading experience that will leave you
breathless.

771760

Printed in Great Britain by
Amazon.co.uk, Ltd.,
Marston Gate.